*Totally Bound Publishing books by A.B. Wilson*

**The Shellenberg Brothers**
The Role

I0598554

# The Shellenberg Brothers

# THE ROLE

## A.B. WILSON

The Role
ISBN # 978-1-83943-734-2
©Copyright A.B. Wilson 2021
Cover Art by Erin Dameron-Hill ©Copyright August 2021
Interior text design by Claire Siemaszkiewicz
Totally Bound Publishing

Published in 2021 by Totally Bound Publishing, United Kingdom.

Totally Bound Publishing is an imprint of Totally Entwined Group Limited.

# THE ROLE

# Dedication

To Mr. Wilson. You're simply the best.

To A.L., M.B., and I.P. –
you know what you did. Thank you.

# Chapter One

*Alina*

"Cut! Again, from the top!" Michael Burch's exasperated demand echoed through the hot, humid Savannah night. Again. In that very specific *tone* that always led to threats of firing, alligator tears and requests for cold compresses. We weren't going anywhere until his perfectionist, directorial ass was damn well satisfied. It could be hours.

We'd been on set since five in the morning and it was going on midnight. Cast and crew alike looked like they'd been ridden hard and put away wet. To be fair, we should have known it was going to be a rough one when he'd demanded that we "*seize the day and chase the light*" as we assembled before sunrise, clutching our coffee cups like zombies.

I glanced around and found everyone staring at me. Humidity-induced split-end halos around everyone's head and sweat stains for days. *Alina, save us. You're our only hope*, they silently implored.

They weren't wrong. In addition to being one of the underpaid, overworked assistant producers for *Southern Gods*, Michael had decided that I was his 'official' muse of the season and thus responsible for inspiring him. All because I'd given him a small handful of ideas that had played well with the network folks and he'd decided that having a muse meant he was a legitimate artist. It was truly ludicrous, but as one of maybe two people Michael listened to these days, I was probably the only person within a hundred miles who could come close to putting out tonight's dumpster fire.

The last few weeks on location in Georgia had been brutal with the unrelenting July heat and an unfortunate, possibly sexcapades-based injury that had sidelined our lead actor. With him out, I'd scrambled, shuffled and sweet-talked the senior producers to rush a much-anticipated guest star to the set two weeks early. The crowning jewel for the season—German actor Markus Shellenberg, total A-lister and critics' darling.

Getting Markus onboard in the first place had been an absolute genius move by Michael. The show was floundering and there were rumors running rampant that the network execs had us on the chopping block. We were hoping that this superstar guest appearance would keep us limping along for another season.

Accompanied by the sighs of relief and muttered prayers for sanity and hope from my fellow crew members, I approached Michael, rubbing my gritty eyes. "Michael, boss man, we've got to call it. The level of overtime we're handing out is going to get us in heaps of trouble with the network, there is zero moonlight for us to work with, and I think we're all hallucinating."

He laughed as he laser-stared us all down. "Lazy asses," he said semi-affectionately. "Fine. I hate overtime and you're all useless anyways. We'll pick it back up in a few hours."

Muted cheers followed. Everyone started to disperse to break down the set before heading to the trailers, rentals and hotel for showers and much-needed sleep.

As the last person filed out, Michael turned to me with a stern look in his eye and a twitching vein in his forehead. "You were right this time, but don't ever undercut my authority again. We are way fucking behind here, and Markus is showing up tomorrow. Do you have the updated shooting schedule ready for me?"

Inured to his rapid mood swings at this point, I responded, "You've got it, boss. Dropped it to your phone. Do you want me to forward it to the rest of the cast once you've approved it?"

"No, I've got it. Jesus. Go get some sleep. You look like death."

"Thanks," I muttered. "See you in a few hours. Five o'clock again?"

"Seize the light, Alina. We're gonna seize it by the fucking balls, twist 'em, and make that light our bitch." He flounced off and I was left shaking my head trying to dislodge the disturbing visual that I knew would be bouncing around my brain like a ping pong ball, keeping me awake.

After another hour tidying up, I checked out Markus' soon-to-be trailer to make sure it was set up correctly. It looked like his extensive rider had been fulfilled — one of the assistants had even managed to track down the weird German muesli and kefir — and I quickly buzzed security to make sure that protocols were adapted for Markus' arrival. They confirmed and

I considered passing out for the four hours until the morning's call on the micro-suede couch in the fancy-schmancy trailer. *Maybe for a second. God, I'm so fucking tired.*

I slumped down and began to work out the knots in my neck with my thumbs. The last two years had been a brutal effort to climb the ladder in a completely new field and build a life in Los Angeles, a city that was equally beguiling and terrifying for this girl from the Windy City. It hadn't been easy, but I'd clawed my way up from minimum-wage production assistant to assistant producer on *Southern Gods* in record time thanks to a previous connection to Michael.

After next season, for which he'd offered me an assistant director credit in lieu of my current title and muse status, I hoped I could finally cut ties with Michael and get out on my own. I wanted to focus on horror and action films — not genres that women were typically known for — and that A.D. credit would catapult me above my competition for jobs. It was rare to achieve it in as little time as I had, but I'd worked my ass off and refused to feel guilty about maxing out my connections to support my efforts.

*Ping!* A text from my best friend, Candace, a makeup artist on the show, pulled me completely away from the half-assed neck massage that had almost put me under.

*Hey girl, you coming home soon? Wanna warn you that Ethan and Rory are here tonight. Put your earplugs in. ;)*

Jealousy, amusement and exhaustion warred within me when I read her message. I loved my roommate and her completely open poly life, but the last thing I wanted to hear that night was anyone having sex. It stood to reason that if I was on a two-year hiatus from dating, everyone else should be too.

Me: Ugh, fine. Don't they each have large personal suites for y'all to play in?
Candace: Yeah, but our place has better ambiance. Ya kno, nevermind. We'll go to their place. Sorry for bugging you.
Me: All good. Finishing up with Markus's trailer. Home soon.
Candace: Oooh. Maybe leave him a naked picture to welcome him? You need to get laid, like yesterday.
Me: Hiatus, remember? Men are untrustworthy assholes, relationships are for the weak. You know it, otherwise you'd be locked down with your two himbos.
Candace: Giiiiirrrrllll...watch it. Me and my himbos can still come to our place. Haha. Get some sleep, see ya in the morning – ily!

After sending her an eyeroll emoji, I pocketed my phone, stood up and stretched until my joints popped and eyes watered. My shirt rode up and I tugged it down self-consciously, not that anyone was around to see the muffin tops that had formed as I ate my way through the heavenly culinary scene in Savannah. I needed to figure out a way to get out for a hike or some climbing on my upcoming morning off, and whipped out my phone again and made a voice memo for one of my eternally updating list-making apps.

With a sigh that could have moved mountains, I reminded myself that everything was going to be fine, that these hiccups and delays, the minor catastrophes of the last week, were about to be resolved. Hopefully. Along with everyone else on set, I had been infected by a weird sense of excitement the minute we'd received confirmation that our guest star was on his way. Markus Shellenberg was a massive deal in the industry and I would have been a total liar if I said I hadn't at least considered his droolworthy characteristics. I mean, he'd alternated between an outright win and a much-contested second place for *People* magazine's Hottest Man in the World for the last five years running — and we all knew those alternating runners-up were just to be nice to the rest of the masculine universe.

I shook my head to dislodge the Shellenberg-induced cobwebs and finally made my way out of the door and into the night. So this was where my life stood — masquerading as a muse to get a step up on the ladder, battling stress pudge and the ever-changing whims of a certified artiste, and an exciting new colleague who was the hall pass for pretty much anyone and everyone attracted to men. *Woof.*

# Chapter Two

*Markus*

Even through my headphones, the shouts and laughter of the trailing media horde echoed in my head, sending my shoulders right up to my ears and my sunglasses down into the collar of my shirt.

"There he is! Markus, hey, tell us about the George Sellers movie! What was it like to work with him? How badly did he kick your ass?"

"Markus! Where's Kate? Should we wait and help her with her luggage?"

I shook my head as I ducked into the car Michael had sent for me, delighted that my team had managed to keep my relationship implosion under wraps.

Everything was shit. I looked like shit and felt like it too. I hated doing television work and usually had more time between projects to recover. My girlfriend, Kate, had broken up with me on-location in Cambodia in a series of fights and histrionics that practically cost me my role in the film I'd recently wrapped. A role that was looking more and more like it was my last for a while, since my status had changed from star to 'uncastable'. Or so my agent said.

Our on-set NDAs might have kept the news from going public, but industry people still gossiped. Everyone who was anyone in Hollywood had probably heard the story of Kate crashing the Sellers set with her screeching accusations about my sexuality and infidelity. We hadn't been quiet when we'd fought and I was now a potential liability, deemed too emotionally unstable, too risky to hire.

Given the darkness of my current mental state, I appreciated the fact that my character on this absurd show was relatively minor and destined for a quick death. That being said, I *needed* this role to be successful and not tank my reputation further. Because after this project wrapped, I had nothing scheduled, and that freedom was terrifying. I'd never been without the prospect of steady work, but maybe it would be a good thing. Time to heal from the break-up and very nearly losing my job.

"Sir? We're here. Let me get your bags." The driver interrupted my depressing line of thinking with his pleasant Southern accent. I got the feeling that he'd been trying to get my attention for a while and felt a momentary stab of guilt.

"Thanks, man. Listen, can you stick around for maybe fifteen minutes? I can check in and drop off my bags, then you could take me to the set?"

The driver frowned at me, probably having trouble deciphering my accent, which always got thicker when I hit peak exhaustion, and even I could hear the slight slur in my words.

"Sure, not a problem," he said. "Uh, if it's not too much trouble, do you think I could get a photo with you for my niece? Big fan of yours, Mr. Shellenberg."

"Yeah, when I get back down. You want a coffee or anything while I'm in there?"

"That would be great, but don't put yourself out. I'll still be here."

I nodded, told him I didn't need a hand with my bags and slid out of the car. Sunglasses back on, I stumbled into the hotel lobby and shrugged off the valets.

"Checking in for P. Collins, please?" I asked the clerk.

*That's right, Phil Collins, the maestro and my musical hero. We can all feel it coming in the air tonight, hang* —

"Your card, sir? For incidentals." The clerk gave me a professional smile and finished checking me in, all the while pretending she didn't recognize me — or maybe she actually didn't, given the fact that I looked only slightly less dead than the roadkill raccoon I'd seen on the way from the airport — and I headed upstairs with my bags.

My suitcase and duffle landed on the floor of my room with a definitive thud, like this was the end of the road for them and me. I dropped my backpack on a chair, pulled out a clean shirt and went to the bathroom to splash some water on my face. As I shrugged on the shirt, I caught a passing glimpse of my reflection and winced. I looked like Christian Bale's character in *The Machinist*.

The ride to the shoot location was relatively uneventful and the driver rambled on about the history of the neighborhood. Trees with hanging moss and Victorian mansions behind mysterious iron gates flanked both sides of a shadowed boulevard. It was gorgeous, to be sure, but jet lag was starting to set in and everything seemed slightly surreal. When we pulled up to a gated compound, the driver gave the guard our IDs and we were waved through.

"This is fine. Let me out here."

"Do you want me to come back later, Mr. Shellenberg?"

"No, I have no idea how long this will take. I can get a ride back from someone later."

"All right, well, a pleasure meeting you and driving you. Here's my card if you need a regular driver while you're in town. Don't hesitate to call!" He beamed at me with a practiced, professional smile.

"Thanks, Beau," I muttered after a quick glance at the card in my hand.

\* \* \* \*

Like every set, this one was chaotic, with people running around, the acrid smell of burnt coffee polluting the air and the sounds of a million egos vying for attention. I scanned the crowd, searching in vain for the tiny figure of Michael, but he was invisible among the comparative giants striding around purposefully. No one paid attention to me as I ghosted through the set, hat and sunglasses on, hands in pockets, searching for the swirl of energy and noise that I knew would contain Michael at its center.

I wasn't really focusing on anything when a figure in my peripheral vision stopped me dead. That wasn't right, though. It wasn't really seeing — more of a visceral experience. Like I'd taken a punch to the jaw, my head literally jerked in that direction. It was a compulsion. And when I obeyed it, I saw *her*.

The entire set seemed to go low-res and fade to the back while she glowed, standing out from the foreground in sharp contrast. She was bright, detailed—down to the tiny freckles on her nose and cheeks, which I shouldn't have been able to see from so far away. Except I somehow could. Dark-brown hair was pinned on the top of her head in a messy knot, the line of her slender neck bisected by the mic arm of a headset. Her green eyes flashed out from under thick, choppy bangs as she smiled at someone while tucking a wayward curl behind an ear.

She was tall, a few inches under six feet, with the lithe build of a former athlete. Her mischievous grin immediately conjured an image of her naked and laughing on the rumpled sheets of my hotel bed. I shook my head, trying to remember the last time I'd had an even remotely sexual thought—definitely before Cambodia, probably even months before that given the emotional minefield that had been my previous relationship.

The woman twirled around like a dancer to speak to someone beside her and tugged her T-shirt down. As she crouched to listen to the response, it was clear that she was totally unaware of the way her magnetism seemed to redirect the flow of the crowd around her. I drifted toward her in concert with the rest, not realizing that I too had been caught up in her current until someone crashed into my chest.

After disentangling myself from a blushing and apologetic production assistant, I whipped around in search of the enigmatic woman, but she had disappeared back into the crowd. I shrugged, wiped the sweat off my brow and turned back to my seemingly endless quest to find the elusive conductor of this chaos. Maybe the woman had been a mirage, a strange, anomalous, attractive mirage. *And maybe I'm losing it completely.*

"Where the fuck is Michael?" I muttered in frustration.

"Ah, over there...talking to his M-U-S-E," a man's amused voice replied from behind me. "What the hell happened to you, Shellenberg? You look like complete shit."

I whirled around and pasted on a vague smile as I stared at a semi-familiar face — Rory Something-or-other.

"Hey, man. Sorry, Rory, yes? How's it going? Didn't know you'd be here too."

"Yeah, it's a pretty good gig, been around since the first season. Came for the role, stayed for the eye candy." He raised his eyebrows at me.

Ah, yes, now I remembered. Rory Sullivan was what my grandmother politely called "a ladies' man" around Hollywood. Not that Rory really gave a shit. He was completely open with how he lived his life. The freedom to live so authentically was alien to me after the last five years I'd spent playing the role of Kate's dutiful boyfriend. I knew how people saw me, how they'd seen us as a couple, but it had all been a pack of lies in the end. For one moment, I wished I could live as freely as this guy, or even my younger brother Matti, whose ability to give a shit about anyone else was practically nil.

I tossed Rory a noncommittal salute over my shoulder as I started to move past him in the direction he'd pointed. He jogged a few steps to keep up and stopped me again with a hand to my arm. "Dude, you're not looking so hot. Is everything okay with you? I don't know if you remember, but we worked together on a film a few years ago when I was starting out. You were super chill with all of us noobs and I've never forgotten it."

For a second I was touched that he remembered, but then I realized that it meant he felt entitled to share with me. Like he knew me and could ask intrusive questions without fear of reprisal. Not that he was rude, but... I was rusty at human interaction outside of a terribly limited group of people, especially after the last three months. A classic 'it's not him, it's me.'

"I'm fine. Just a bit jet-lagged after a rough flight and shit three months filming in Cambodia with George Sellers." I scrubbed a hand through my chopped-off prison haircut beneath my hat and sighed. "Sorry, where did you say Michael is? And what is this 'muse' nonsense?" I asked. The muse thing was new for Michael, who had never been short on artistic vision, and I couldn't help making the air quotes with my fingers as I said the words.

"He's over there, by the tent. Talking to the tall chick with a headset and clipboard. That's his 'muse'." Rory rolled his eyes as he made the same air-quote gesture and I immediately visualized the gorgeous mystery woman from a moment before.

Not realizing he'd lost me, Rory continued yammering, "She's one of the assistant producers, but Michael cannot keep away from her. Says she's his inspiration for the entire season and refuses to make decisions without her. She does everything for him, probably wipes his ass."

"They hooking up?" I asked, still trying to see around the crowd to the tent.

"I don't think they are, but I wouldn't be surprised if he tried to get with her and she shot him down. I mean, she laughed and patted me on the head when I tried to shoot my shot," Rory said, not at all embarrassed.

I raised an eyebrow at him and asked, "She's that special?"

Before he could answer, the crowds parted and I finally saw Michael. I saw *her* as well, standing in front of him as he gestured and hopped around like an animated cartoon character. Again, everything dulled to a low buzz and faded away while she burned out in high relief.

"Oh-ho! Mr. Super Famous Serious Actor with the Serious Girlfriend sees something he likes!" Rory crowed.

I tried to deflect with a dirty look. "Don't be a dick, man. I need to talk to Michael. See you around." My fingers tingled with anticipation but my limbs were rigid as I moved robotically in their direction. I felt unprepared and vulnerable for what was to come—a job I needed to ensure future work and now this mystery woman who was yanking me toward her like a tractor beam. This was nerves, plain and simple, I realized belatedly. Something I hadn't dealt with in years.

I was almost to Michael when I heard Rory yell from behind me, "There's a pool going on who gets to bang her. Let me know if you want in!"

For a second I considered turning back and punching him in the face—like, how dare he take such a derogatory stance—but that wasn't going to do me any favors, and I needed this job. Besides, he sounded like he felt sorry for me more than anything.

As I made my way toward Michael, I noticed people pointing at me and whispering. I heard a woman say, "I thought he'd be bigger," and another respond,

"Yeah, I thought he'd be hotter. He looks like a homeless person."

I turned and gave the two a dirty look, but couldn't help flushing in embarrassment. This was why I hated my job sometimes, why I hated Hollywood. The fact that they'd gossip pretty much right in my face was a red flag, at least to me, about how things were going to go on set.

Michael turned as I approached him and his 'muse' and shrieked in my face. "Ah-ha! Shellenberg, you made it! You look like death. What happened to you?!"

I winced as he said, "Sorry, sorry, sorry. I forgot — Sellers, right?" At my nod, he went on more sympathetically. "Well, anyways, I'm glad you're here. Meet Alina." He gestured toward the woman who had pretty much stopped my heart a moment ago. "She's one of our producers, probably the single most important reason this season is going to be a success, and my muse!" The woman's eyes bugged out, like she was choking back a laugh so hard it had rebounded into the upper reaches of her skull as she extended her hand toward me to shake.

For that matter, I was struggling to keep my mouth from doing much more than twitching. It was almost adorable how proud of himself he seemed, like a true artist with his 'muse', and he continued to ramble about her amazing work ethic and other stellar qualities. But he was serious, and it was actually kind of…reassuring.

She was a serious person then, not someone he'd hired as a pretty distraction. And from the way he rambled on, it spoke volumes about her abilities and potential that she'd earned his trust. I'd known Michael for years and I'd never seen that level of reverence he'd directed at her with his introduction — and I'd officiated his last wedding to the love of his so-called life.

It also didn't hurt that she was so otherworldly gorgeous that an entire sublevel of my brain started to contemplate what it would feel like to have her ridiculously long legs wrapped around my waist while I drilled into her. I wrangled my focus back to the hand outstretched in front of me and wrapped my fingers around hers, squeezing carefully. I hoped she couldn't feel the tremor.

"Hello. Ah-lean-ah." I said her name carefully, rolling out the syllables. "Nice to meet you." I turned back to Michael, trying to block her face from my immediate view. "So, we need to discuss my role, yes?"

I knew I sounded curt and dismissive, but I couldn't help it. I needed to get out of there and away from her before the hot prickles of anxiety turned into something worse. Too many people in too short a time. Too much interaction compared to the last three monastic months after almost losing everything on Sellers' set.

Oh, and of course there was the fact that an unwanted chemical attraction had taken hold the minute I'd seen her. Some gut-level instinct warned me that this was one of those turning points in life, that she was a new star to orbit in my limited universe.

She stepped back, big green eyes widened in surprise at my abrupt dismissal, clearly broadcasting the whole, "I didn't think you'd be such a complete dickhead," feeling. Out of the corner of my eye, I watched her eyes narrow as she shook her head and exhaled hard to blow her bangs out of her face.

"No worries, I was on my way out. Michael, I'll drop off my edits later," she muttered and stomped off.

Michael looked at me curiously. "What was that about? You're not usually an asshole."

"I'm sorry, a bad reaction. Listen, I'm incredibly drained. I only wanted to check in in person, let you know I arrived and see if you might want to grab dinner or a drink later after I catch a nap. No problem, though. I'll see you tomorrow morning. Seven-thirty, right?"

"Yeah, seven-thirty. But let's get that drink—how about ten-thirty tonight? Hotel lobby?"

I nodded and strode off, briefly considering whether or not I should find Alina and apologize. I didn't know what I'd say, though. Maybe, 'Sorry for being my dysfunctional self, I need a quick nap and let's try this again later?' I should have realized that the unexpected compulsion to find her, to explain, apologize, was a sign—this woman was going to change everything.

# Chapter Three

*Alina*

Michael's ongoing outrageous behavior, along with Markus Shellenberg's brief initial appearance on set and professional brush-off, established the tone for the following day, which had to be one of my worst in the last two years. I rarely felt so professionally insignificant and couldn't for the life of me figure out why Markus' less than effusive greeting had affected me so deeply.

Even though we'd started at the ungodly hour of five o'clock in the morning, everything — at first — seemed like it was clicking smoothly. Craft services had brought in Krispy Kreme, which they never did because actors are processed-sugar- and carb-phobic. The set's resident caffeine connoisseur had made nuclear-grade coffee, and Michael was in a happy mood. The muse crap was working in my favor — for the second day in a row.

The bad began to outweigh the good only two hours after we started, when Michael asked what I thought about using a heavier hand with foreshadowing the demise of Sebastian, Markus Schellenberg's character. His character, although relatively minor, was a perfect foil for Ethan Thomas' slightly more significant character, Joseph, and their battle to the death would be the season-ending cliffhanger.

Markus was only doing a very brief arc on this one season, so I figured we should obviously foreshadow his character's death — partially for plotting purposes, but also for insurance and publicity. Since he was only doing this one season, we did not want to deal with Markus Shellenberg-itis from the press or fans of the show. He wasn't coming back, and we couldn't afford to alienate viewers by making his 'death' seem less than one hundred percent certain. My reasoning did not sit well with Michael.

"Alina, you've got to be kidding!" Michael shouted, loudly enough to be heard from five miles away. "That's the stupidest reason possible. You have no concept of art, of plot pacing, of…of…of the beauty of death and surprise. How could you even think that would be an option? Christ, this shoot is a mess."

The set went completely silent. Shocked looks ricocheted around the groups of people standing by, waiting for direction. Michael may have been an asshole to most people, but he rarely targeted me this publicly, or with such a violent response. This was not normal.

I yanked him off to the side and snapped, "Michael. You asked what I thought. I told you. Not sure what your actual problem is, but you better figure it out."

He nodded stiffly, but his eyes still glittered with repressed rage. "Fine, yes, you're right. I'm sorry I snapped. It's not you, it's the network suits—fuckers. Markus being here isn't enough to satisfy them. They want more or the show is done." He scrubbed a hand over his face and wiped off the sweat before cupping a hand around his mouth like a bullhorn to yell, "Break, everyone. We'll pick it back up in ten."

On my way out, I dumped my headset and mic pack by the monitor station without acknowledging the sympathetic and curious looks from my colleagues and headed over a small rise behind the tents that shimmered through the early morning haze. I slumped down on a bench beneath a tree and finally allowed myself two minutes of deep breathing exercises. I even set a timer.

By the time I'd pulled myself together, it was a little after seven-fifteen in the morning, Markus was due on set for his first day of shooting and I needed to triple-check that his last-minute espresso machine request was in his trailer. I also needed to publicly make nice with Michael and shut down the inevitable gossip about his meltdown. We couldn't let the threat of cancellation get out or we'd lose everyone. I also didn't need people speculating about our nonexistent personal relationship again. I heaved myself to my feet with all the grace of an eighty-year-old elephant and started plodding back to the set. The low buzz of a hundred voices issuing and taking orders sucked me right back in.

"Where is he?" I spat out as I grabbed the first production assistant to cross my path.

"Who?" she asked while batting her eyelashes at me, trying not to laugh.

"You know who. Don't give me that shit and I won't tell Rory that you stole a pair of his underwear from Wardrobe to auction on eBay."

"Jesus, Alina. He's right over there. Waiting for his guest of honor by the monitor bank," she said, her voice truly annoying in its singsong pitchiness.

"Thanks." I dropped her arm and reluctantly turned toward Michael.

I was within a few feet when I noticed a fuss over by the entrance — hopefully a fire that could wait to be put out. Ignoring it for the moment, I got right in Michael's face. He looked at me with sad puppy-dog eyes, pulled a theatrical frowny face and slung his arm around me. I sighed, resting my head on his shoulder, and we chorused, "I'm sorry." I was pretty sure he meant it. I didn't.

When Michael stepped away to confer with some of the lighting crew, I turned back to see what had caused all the excitement earlier. The set continued to buzz like a disturbed beehive as the swirls of crew and talent split and coalesced in new directions. It was like the center of gravity had shifted and realigned in a split second. I wasn't sure what had happened until I saw a very tall, very thin blond man with a baseball hat gliding through the crowds. Markus Shellenberg, again, in the flesh. The fine hairs on my arms rose as if a lightning strike were imminent. I could practically smell the ozone in the air.

He was still far enough away that the features beneath the brim of his hat were shadowed and indistinguishable, but his visual impact was undeniable. Even if he looked less than his best, he was still Markus. Fucking. Shellenberg. I saw one woman stumble, a man drop a boom mic and two of the younger assistants smash into each other. The coffees they were ferrying to their various overlords flew into the air and rained back down in a steaming brown shower that suddenly struck me as an apt metaphor for my shitty, shitty day.

I worked my jaw back and forth as it tightened with the beginnings of a tension headache. Everything on set felt like it was changing with his arrival—from Michael's stress levels to the way everyone was ready to drop anything for this guy. And I was one of them, which annoyed me even more. Christ, I was crabby, but I wanted to yell at the sheep, 'Yes, he's pretty. But he's a rude fuckface and doesn't deserve your adoration.'

Everything I'd heard about him seemed to have been way off-base—he wasn't kind or respectful. More like impolite and disinterested. Those were the words I would have used to describe him going off the previous day's meeting.

He was different from how he appeared in photos and interviews, too. As he navigated the crowded set, his hands were stuffed into his pockets and his shoulders shrugged up to his ears while he looked around furtively. His bone structure was sharp enough to cut glass, and there was a grayish cast to his already pale skin. While he seemed to have lost a surprising amount of weight since the last time I'd seen him in a photo or video, his shoulders were still broad and his frame hinted at the body the world had last seen in all of its cut, full-frontal glory about a year ago in *Untimely Justice*.

It was a real pisser that—despite his unexpected rudeness and the changes to his appearance from his last role—he was still one of the Beautiful People. Maybe he wouldn't have won "Hottest Man in the World" this year, but he still would have been in the top ten with his unique swagger and distinctive features. His deep-set navy-blue eyes, albeit currently ringed in red, coupled with cheekbones and a jawline that Renaissance sculptors would have killed to depict, marked him as someone to watch. The jagged edges of dirty-blond hair that peeked out from under his baseball cap did nothing to disguise him.

It was wild how he drew the eye of everyone and managed to keep their attention focused on him. He had that level of charisma that all of the popular kids seemed to have growing up. No one could ever put a finger on what about them was special, but everyone knew they would probably walk off a cliff if one of the cool kids suggested it. Pure magnetism.

As I looked down at the clipboard in my hand and fidgeted with the paper, his gaze skated over my face with a tangible gravity then dismissed me to focus on Michael. Stuck in some sort of fugue state, I was vaguely aware of their bro-y greeting.

"Well, anyways, I'm glad you found your way back. You remember Alina from yesterday, right?" He waved his hand at me like a magician about to pull a rabbit from his hat.

I thrust my hand in his direction and mumbled somewhat resentfully, "Hey, nice to see you again."

Markus hesitated before taking my hand and shaking gingerly. I registered the same slight electric charge I'd felt in his hand the day before. His touch lit my entire body on fire from the inside, and the muggy Savannah air was almost a relief from the sudden hot flash. Fucking Beautiful People.

"Likewise." His voice was rusty, as if he had woken up two minutes ago, but there was some sort of amusement in it.

*Probably because I'm still shaking his hand.* I quickly dropped it and started fiddling with my headset. "Uh, yeah. Hope everything is to your liking in your trailer. Let me know if you need anything on set and I'll take care of it." I managed a professional nod and glanced at Michael. "I've got to run. Text me if you need anything."

I made it around the corner of the craft services tent, walking fast and breathing like I'd run a mile in the heat. A blush climbed its way from my chest to my face. I was on a permanent hiatus from men — almost two years of unintentional but self-imposed celibacy — and my career was all that mattered. Markus Shellenberg was an entitled douchebag actor who hadn't even bothered to apologize for his rudeness. Still, I was ninety-nine percent sure that even a corpse would have reacted to him.

* * * *

The caterwauling wail of an antique air horn cut off abruptly as I slid into a temporary shed behind the Wardrobe trailer and gingerly shut the door. My breathing evened out slowly as I leaned against the sun-warmed wall.

"Alina, right?"

Hearing his quiet, lightly accented voice from the shadows of the shed made me jump. Between the low light and seemingly random groupings of rolling wardrobe racks, I hadn't even noticed the other person in the room with me. And I should have, because Markus Shellenberg's presence was so big it seemed to suck up all the available air in the tight space.

"What was that siren for? Did I hear the announcement correctly? A *lockdown*?"

The low, precise voice had barely said anything, but it was doing a number on my stomach, making it flip over as I contemplated the very simple question that I was unable to answer immediately.

"Look, I'm sorry if I'm bothering you, but I don't really get what's going on. What are we locking down for? Not that that makes sense grammatically, but, hey! Anyone home in there?"

He was still there. Still talking. Waving his hand at me, trying to get my attention and staring at me like I might be broken. Crickets were chirping.

"God, no, I'm sorry. I was completely spaced. You didn't hear incorrectly—there's a lockdown. One of Michael's efforts at generating 'spontaneous creative energy', which I think he's confused with fear. For the most part we pretend to be scared—maybe this will be the time that the big bad wolf, or tornado or something will be out to get us when the alarm goes off. Not that you'll need to try hard to play along. I hear you're a pretty good actor."

I was talking too fast, the words tumbling over one another, completely out of control, like one of those log flume rides where people go flying, flail into a massive splash then get jerked to an abrupt halt.

"Ugh, sorry. It's your first day on set and I'm being a sarcastic asshole. You're a great actor, even if you were kind of a dick the other day."

For a second I wondered if the explosive verbal diarrhea he inspired could have a clinical name. Maybe the Shellenberg Effect. The punch this guy could pull with his mere presence was enough to make a nun reconsider her vows.

His smile was faint, the dimple barely popping in his left cheek, but it was there. I swear.

"It's fine. I see why Michael likes you so much. You don't hold back, do you? And you're right. I *was* a bit of an asshole and I'm terribly sorry. I was going to try to find you to apologize but you seemed to have disappeared when I was done talking to Michael."

I nodded, only slightly mollified.

He frowned for a second, like he had more to say on the apology front, but then he gestured for me to join him on the floor behind a rack of musty wardrobe changes. "Come on, sit with me. Unless we're supposed to be somewhere specifically?"

"No, we're good here. Everyone knows the drill. No one's going to come looking for us. Not that that doesn't sound like something a serial killer would say." I shook my head and tried to calm my nerves. "Anyways..." I dusted off a patch of floor near him and plopped down, tucking my knees up against my chest so I would have a place to rest my chin for however long Michael's theatrics would take. "Why are you hiding out in here? We're a little off the beaten path."

"I don't know, to be honest," he murmured. "I was wandering around, listening to an audiobook, when the announcement and siren started blaring. This was the first open door I found. How long is this going to take?"

I waved my hand like a seesaw. "Eh, depends on Michael's mood. We had one that was an hour and a half early on, but the last one was only seven minutes."

He chuckled quietly. "Sounds like Michael. What a drama queen."

I laughed, and we sat in a strangely comfortable silence for a few minutes.

"So, since we're stuck for the moment... I've worked with Michael before and never met you. He usually keeps a consistent crew from project to project. Where'd you come from? And what is this muse thing everyone is talking about?"

Maybe I wasn't the only one with the verbal diarrhea challenge.

"Oh, that. Everyone is talking about it?" I groaned as he nodded.

I sighed and looked to the ceiling for help. The dim light in the shed, the occasional dust motes winking out in stray beams of sunlight through the cracks in the slats and the grandmotherly scent of musty polyester lulled me into a confessional mood. That, combined with his deep, lightly accented voice, sent me back to sixth grade, when I had my only experience with Catholic confession — and that priest had been ancient, with wiry ear and nose hair, not an insanely hot, international sex symbol.

Which was really my only excuse for spilling my guts, and I was mildly horrified as the words kept coming out. We started with the death of my parents back when I was in college all the way up to my filmmaking dreams. A nice little pitstop to discuss my cheating ex back in Chicago, who'd hooked up with my now estranged sister, a brief soliloquy about some recent unwanted attention from asshole actors and a final drabble regarding the loneliness of starting over in one's late twenties. Every boring beat of my workaholic life through the last eight years.

To his credit, he only listened, nodding occasionally, seemingly stunned by my endless spewing of words. I swear I tried to hold back, but there was something that was so elementally compelling about him, how he cocked his head at me as if assessing my words and worth. The fact that he hadn't already won an Oscar was clearly a total travesty.

"You know, it is good that we're getting to know each other. I'm terrible at meeting people on sets and it's nice to talk to someone normal. A little ridiculous that a fake lockdown was the reason, no? Maybe we need to try this again sometime in a slightly more traditional setting," he said with another faint smile.

I looked at him blankly, not sure if he was hitting on me or if I was dreaming that the most handsome man in the world was planning on spending time with me in the future.

"You know, because I need more friends? Seeing as how I'm a 'rude dickhead', right?" He snorted when I remained quiet.

His deadpan sarcasm failed to register. He was a cipher, hard to read in the best times, impossible here in the dim light. I changed the subject. "Anyways, yeah, enough about me, tell me about you. You're not what I expected. I mean, I'm not sure what I was expecting, but you don't seem okay. Is everything all right?"

"All right is a relative term. But no. No, I'm not really okay." He disdainfully sounded out the individual letters in the word and made a face.

"I just finished that Sellers movie—you heard Michael yesterday?" he asked and waited for my nod. "So it was a movie about a French journalist who was shot down over North Vietnam during the height of the Conflict. He was held hostage as an accused spy for many years with no one able to get him out. Everyone in his life forgot about him. I was the journalist, and Sellers pretty much kept me in a hole in the ground for the last three months."

Markus shuddered as he related the experience. "It was terrible. I barely saw sunlight, ate only what prisoners would have eaten during that time period and was stuck in filthy rags. There was too much time for introspection with only me and a camera that tracked every movement. It probably didn't help things that my girlfriend broke up with me halfway through.

Sometimes I feel like I'm still down in the hole and this is a dream."

"Oh my god, how are you comfortable in here?" I interrupted him. "Maybe we should leave."

"No, it's fine. I'm fine here." He waved me off. "This is cozy compared to where Sellers stuck me. Positively plush." He shook his head. "I apologize. My head is not in a good place right now and I can't seem to stop talking. Maybe I should go see if this lockdown is done yet—there's no need for you to hear the rest of my sob story."

"No, no. You can stay, I'll go check. But wait—Kate—I mean, your girlfriend, she broke up with you? I hadn't heard. How does no one know about that? Fuck, man. That's seriously rough."

"Yeah," he admitted ruefully. "And I didn't handle it well at all. Five years of my life, gone." He inhaled aggressively, like he was trying to hold back a strongly worded statement about the situation. "Perhaps we can change the subject now, though. Something slightly less personal. How do you feel about yellow mustard versus Dijon? I think it's gross, personally."

I gagged and laughed at the same time. "You had to pick mustard? Blergh."

His rusty laugh twined around my own much more breathy one. Maybe it was the darkness and the closeness of the rolling racks, but everything about that moment seemed out of time. The level of vulnerability and openness he shared with me was surprising considering his earlier rude standoffishness.

"Sorry, didn't realize mustard required a trigger warning," he said once his laughter had died down to the occasional hiccup-y giggle. "Since we're stuck here, do you want to run some lines with me? I know I'm only in a few episodes, but we're supposed to be shooting all of my scenes in one big chunk and I've barely looked at the script."

"Sure?" I couldn't help my response coming as more of a question than an affirmative answer. Hardly anyone on set asked me to run lines with them. In fact, the divide between cast and crew here was especially strong. I'd worked on one indie film previously and it had been a much different story—I'd run lines with more than a few of the actors on that project.

"Great, thank you." He rolled onto one hip and pulled a flattened tube of papers out of his back pocket. "Here," he said and thrust it at me. "I think I've memorized most of today's scenes, but let's start on page eighteen."

I flipped the pages slowly and noted all of the annotations he'd made, most of them in German. I had no idea what they meant, but there sure were a lot of exclamation points and question marks. "Okay, you ready?" I glanced at him and he nodded expectantly.

"Sebastian, we need you to take on this task. You are the only one who can convince them to join us," I read slowly and clearly. I didn't bother trying to emote. I was merely a backboard for him to shoot off of.

"Vivian, I can only try. You know it's not going to be that easy. They may—" He paused, as if frantically racking his memory.

"Try something," I inserted.

"Yes. Try something," he muttered, then started speaking again in the deeper, in-charge voice of his character. "We need to be ready for anything."

We went on like that for a few more scenes and he only got tied up one or two other times. I couldn't help but think that if this was an unprepared Markus Shellenberg, a prepared one would be a director's wet dream.

"Okay, that's good enough. Those are the scenes we're doing today and I think I'm ready. Would you have time to do this again sometime? Maybe not today or anything, I'm sure you're busy. But some day?" he asked a little tentatively.

I grinned at him in the half-light. "Not bad, huh. Sure, I'd love to. This was fun." He was so talented, even sitting on his butt in a dark dusty space, that I'd started to fall under his spell. Suddenly, the script seemed less silly to me and much more real. I stood and brushed myself off.

"Great, I'm going to hold you to that," he said with a smile. "Let's go check to see if we're free to get back to work."

"Cool—you're supposed to be over at the big house today, do you know where that is?" I asked as I scrambled through my set schedule.

"Yeah, I've got it. Thanks, Alina. See you around?"

"Definitely," I said and laughed. I had a date—well, not really a *date*—with Markus Shellenberg to run lines. Not that I was starstruck at all.

He walked out and I waited a beat to leave a few steps behind him. That ass was a lovely view on an even lovelier day.

# Chapter Four

*Alina*

"Nooo, no, this isn't happening," I whispered as I attempted to wipe my bangs back with a sweaty forearm. "I am *not* stuck on a tiny overhang without a way down, please, no."

I frantically re-scanned my surroundings — a thin ledge on the rock wall I was climbing, well over ten feet from the bounds of my crash mat. I closed my eyes for a moment and opened them to look briefly down. Nothing had changed, despite my desperate wish otherwise. I blew out a pissed-off breath and my sweat-darkened bangs floated up only to decisively flop back into my eyes.

The faint sound of bees buzzing around the sweetly scented yellow flowers that clung tenaciously to the little divots in the cliff mocked me with the insects' ability to fly, fly away. A knight in shining armor — even semi-tarnished armor — would have come in handy right about then.

"Go climb the little bluff from the guidebook, enjoy the peaceful meditative properties of nature in splendid isolation, work off those extra helpings of mac and cheese. You're an expert boulderer, never fear. All will be well." I snorted at my earlier optimism about this little jaunt.

I shifted my weight tentatively and froze as the shale beneath my feet crackled. The dry smell of the flaking shards rising up around me threatened to make me sneeze. I held my breath, trying to trap it in so I didn't blow myself straight off the ledge, and started plotting a return route toward my crash pad.

A massive crash near the base of the cliff accompanied by furious swearing in a foreign language broke me from my careful planning and I nearly toppled off the wall altogether. Whoever it was, he was big and clearly male, plus within hearing range of me — a nice bonus. The swearing continued and the underbrush shook as he kept moving in my direction. Within moments a very confused and scratched-up face appeared through a bramble, followed by two arms, then the trunk of a man who'd been running without a shirt. A very attractive man whom I immediately recognized from our interactions on set. *Not that I stare at him or could spot him a mile away or anything.*

Wireless earbuds were stuck in Markus' ears, and he clearly couldn't hear anything but his music. As he pulled himself free, his left leg seemed to catch in the twisty roots of the shrubbery and he fell, barely saving himself from landing in a heap of twisted ankles and broken kneecaps. He got both feet on the ground and stood there for a second, still shaking his head angrily and muttering to himself.

I continued to watch in amusement as he did a massive double-take when he finally noticed my pack and gear pile. He swung around wildly before connecting his proximity to a cliff to the backpack, climbing gear and crash pad and slowly looked up and met my eyes. I waved uncertainly. He stood there with his hands on his hips, smiling at me like he had a secret. I hoped it was the secret to the way down.

Markus popped an earbud out, wiped his sweaty face on his arm and yelled up at me, "Fancy meeting you here. Any thoughts on where the trail is?"

I grinned and shouted, "I'll get you back there if you wouldn't mind shoving that pad over here so I can jump."

"Maybe I'll leave it where it is and take a nap in the shade," he teased. "Looks quite comfy, and running in this humidity was not my smartest decision."

Ah yes, the man was glistening. He might have lost muscle tone since his scary hot part in *Untimely Justice*, but the warm flush on my skin could no longer be chalked up to the humid Georgia morning.

I cleared my throat. "Yeah, you could do that, but then my broken limbs would be on your conscience when I finally get up the courage to jump so I won't be too late getting back to the set."

"Hm. When you put it like that, I guess I can help." He grabbed the foam mat then dragged it over to lie beneath my ledge. "Do you need me to hold this? How'd you even get up there, anyways? There's, like, nothing to hold on to."

I twisted around to double-check the placement and grunted. "Tiny little toe and fingerholds. Now, get out of the way, coming down!"

He applauded my not-so-graceful landing-slash-collapse onto the sun-warmed mat, then leaped on top to lie next to me, propping his face up on his fist. The sweaty smell wafting off him was almost reassuring — thank god the Beautiful People still stank like the rest of us after a run on a Georgia summer's day. He grinned at my obvious disgust and tapped my nose with one sweaty finger. "That was badass. I can't believe you jumped off a cliff." I reached out and flicked him, hard, in the forehead. Or it would have been hard, but he was so damp that my finger slid off ineffectually.

My ears grew hot as my embarrassment over that familiar gesture got the best of me. "Uh, thanks? But it was amateur hour getting stuck up there in the first place. I don't know what I would have done if you hadn't come along."

He smiled and fluttered his eyelashes at me. "I love playing the hero."

I rolled my eyes at him and retreated to sarcasm to quell the flirtatious flush that rose up in response. "Well, bless your heart. And I so appreciate it, whatever shall I do to repay you?" I elbowed him in the side and he huffed out a gasp in surprise. "Now, do you want company on the way back? I've got to get back to the set."

"Yes! I was on a trail, I swear, but it disappeared. I've never been good at directions and have no idea where I am."

I laughed. "Well, you're not too far off. Let me grab my bag and gear. We can walk back together. How'd you get out here anyways?"

"Oh, I hired a driver," he said as he stood up and grabbed an ankle in a quad stretch. He switched legs and extended a hand to pull me up.

My jaw dropped and I barely escaped inhaling a slow-moving fly. "You took a one-way trip to a state park? To go running? How were you planning on getting back to the hotel and set? There's super minimal cell service out here."

He looked sheepish and toed a shoe in the dirt before nodding at me. "Yeah, didn't really think that one out. Figured I could call someone when I was done and I needed to start working out again. My brain feels better when I'm physically active—like I'm in control."

"Totally get that, it's why I'm out here too. That and I really enjoy cornbread and mac and cheese." I sighed mournfully. "Anyways, let's go find my car. I can be your driver for the afternoon."

"Now who's the hero?"

We shared a small smile and he helped me fold my mat then tied it to my backpack as I traded out my climbing shoes for trail runners.

"Want to race? I'll give you a head start since you only vaguely know your way back."

"Uh, no. Some of us—i.e., you, Ms. Sporty—may have an infallible sense of direction and be extraordinarily in shape, but others of us—i.e., me—smoke too much and haven't run in months. So, no. We're walking. Together. Now hand me your pack. It's the least I can do."

He easily swung my bag over his broad shoulders and I gazed, transfixed, at my climbing shoes swinging back and forth like a metronome as he started to walk back to where he seemed to think the path lay.

I hurried to catch up. "Ah, my knight in semi-tarnished armor."

He turned to wait for me and shot me a massive shit-eating grin. "Friends, then? After everything I told you during lockdown and now this rescue, I feel like we need to formalize this arrangement or you'll abandon me when it's convenient for you." He kept a mostly straight face as he held up a pinkie finger.

I laughed and wound my own pinkie finger around his. "Best friends. And that means that you'll forget all about me getting stuck on a ledge. Got it?"

"No promises, friend."

We made it back to the car without issue and immediately started bickering about music choices. He was an Eighties synth-pop fan and I felt equally strongly that Americana was the answer, given our *Deliverance*-level nature experience. We finally compromised on Taylor Swift, as one does.

As we drove, I couldn't help but notice that he was sneaking little looks at me as he leaned against the open window, his damp blond hair lightly fluttering in the breeze. His fingers tapped a silent rhythm on the 'oh shit' handle above his head. Maybe the chemistry wasn't so one-sided, then, or maybe he was relieved to have found a friend — not exactly a common occurrence in adulthood, especially on a Hollywood set. I couldn't decide which option was more desirable and it was annoying to be this attracted to someone when work should have been my main focus.

"Do you want me to drop you at the hotel?" I asked as we wound closer to the set. "I've got a few extra minutes."

"Nah, that's okay. Can you take me to the set with you? I can shower there. The cleaning staff is usually in our rooms right now and I don't want to get in their way."

"Sure, but you're going to have to wait for me at the crew house before we head to the set. I don't have a fancy trailer with a shower and wardrobe."

"Or I can run from the crew house over to the set. That should work as well."

"Whatever is easiest — "

His phone rang and interrupted me. Markus glanced at the screen and swore. "I need to take this. My manager. Do you mind?"

He gestured for me to keep it down and I raised my eyebrows at his presumption, but nodded in response to the silent request.

"Markus, my man. How are things in Savannah?" crackled a booming voice through Markus' phone. Clearly his manager was one of those guys who could work a room on sheer volume and force. I'd have hated to sit next to him in a meeting.

Markus side-eyed me as I kept driving, face forward, pretending I couldn't hear. "Yeah, it's good, thanks, Will. Listen, I'm kind of in the middle of something here. Do you have anything in the works for me?"

"Well, here's the thing. The short answer is no. Kate's blow-out on Sellers' set and your slip-and-slide spiral down is getting around the studios and streaming services. I've talked to a few people and everyone thinks it's a risk to take you on right now." Will paused and I saw Markus wince out of the corner of my eye. He pinched his brows and blew out a deep breath.

"There's nothing you can do, then?" he practically whispered.

"Nah, man. Not at the moment, but you know how this industry is. It's cyclical. Before this you had a great reputation as a professional — could handle anything, not a pain in the fucking ass to work with, no diva shit. This is an aberration, right? It will pass. Let them forget and I'll keep my ear to the ground for you."

"Will, come on. I get it, but isn't there *something*? I need to have work in the pipeline, I can't sit around. A break is one thing, but..." He trailed off and started futzing with a loose thread on the hem of his shirt, tugging on it until a few inches of thread unraveled. We were stopped at a light and I watched as he compulsively started winding the loose thread around his thumb till his finger turned purple, then he let go and watched the blood flow return to normal.

"No, Markus. Look, do your job with Michael and do it well. You're tight with him, maybe he can work something for you. Would you want to stay on? I mean, it's not your usual type of role, but series work is solid and steady."

Markus glanced over at me again, clearly wishing that he were anywhere else but stuck in the car with a random person he'd only recently met, before saying, "I mean, sure. If he'd have me. It's a small part with potential to grow, but it would keep me busy. I need to stay focused. I can't spiral again."

Will chuckled. "You're damn right about that. We can't clean up another mess. Not that your mental health isn't super important and we don't care about you, buddy. Heh, heh. Speaking of, Claire's got a few therapists' numbers if you want them."

Markus flushed and I determinedly kept my eyes forward. "Tell Claire to stick to P.R. and let her know we're good to release the initial messaging about Kate and me. Good?"

"You've got it, boss, we're on it. Take it easy, man, and have fun in Georgia. Talk to Michael, feel him out on staying, then let me know what you want to do. At this point you're more in with him than me. All right?"

"Sure, Will. Got to go. Will let you know what I hear from Michael."

Will whistled cheerfully. "Later, gator. Don't get in any more trouble out there!"

Markus stabbed the red End Call button and turned to me. "I know you heard everything, so don't try to pretend you missed that. Will's got this voice that projects beyond anything I've ever heard. Can I trust you not to talk? Especially about the job?" His worried look made the shallow wrinkles in his forehead and the corners of his eyes deepen.

My stomach turned over at the lack of trust in his voice, but I kept my eyes on the road and my voice neutral. He didn't strike me as someone who wanted my pity. "Of course, Markus. I promise. Is there anything I can do? Talk to Michael?"

"No. It's fine. I'll be fine." Despite his reassurances, the tension in his forearms and the vulnerable look in his blue eyes told a different story.

"Okay, well, if you ever want to talk... I might not be a therapist, but I'm a decent listener."

"And now I know where to find you." He threw me a lost-boy smile as he scrubbed a hand through his hair. My heart beat unevenly as a tiny dimple in his left cheek winked at me.

We pulled up at the crew house and parked. I pointed to the back gate, where Candace was stepping out. "That's me, in case you need anything."

"Thanks, Alina. For the ride and everything. See you on set?"

"Of course, and thank you for the rescue. Later, best friend."

He flashed his famous smirk at me as he plugged his earbuds back in. I watched him jog away and fanned myself. There went a ton of baggage in a very pretty package.

"Ooh, Alina! What kind of sweaty sins would you like to confess to Mama Candace?"

My friend slipped past the gate and we silently watched him run away from the house in easy loping strides, ogling him from behind. One of those moments of pure female solidarity.

I sighed and nudged her. "Oh, shut up, you. He was out at the park where I was bouldering and we happened to run into each other. I gave him a ride back. Mama Candace needs to mind her own business."

She grinned. "Sure, that's all it was. Like, no 'oh look, we're alone amidst the beautiful bounty of mother nature, let's hook up in this field of flowers'?"

I laughed and nudged her again in the shoulder. "Why are you like this?"

She crossed her arms across her chest and stuck her tongue out at me. "Born like this—sexy, sassy and supernaturally good at makeup and hair." We giggled together at her alliteration. She glanced one more time at his receding figure, then back at me and winked. "Yeah, well. That's one sexy man."

I could only nod in agreement. "Too hot for his own good. See you on set."

She gave me a little finger waggle as she hopped onto her bike and disappeared in the same direction as Markus.

*Yep, a very pretty package that now knows where I live, and maybe he'll be all about a late-night visit sometime.*

I slapped myself upside the head.

*Remember taking that hiatus from sex? Must. Not. Forget. Hiatus.*

# Chapter Five

*Markus*

A few days after Alina's and my outdoor adventure, I woke up with a shout as I struggled out of the tight cocoon I'd made of my covers. My nightmares had been getting worse over the last few weeks, and now they haunted me for at least a few hours every morning.

The low-level anxiety that had been my constant companion since leaving Cambodia ratcheted up another notch and I quickly got into the shower, hoping the steam would wash away the sticky residue of the night. But the pinpricks of panic continued to push into my skin as the water heated.

I needed to talk to someone who had some perspective, who could help me figure out what was wrong with me. Was this creative exhaustion? The well being tapped out, so to speak? A late-manifesting anxiety disorder? Post-traumatic stress from the conditions on Sellers' set? The problem was, I didn't really have anyone I could ask those questions, and that realization slammed into me like a ton of bricks. I slid down to my knees on the cold tile and rested my head against the wall as I watched the water droplets roll down the shower door. Maybe I should have taken up Will's suggestion to let my P.R. agent locate a few therapists.

Over the past few years, my life had narrowed to work and Kate. It'd happened so slowly that I hadn't even noticed. My ties had been cut as Kate reassured me that most people only wanted me around for what I could do for them. I'd never been very social or outgoing, but this was a new level of isolation. I vowed to make a better effort at connecting. That morning, it felt especially critical.

The first person I saw on set when I arrived late was Rory—not my top choice for an empathetic ear, but I had to try. I'd promised myself I'd be better about making connections with people on this set, and if I wanted to make a case for myself as a regular, I needed to fit in with the rest of the cast.

"Bro, you need to get your ass to Wardrobe before Michael loses his shit. Wait. You look sick. Do you need to go back and rest or something?"

"No, I'm not sleeping well and feel really off. That last role is sticking with me—break-up probably doesn't help either. You know?"

"Whoa, dude. I'm sorry. That's seriously rough. I've always been able to shake off roles, so I can't help there." He said it so blithely that I bit back a comment about how he would never have that problem, given the shallow roles he always took. "But woman problems are more up my alley. What happened with Kate? How did I not know you broke up?"

"I don't know, things got complicated. She wanted more from me and I couldn't figure out what. Then she started acting strangely, showing up unannounced on my sets to pick fights in front of everyone, telling them that I was a prude who couldn't satisfy her, demanding to find out who I was sleeping with, that I'd talked shit about whatever project I was working on. It was terrible."

"That's messed up. I didn't know any of that."

"Yeah, my lawyers don't fuck around and we've managed to keep it out of the gossip cycle for now, but we're about to announce that we're no longer together and it's going to get messy. But whatever, you're right, I'm late. Maybe we could grab a beer or something tonight?"

"Shit, yeah. Sorry again. Let me check with a few people, maybe we can get a group together." He wandered off toward the catering setup, sniffing the air like a bloodhound.

*Progress, definitely progress. I can do this, make connections, establish myself. I've got this.* I whipped open the door to Wardrobe, almost colliding with Alina, who slipped out with a mumbled thanks, face buried in her clipboard.

"Hey!" I said as she quickly slid around me.

"Oh, sorry. I didn't see you. Everything all right? Good, I'll see you around—Michael's got me searching for a lost mic pack and I've got to run." She rushed off without waiting for my response.

The rest of the day went about as well as that encounter. It was frustrating, like I was stuck behind a glass wall. I could hear and see everything happening, but I was completely separate from it all. Rory was cool, but Michael was spinning out of control and running

Alina into the ground. Every time I saw her, her sunburn had gotten redder and her shoulders more hunched as she raced around on Michael's behalf.

By the time I was done for the day, it was ten o'clock and my skin felt like it was about to crawl off my body. Rory had cancelled on our drink. He had a hot date, apparently. I was wearing a trail in the carpet in my suite with my pacing, considering whether or not a haircut would be a good idea — *some* sort of change seemed necessary — when my phone chimed with an incoming text. From Kate, of all people. I didn't want to look, but it was followed by a second ding that had me swiping open my messages before I could stop myself.

*Hey handsome, how's my leading man?*
*I hear you're busy down there, playing nice with the production bitches. Trying to make me jealous?*

"What the actual fuck?" My internal monologue went audible in surprise. I didn't want to respond, didn't even know what to say. We were over, done. She'd driven the nail into the coffin. My phone chimed a third time.

*MARKUS, wtf is your deal? You know Vanessa and I are friends, I can't even believe you'd do this to me.*

For a second, I didn't even know who she was talking about, but then I remembered Vanessa, a completely incompetent actress, and her on-off husband, Terrance. Both had small parts on the show, but I hadn't been in a scene with either of them yet. A fourth ding.

*I mean, I know we're fighting, but this is just a bump in the road. Sow your wild oats, I guess, we'll talk more when you're home. Love you!*

I threw my phone so hard onto the bed it bounced twice. No way was I responding. I couldn't get involved with her mind games. But I also couldn't stop thinking, remembering, how good we'd once been. What we'd become, though, was a different story. I tried to pull my racing thoughts away from the Kate whirlpool that was only going to drag me down, and flipped on the TV. I rapidly scanned through channels, searching frantically for something to distract me. *Oh!* British Bake-Off! *Perfect, I haven't seen —*

*Ping!* A fifth message from Kate, but this time a video clip with no message attached. My index finger shook slightly as I tapped the play button and was immediately treated to the sight of her going down on someone with a very thick, slightly crooked dick. She waved cheerfully at the camera and mouthed, "Hi, baby," before licking him from balls to tip.

I threw on my running gear, forced my phone into an armband, paired my headphones and ran out of the room. My feet pounded the pavement as I tore off, unseeing.

\* \* \* \*

When I came back to awareness, I was dripping with sweat and bent over outside the crew house where I'd left Alina after our previous disastrous run-in with Mother Nature. My phone indicated that I'd left the hotel over an hour earlier and I had no idea where I'd been or what I'd done since then. My music was playing and I was standing there, shaking, when a hand tentatively gripped my shoulder.

"Markus? What are you doing here? Did you hurt yourself?"

I looked up into Alina's concerned face and silenced the music. "I don't know." I swiped my cheek, realizing there were tears mixed in with the sweat. "No, that's not right. I didn't hurt myself, but I can't get a handle on what's happening to me."

My breath was a series of uneven, jagged gasps. The soupy Georgia air felt like it was suffocating me, but I couldn't stop talking and the words poured out in uneven patterns that only barely made sense. "Kate's been texting me weird stuff, acting like we're still together, and, an hour ago, a fucking video clip of her giving some guy a blow job. Why is she doing this?"

I dropped to a crouch with one hand on the dusty driveway, propping me up. Little puffs of clay dust started to turn to mud as they mixed with the sweat and tears on the backs of my fingers. "I can't go through this again with her. I can't. I need this job and I can't let her wreck this for me too. Did you know she knows Vanessa? They've been talking and I fucking hate this."

Alina gently squeezed my shoulder and knelt in the dirt next to me. She brought her hand down to rest on top of mine and intertwined her fingers with my own. It was so gentle, like she thought I might break if she pressed too hard. The tears and panic started to ebb as she pulled me up to stand, wrapped her other arm around my waist and tucked herself into my side. The comforting warmth of her body slowly brought my heart rate back down.

"Come on, let's get out of the yard. We can talk more inside if you feel like it, and if you don't, you can sit on the couch and be all sweaty and broody."

The last was said with a gentle smile as she reached up and cupped her hand around my chin. She tightened her grip and tugged me around to face her. "Stop running and come in. Candace is out on a date with Rory and Ethan. Talk to me."

I let her lead me in, suddenly noticing that she was wearing sleep shorts and a tank top. Her hair was haphazardly tied in a knot with a pencil through it, face glowing like she'd only recently finished some sort of skin care routine. She'd probably been getting ready for bed, and everything about her felt safe and calming, like a balm to my anxiety.

"Oh. So that's why Rory skipped out on a drink with me. Huh. If I could indulge in the distraction—what is going on with those three?"

She shrugged. "If you're asking romantically, I think they're casually dating each other. Sexually, yeah, they're together most nights. It works for them." Without asking, she handed me a steaming mug of tea and gestured for me to drink up. "Here, for you, I'll make another for myself. It's chamomile."

I looked down at the tea. Little drops of honey that hadn't been fully stirred in bobbed on top. "That's one reason why Kate broke up with me. She said that I'm too boring for her in bed and that I'm emotionally closed off. I don't really think I am, though. I've been with men and women in the past. In groups, one-on-one. I prefer being with one other person, regardless of gender." I glanced at her and asked, "Do you think it's boring?"

Alina looked stunned at my abrupt disclosure. "Uh. Hm. Honestly? No. But I've never tried the group sex or open relationship thing. I mean, it's definitely intriguing, but I have a hard enough time turning off my brain with one person. I can't imagine how bad it would be with more."

She started ticking off her worries on one hand. "Like, have I kissed Person Two enough? Maybe they're feeling left out. Or shit, does Person One like nipple twists, or was that Person Three? I'd be the most annoying person in a three- or moresome. Everyone would hate me, and then I'd need to move to a deserted island. And don't even get me started on how crappy it would feel to miss both of my boyfriends' birthdays."

"How do you think so much during sex?" I asked, genuinely curious. "That makes no sense to me. It's not even possible."

"Oh, it's possible, all right. Usually I think myself straight out of an orgasm." She slapped her hand across her mouth, horrified. "I shouldn't have shared that."

I laughed, and the residual tension rolled away. "Oh, I don't mind. Apologies that you've never had good sex though. That's truly a tragedy."

"Screw. You." She threw a couch cushion at me and laughed. "You don't know me." Humor looked good on her—cheeks flushed, a little embarrassed, but not taking herself seriously.

"I'm so sorry for intruding tonight. I don't think I said that yet. You look like you're ready for bed and I feel like I barged in. I've never had a panic attack that severe. I thought running would help. It usually does." I tried, unsuccessfully, to explain my sweaty presence outside her house as I twisted the now empty mug in my hands.

"It's okay. I really don't mind hanging out with you. Do you want to talk about what happened with Kate?" Her brow furrowed in concern, she reached out, plucked the empty mug from my hand and set it on the table.

"It's easier to show you," I said, and handed her my phone with Kate's messages pulled up.

"Oh my god!" she whispered. "I almost didn't believe it when you told me outside. I seriously think you should report this, file for a restraining order. Maybe re-think your manager's recommendations on therapists." She reached out again to touch my arm, this time grabbing my hand tightly in commiseration.

"Look," she said, "you don't need to stay in Savannah. Tell Michael that there's an emergency at home that you need to deal with — you guys are friends, tell him the truth, this *is* a bit of an emergency. The remainder of your scenes can be shot on a stage. I'm on a direct flight to LAX tomorrow morning and heading to the airport at six. You can hitch a ride if you want."

I started to protest, but she cut me off with a wave of her hand. "Seriously, if *you* say you need to get home, I guarantee he'll bring everyone back to shoot the rest on a stage. A few camera guys can stay here and collect b-roll if needed."

I nodded along, feeling the pressure to be decisive. "Fine, let me call the airline and see if I can get on that flight. Then I'll text Michael. Would you be able to take me back to the hotel after, or should I call someone?"

"I can take you back. It might take a while to get a car here given the time. I'm mostly packed, was going to zone out with a movie and then head to bed."

Alina wandered off while I made the call to the airline and booked the flight. I was about to hang up when I caught a glimpse of her dancing around the kitchen, loading our mugs into the dishwasher. Her off-key attempt at singing along with her playlist was innocently charming. But that sinuous hip movement that all women could somehow do that made them look like every bone in their bodies melted to conform around a dance partner looked more than fucking good when she did it. I shifted uncomfortably as my cock decided that this was a perfectly acceptable time to wake up after its long hibernation.

On the phone, I asked the airline rep if they could upgrade a fellow passenger to first class, and after a little finagling, Alina was set up next to me. I figured it was a nice thank-you for everything she had done tonight. I hung up and texted Michael to let him know my change of plans and exactly what had precipitated the change. Alina had been right. He understood. Then I tried to think of natural disasters and painful dental surgery in an effort to lose my irrational hard-on.

She strolled back in. "You good? We road-tripping tomorrow? Because if so, I've got dibs on music and snacks. And tagalong buddies get no say."

"Do road-trip buddies get a vote when it comes to which truck stop adult toy stores we visit?" *Why do I say such stupid shit? I sound like someone's perverted uncle.*

Her jaw dropped and she shook her head, then lost it and doubled over laughing. "Well that escalated quickly. Now, are you coming—oh, god. Don't say anything. Get in the car."

I grinned and snagged my headphones from the table, grateful that I hadn't offended my only friend and ride out of here. "Thanks for tonight. Really, you didn't have to do any of this. You could have sent me home. Thank you for being here."

She looked at me like she was about to say something, but she shut her mouth. "Absolutely. Now let's get you back to the hotel. Someone needs his beauty sleep. And some professional help, but we can talk about that in the morning."

# Chapter Six

*Alina*

Given my addiction to punctuality and general manners, Markus earned a few bonus points for already being outside the hotel when I pulled up the next morning. He was sitting on a suitcase, with a backpack, hat and sunglasses on. As he drummed one hand on his thigh, the other brought a cigarette to his mouth for a long drag. The habit was gross and I rolled my window down in preparation for the stench.

"Hey, get in the truck, handsome."

Markus startled, looking around. I rolled my eyes. *Give me a break. Who else would I be talking to?* His lack of ego and occasional insecurity continuously endeared him to me. The way his eyes lit up as he caught my own didn't hurt either.

"Ah, Alina. Thank you for the ride," he said somewhat formally as he threw his bags into the back seat after hurriedly grinding out his cigarette in a nearby ashtray. "I'm so glad that you suggested taking the earlier flight. Truly, I need to get out of here —"

"Shut up. Seriously, it's okay. I'm glad we're getting you home before you completely lose your shit. I wasn't kidding last night when I said that you should look into professional help. I'm a decent listener, but not a therapist."

His face fell, going from hopeful to hurt, and his hands knotted into fists.

My attempt to backtrack was pathetically awkward. "God. I'm sorry. That came out way harsh. Let's get some coffee. I'm an asshole until I've had my first cup." I started to reach toward him and dropped my hand as I watched him buckle up and lean into the window, as far away from me and my thoughtless words as possible. "Markus, really, I didn't mean it. You're going through some serious stuff and that was insensitive. I apologize."

A tiny muscle in his jaw twitched as he tugged his hat lower and crossed his arms across his chest. "It's fine," he said, still refusing to look me in the eye. At least he uncurled a bit and shifted away from the window completely.

As we pulled into a Starbucks drive-through, he muttered, "Besides, you're not wrong. I was thinking about it a lot last night. What I should do when I get home, et cetera, et cetera."

I ordered, then as we pulled up to the window I asked, "And what did you decide?"

The lady handed me our coffees, doing a double take when she saw my passenger.

"Hey, isn't that —"

I pulled away, screeching the tires, before she could finish.

"I didn't decide anything definitively, I guess. I mean, other than the fact that I won't be responding to Kate, and that you're right, I probably need more help than I thought I did." He shrugged, opened the lid of his to-go cup and blew on the hot liquid in a vain attempt to cool it down.

"I did realize, though, that I need this job, and maybe there's a way for me to make it more than a bit part. Before yesterday, I was only halfway considering talking to Michael about staying on, but now I think it's imperative. I can't sit around my house having a breakdown. I need to fix myself and be out working, showing everyone I'm still bankable."

I hummed in agreement. "Anything I can do? Really, let me know. I can sound out Michael, maybe the screenwriters, and see what they think. Not that it would be a hard sell or anything — pretty sure the network will greenlight us forever if they get wind of you wanting to stay on."

"No, thank you," he said more easily as he reached over to turn up the volume on the radio. "I'm going to see if Michael can meet with me tomorrow. It would be interesting to help him define a role within this show's weird world."

I nodded and smiled at him. "Good. Like I said, let me know. Happy to help you out — you know, since you're my knight in semi-tarnished armor and all."

He grinned back at me, a little dimple in his cheek shyly peeking out at me for the first time since he'd rescued me at the park, and settled in after taking a sip of his coffee.

\* \* \* \*

The ride felt shorter than usual given the early hour, and we pulled into the rental car return about thirty minutes ahead of schedule. I gently shook his shoulder. "Markus, we're here. Wake up."

He grabbed my hand and pulled it over his chest as he tried to roll to the side. "Five minutes," he muttered.

At least I assumed that was what he said. It was in German. And it was clear that he wasn't awake at all. I tried shaking him again. "Markus, we've got to go. Time to go home."

He mumbled something else in German with his eyes closed and brought my hand to his face, kissed it gently and shook his head. "Nein."

My stomach did that weird flip thing again. His soft lips on my palm were a stark contrast to the rough stubble on his cheeks. But now the rental car guys were staring at us curiously. I wrenched my hand loose from beneath his cheek and shook him a little harder. "Markus, now!"

Still no response, so I decided it was time to pull out the heavy artillery. Crossing my fingers that he wouldn't wake up swinging, I stuck my finger in my mouth and quickly dipped it into his ear. My eardrums nearly ruptured as he shrieked out some sort of Viking war cry.

"Argh! What was that?" he yelled at an unholy volume, shuddering and pawing at his ear. His sunglasses were askew and he stared at me with eyes that threatened to shoot laser beams at me.

I shrugged. "Wet willy. Had to go nuclear. Now get up. We're at the airport." The last was somewhat unnecessary, as he was violently twisting around, scrambling to get out of his seatbelt and the car.

"What the fuck is a 'wet willy'?" he muttered from behind me, still pawing at his ear while he grabbed his bags.

I winked at the laughing car return guys and grabbed my own stuff, including the all-important memory cards containing the raw footage for everything we'd shot to date in Savannah. I smirked. "Let's go, princess."

We weren't running late, but Markus' long legs were eating up the walkway to ticketing faster than my own could go. It wasn't like I was short or out of shape, either. He was hauling ass like he was trying to run away from a burning Target on Black Friday with the last eighty-inch flat screen and a horde of overzealous Midwestern soccer moms on his heels.

"Dude, c'mon. Don't be all pissy. Wait up, please?" I called out.

All I got was a dirty look thrown over his shoulder as he continued at breakneck pace down the walkway.

"Fine. Stupid, overly sensitive man. With stupid long legs," I muttered, deliberately slowing my pace. It wasn't like he needed my help getting through security or anything. He was a semi-functional adult. Shrugging off the cold shoulder and my overwhelming mothering instinct, I shoved my earbuds into my ears to tune out the terribleness of ATL and lined up with the other suckers in coach to check my bag.

By the time I got to the front of the line, Markus had disappeared. I briefly considered whether to call him a dick or a weiner schnitzel when I caught up with him. The more time I had away from him, the more irrationally irritated I became. So when the ticketing agent at the counter told me there was a problem with my reservation, I started to lose my mind.

"Apologies, ma'am. Perhaps *problem* wasn't the right word," the nice lady drawled. "Your previous reservation is still here, but it looks like someone upgraded you sometime late last night after you checked in. You're now sitting in first class. Congratulations?"

"Oh god. I'm sorry, thank you. It's been a stupid morning and my stupid friend is pissed at me for a stupid reason and I'm just really stupidly cranky right now." I handed over my bag, which got a fancy 'First Class' tag slapped on it before being tossed down the conveyor belt.

I clutched my golden ticket and headed for security with an uncomfortable feeling of guilt turning my stomach. I resolved to buy Markus a drink sometime in thanks, and also promise to never wake him with saliva in the ear again.

Outside security, Markus was sitting hunched over on a bench with his backpack at his feet as he waited for me.

"I'm sorry I woke you up with spit," I said, plopping down next to him. I leaned my head on his shoulder for a moment, the gesture surprisingly natural for how little we truly knew each other. "Let's head to the gate. Thank you, by the way, for the upgrade. You didn't have to do that."

He sighed and rested his head on mine. "No, it's fine. I don't wake up well either, and I'm on emotional overload. You know those women who always got tied down to train tracks by the evil villain in silent movies? I feel like those women, waiting and watching for the inevitable train, you know?"

"Okay, drama queen." I nudged him and was delighted when a teensy grin sparked across his face. "I get it, not quite there, but I've not been at my best lately, either. This has been a really hard season to film with the network breathing down our necks about the ratings slipping."

He nodded silently and we watched people hurry past us for a while. I elbowed him again. "Hey, it's going to be all right. For both of us, I promise. We'll get through this. Take things one step at a time, okay? And I'm sorry, again, for being such an insensitive jerk this morning."

He tipped his head down in acknowledgment and shoved his sunglasses back onto his face as we stood and joined the flow of the crowd. We drifted along, separate but together, and found two seats next to each other by our gate. I pulled out my tablet to read my latest favorite historical romance while he stared off into space.

It was strange, I'd never felt so protective of someone before, and all of my irrational anger from this morning shifted over to his current relationship and work woes. It really wasn't fair. He was incredibly intelligent, sensitive, and such a genuinely *nice* guy — once I'd gotten past the barriers he posted in self-defense. Obviously hot as fuck, but that wasn't the point. He was a *good* person who was clearly struggling mentally, and I'd been there too, hostage to a brain that wasn't wired normally and incapable of breaking free. It sucked. Lost in my own thoughts, I barely heard the gate agents announce the boarding call for our flight to LAX. I nudged him. "Time to go, big guy."

He nodded again and we headed wordlessly to the counter.

"Markus Shellenberg? I loved you in *Untimely Justice*. You were so amazing," the gate agent practically shrieked as she scanned his ticket.

"Thank you," he said, and shifted back and forth, clearly a bit uncomfortable being the center of her enthusiastic attention.

As she opened her mouth to continue to gush, I stepped up behind him and knocked him off to the side to thrust my boarding pass at her. "Sorry, he's flying under the radar. Can you please let us on the plane?"

She frowned at me. "Are you his bodyguard or something?"

"Yep, now give me my ticket back and let us get on the plane."

Markus' faint chuckles transformed into a full-on howl as we walked down the boarding ramp. "Seriously? My bodyguard? Thank you. I needed that."

I was slightly mortified and winced at how that must have looked. "I know, I have no idea where that came from. Are you okay, though? I pushed you kind of hard, and sometimes I don't know my own strength. Because I'm way stronger than I look. Shit, if you get hurt, Michael is going to fire me, and then I'll never find another job. You better be okay."

The Shellenberg Effect was back, and I was babbling again.

"You? Hurt me? Ha. I like this look—you're very cute when you get all ferocious. Like an irate Chihuahua or something." He laughed again and slung one arm around my shoulders. "Now, let's go get a drink to celebrate going home. Free ones always taste better." He squeezed me tightly before letting go as we moved in single file for the last few steps to board the plane.

I was speechless as he grabbed our carry-ons and shoved them into the overhead compartment. As he slid into his window seat, he shot me the most heartbreakingly happy-go-lucky grin while I stared at him in confusion.

"Oh. Are you good with the aisle seat?" he asked, mistaking my blank stare for irritation. "It will be easier, if you don't mind, for me to hide a little from over here. People aren't likely to try anything with my bodyguard blocking them from asking for photos and stuff."

I supposed his complete mood one-eighty, the joking around and all of those little touches were good signs, but they made me horribly uneasy. Like I no longer knew who he was or how I was supposed to relate to him. Apparently he had been operating at maybe fifty percent capacity the entire time I'd known him. The full-on version of Markus Shellenberg was a lot to take in, and I wasn't sure I'd survive it if he turned one hundred percent of his charm on me.

"Uh. No, it's fine. This is fine," I muttered as I tripped and fell into the aisle seat. "What's the deal with the sudden good mood? And when can we get those drinks you promised?"

"Oh, they'll be around in a second. But good mood? Maybe because we're going home and things will finally get back to normal?"

I wanted to roll my eyes. He needed to figure out how to manage expectations and regulate his emotions independently. Not count on some sort of external force or change in environment to stabilize him. Going home wasn't going to help anything unless he started figuring out how to help himself. For heaven's sake, he'd been practically catatonic not even twenty minutes ago.

The flight attendant came by, batting her eyelashes. "Glass of wine for you and your friend, Mr. Shellenberg?"

He nodded briefly before looking at me, eyebrows raised.

"One for me too, white, and maybe a coffee."

She nodded, left with slightly pink cheeks, and returned with our wine in record time. We downed our drinks and started outlining a ridiculous plan to rehab his reputation and get the roles of his dreams going forward — starting with figuring out how to make his current role permanent, a plan that looked better and better the more I drank. If he were to stick around for a year, the ratings would be huge and it would be my first season as an A.D. Pretty great fucking timing, and amazing for padding out my resume.

I scrawled down his ideas, and my corrections to them, on cocktail napkins emblazoned with the airline's logo. When we finally finished, I wadded up the napkins and thrust them in his direction as I reclined my seat and curled up in a ball. "Here, you hold on to this. We'll need it when we get in and have to execute the plan."

He nodded, staring at the napkins clenched in his fist. "Thank you, Alina. I'll wake you when we land."

My eyes had barely closed — or at least that was how it felt — when someone gently stroked the hair away from my cheek and nudged my shoulder. "What was that you said this morning? Wakey, wakey?"

I frowned as I recognized the voice and burrowed deeper into whatever comfy pillow I had landed on.

"Rot in hell, Markus Shellenberg. You're not the boss of me."

His breath tickled my neck as he laughed and murmured from somewhere above my head, "Ah. Payback's a bitch, no?"

Then I felt it—the cold, wet, descending hand of god. In my ear. I'd taught him too well and I was going to make him pay for that later.

# Chapter Seven

*Alina*

"Hey, crabby girl, slow down. I'm sorry I woke you up exactly the same way you woke me up earlier. So miserable, right?" He raised an eyebrow at me as I huffed and puffed my way to the baggage carousel. "Besides, you're really a terrible bodyguard. Pretty sure that falling asleep and drooling all over your client is frowned upon."

"I don't drool!" I hissed at him.

"You do. And you did. All over my shoulder." He pointed at the pretty obvious evidence on his shirt. "Anyways, let me take you home. My driver is right out by the curb. We should go before the paparazzi show up—someone over by that baggage carousel has their phone out."

"Fine! Yes, all right? Please extract me from this situation. I'm in need of another rescue." I groaned. The last thing I needed was to be linked to him publicly.

"Where do you live?" he asked brusquely as he helped me into the car and pulled out his phone.

"Venice," I answered and gave the driver my address. "Thank you, Markus," I said as I leaned back and let the luxurious smell of new leather wash over me.

"It's fine. What do you have going on today, anyways?" He was still texting someone. A cute little groove appeared between his eyebrows as he grimaced at his phone.

"I don't know. My usual Sunday night routine, I guess?" I offered. "Clean the house. Do my laundry. Maybe go for a walk on the beach or to a little bar by my house for dinner and a drink."

"By yourself?" he asked incredulously.

He must have forgotten what life was like before fame. "This may come as a surprise, Markus, but I'm quite good at doing things on my own."

"Fine. The freedom to do things alone is so strange to me. And I'm really not looking forward to checking out the damage at my house. Want to come with?" he asked and I couldn't quite tell if he was messing around. The pull he exerted kept drawing me closer, urging me to help him.

His voice changed before I could respond, becoming more emphatic as he pointed out of the window. "This place is beautiful. Honestly, this is what I thought all of America was like when I was a kid. *Baywatch*, *90210* and all that."

My cheeks heated up, that had been a rhetorical question. He didn't need me. I tried to let it slide. "I know, right? I really, really love it here. I don't even mind the commute. It's too perfect, and I never want to leave. See over there? That's the bar I'm heading to later, Forse. Super cute, right?" I reached across him to point, nearly knocking his hat off.

"Let me guess…wine bar?" he asked, only slightly patronizing as he glanced at the place and adjusted his hat.

"Nah, nothing that pretentious. Just good food and all of the alcohol to make bad days better. Oh, turn here! You can pull over. That's my place right there."

He got out with me to carry my bags and I immediately tried to take them back. The tug of war over my suitcases was embarrassingly one-sided as he quickly leveraged his size and reach while sticking his tongue out at me like a naughty child. I rolled my eyes and tagged after him, fumbling around in my tote before finally finding my keys.

"Look, I meant what I said earlier. It's going to be all right. But I don't know… Do you want my number or anything in case you need to talk later?"

He gulped and handed over his phone. "Yes, please."

I quickly keyed in my info and sent myself a text so I'd have his number. We stood there staring at each other, both of us unsure as to what the proper goodbye protocol was in this setting. Did I give him a hug? Pat him on the ass, like "go get 'em, slugger"? Maybe a firm handshake. I settled on an awkward wave as I backed through my door, dragging my luggage with me to form a physical boundary between us. "Well, good luck, I guess? You can call me if you need anything, but I'm sure you'll be fine. So…see you tomorrow?"

"Yeah." He sighed heavily, then straightened his shoulders and nodded. "See you tomorrow. Thanks again, Alina."

As I walked through the downstairs, opening windows and curtains, I breathed in the slightly stale, salty air of my home. For the umpteenth time, I was grateful to my frugal parents and their dedication to saving that had left me with a small inheritance after they had passed—enough to move to L.A. and start over, even buy this house. I knew I was privileged, but that money was almost gone now and it was all up to me to make it big.

There were so many things that needed to get done before we could wrap this season of *Southern Gods*, but they were manageable. First, I had lists to make and I wanted to start on the small mountain of laundry I had brought home with me from Savannah. Then, figure out the mundane tasks of living that would have to fit around Michael's demands.

The level of organization that I tried to achieve in my life might have seemed ridiculous and unnecessary to most people, but it helped me to feel like I had a semblance of control. Most of my moves over the last two years had been so far out of my comfort zone that I felt perpetually off-kilter. My lists provided structure and helped me avoid conflict and confusion. Offhand, I wondered if Markus had any of those guardrails.

I was worried about him—with his stupidly gorgeous face and rare ability to share his vulnerability with someone new. Plus, his thoughtfulness and the way he teased me about falling asleep and drooling on him. It was dangerous how much I enjoyed spending time with him. He pulled me out of my comfort zone, and that could be a decent thing in small doses.

With one load already in the washer, I started flipping through my bullet journals. I smiled happily at all of the crossed-off items and checked goals from previous lists. Tangible proof that I hadn't made a huge mistake when I'd moved out here so suddenly. My phone rang as I opened to a fresh page to start a new list for the remainder of the shoot.

*Markus. Shit. Not a good sign.*

\* \* \* \*

Forse, Italian for "perhaps", was one of those unpretentious places that couldn't decide if it was a wine bar, a restaurant or a bar-bar. They kept late hours, never stopped serving antipasti and took a more than tolerant approach to pouring wine. The waitstaff had all worked there for ages, cementing the idea that this really was a family establishment. It was my second home.

By the time Markus arrived over an hour later, I had finished my first generously poured glass of wine and ordered round two while plodding through changes to the shooting schedule Michael had sent me for the remainder of the week. I'd waited to order a main even though the rich garlicy-basil scent of their traditional red sauce wafted through the entire space, tormented me with daydreams of gluten-y goodness. At least the cheese plate was still largely intact. I had a feeling Markus was going to need it more than me.

"Alina." His voice grated out through gritted teeth as he greeted me.

"Markus, shit, what happened?" I asked as he slid into the seat across from me. "Need a drink?"

Markus took off his sunglasses, folded them carefully and set them aside. Then he sank his chin into the palm of his hand as he stared at me with slightly manic, glittering eyes. "Yes, a drink. Two Fernet, please. And a glass of whatever you're having."

I practically dry heaved when I heard his bizarre order. We were clearly about to board the struggle bus. Fernet was a very nasty herbal digestif. One did not simply 'have two' for funsies. "Yeah, sure. Do you want any bread too? There's cheese here if you want it. Shove it in your mouth. You'll feel better." I was a helpful, conversational genius.

His fingers twitched on his jaw. "Are you serious right now?"

"I never joke about cheese. That would be sacrilegious."

He grunted and closed his eyes — probably to drown out my jabbering again. The room suddenly felt five degrees darker and colder.

"Sorry. I'm babbling and making bad jokes. It's kind of intimidating when you walk in and ask for one of the grossest drinks ever after what I'm sure was a pretty emotional afternoon." Before I could embarrass myself further, I slipped away from our table.

On my return, I watched Markus slowly drag one hand down his face, pulling his features out of sync. I could hear his sigh from six feet away. Setting down the drinks, I resumed my seat and leaned over so I could flick his forehead to get his attention. "Let's hear it, then."

His face contorted as he sniffed the wine and set it aside with a decisive nod, then brought the Fernet up to hover in front of his gorgeous mouth. "Fuck, I don't know. It was weird being back there without her — I ended up packing up things she'd left behind, got the locks changed so she can't force her way back in, sent her stuff to the hotel where she's staying. She's really gone and that's in my past. I can move on. I think I'm ready to."

He shrugged and smiled uncertainly. "I'm sorry to interrupt your afternoon, but I forgot to tell my housekeeper I was coming home and realized I didn't have any food in the house once I was done packing up Kate's crap and... Well, I didn't know who else to call."

I held back from flippantly suggesting delivery and nodded in sympathy. My nod turned into a full-body shiver as Markus abruptly slammed the Fernet, slid the glass aside and downed half the wine. Looking up, he made eye contact with the bartender and held up his glass to request a refill. "Bring the bottle, please," he called over to the bar.

He took a deep breath and slowly fanned his fingers out on the table, cracking each individual knuckle like he was preparing for a prize fight while we waited for the bartender to refill our glasses. "I know I've still got some things to process, but I feel free for the first time in ages."

I looked at him, not completely sure he was being honest with himself. "I don't know, Markus, it usually takes a while to work through this kind of emotional trauma."

"Yeah, but isn't admitting you have a problem the first step on the way to recovery? I'm ready to leave that behind. And watch this." He pulled out his phone, swiped to the message screen for Kate's string and tapped on her contact info. Then, with me watching and a theatrical flourish, he tapped 'Block Contact' decisively. "There, done."

I clapped while he grinned proudly at me. He was finally taking control and I knew how that felt. That first step *was* liberating. "Congrats, Markus, that's fantastic. Really proud of you."

He shrugged bashfully under my gaze and started dragging his fingers through the condensation droplets from our waterglasses on the table. "Thanks. I kind of don't want to think about it or her anymore tonight — she's not worth the energy." He paused to finish his second glass of wine and looked me dead in the eye. "I sort of want to celebrate being out of that relationship. Can we do that?"

"Hmm. Yes, I suppose." I attempted a straight face, but he was starting to slur as the alcohol kicked in and his accent made him sound like the Terminator. He grinned sloppily back at me and the room seemed to brighten with his excitement.

"More wine? And maybe we should order some food. What do you feel like? Can I get really drunk now, or is that frowned upon?" He was so full of questions.

I laughed. "Yes, yes and yes, we should totally order food."

Things got kind of blurry once we left Forse. There was a lot of stumbling into each other, a kind of loose, casual intimacy growing between us that was beyond the usual touchy-feeliness of intoxication. I had to keep reminding myself who he was, why he was with me and that we weren't a couple. We were friendly blips on each other's radars. I was 'there for him', as the saying goes. Nothing more or less.

Still, we drank soju and sang karaoke at a dive bar in Koreatown. We danced on the table in the tiny private room we were assigned and shouted the words to Tiffany's *I Think We're Alone Now* with our sweaty foreheads mashed together, centimeters away from kissing as he stopped the chorus and stared transfixed at my mouth. The air between us felt electrified, the moment only broken when the lights flickered to let us know that it was last call.

We weren't terribly far from my house at the time, so I pulled Markus into my cab, ignoring his demands to be taken to a hotel. There was no way he was going to be able to get a hotel room in his current state without the paparazzi finding out, and I was honestly shocked that we hadn't already been discovered.

Too drunk to do more than pout about me ignoring him during the car ride home, he slouched down in his seat and dropped his head to my shoulder. When we got to my house he was barely awake and I had to haul him inside. He made it up the narrow staircase on his own, though, and careened into the bathroom attached to the master bedroom.

I pulled out the futon for him in my tiny spare room and made it up with a mismatched set of sheets. Maybe if he passed out on the diagonal, his six-three frame would fit. Mentally shrugging and washing my hands of the sleeping situation, I wandered across the hall into my room and found him sitting on the edge of my bed, head starting to droop.

"The bed is ready for you. I'm sure you're tired."

"I am. Thank you for everything tonight, Alina. That was the best celebratory end of a relationship… Ever." His voice was gritty with put-off sleep, his accent making his words almost unintelligible now that he was drunk and tired. He tugged me closer and kissed my head. "Goodnight," he said as he heaved himself to his feet then staggered away with a heavy list to the right.

I stripped down to my underwear, braided my hair back and grabbed a ratty college basketball T-shirt with cut-off sleeves. The fatigue and emotional overload of the day started to hit at that point and I slid into bed, grateful for the silence and reflecting on the warmth in his stare as he'd said goodnight. The attraction was there, for both of us, but I wasn't sure if either of us would ever be ready to act on it. As I was starting to doze off, I heard quiet footsteps padding into my room toward the bed.

"Alina. *Psst*. Are you awake?" a tired voice slurred. "You weren't kidding. That futon is a death trap. Let me in." A bony finger poked my shoulder.

I scooted over and felt the mattress depress on the other side as a long, lean body slid in and under the covers. "Mmmhm, so much nicer. So cozy," he murmured.

Two seconds later, I heard light snoring from the lump behind me and I reached back to pat him awkwardly on the shoulder as my own eyelids shuttered.

\* \* \* \*

I woke up hot and starving, with the hangover from hell beating into my brain. As a minimal level of clarity set in, I recalled that I was definitely not alone in my bed. A tall, mostly naked, sculpted-from-granite German actor was wrapped around me. The man felt like he had at least eight appendages, all trying to snuggle me to death. Or maybe five, given the hard-on I felt throbbing against my ass. *Fuck, that feels good.*

I bit my lip, trying to hold back a moan as his arms tightened around me, eliminating the millimeters of space between our bodies. I could feel every minute movement, every hitch of our increasingly ragged breathing. His very large, very warm hand slid from my stomach over my ribs to stroke the side of my breast through the gap in my shirt as he groaned, and I swore I could feel the individual ridges on his fingertips.

"So soft," he murmured faintly.

I rolled my hips in response and, as light as a butterfly, he skimmed over my nipple with his thumb, circling it gently as he dropped his mouth to my neck and jawline, where he nuzzled in. My headache seemed to subside with each nip of his teeth on my neck. I arched back harder against him and he growled something in German. While I'd never found that phlegmy language sexy before, I'd also never heard Markus' hoarse bedroom voice or imagined him talking dirty to me. Because that was what I was convinced it was — a whole lot of

He pressed his hand against me and slid from my breast back to my hip with increasing pressure to pull me flush against his erection. The soft cotton of our minimal clothes was almost too rough against my skin — my nerves and senses all felt like they were on high alert, like my fight or flight mechanism had been activated. Only, there was a third option screaming at me to fuck it all. He ground against me while sliding his fingers beneath the waistband of my underwear to stroke through the tantalizing wetness of my arousal. The rough touch of his callused fingers on that sensitive skin shocked me fully awake.

I flipped over to face him. His eyes were already open, pupils blown wide. Slowly, so slowly, our heads inclined toward each other, our eyes closed and our lips pressed together. I teased his lower lip with my tongue and he pulled back abruptly. We considered each other for a heartbeat. "How long have you been awake?" I asked breathlessly, trying to keep my mouth covered.

"Hmm. Not very long. I was having the most incredible dreams. Your bed is very comfortable." He stretched his arms over his head and blinked at me. "That was a lovely wake-up call, too."

"Yes, lovely," I said in distraction as I glanced at the clock and realized that I was going to be late if I wasn't in my car racing toward the studio within the next five minutes. "Shit, I'm going to be late. You don't have to be on set till later. What are your plans?"

"Mmmhmm," he hummed as his eyes shuttered again. "If you don't mind, could I crash here for a bit? I don't have anywhere to be and I still need to get my car back from the bar."

I gave him a long look as he lay there super innocently with his eyes purposefully closed, little tufts of his hair messily scrawling jagged little notes on my pillow. "Uh. Huh. Sure. You're welcome to invade my space for the morning. But you better be on set on time today, and we are talking about this very friendly wake-up later. Don't forget my keys."

"'Kay. See ya later." He turned and burrowed back under my covers, effectively ending the conversation.

I crept into the shower, embarrassed that I could still feel his soft kiss tingling on my lips. What was there even to say? If we allowed this fire between us to burn, I was the one who'd get hurt. He'd walk away unscathed, the typical Hollywood stud who notched off yet another grasping crew member. That was the last thing I needed.

# Chapter Eight

*Markus*

The door slammed shut behind her and a few minutes later her car's tires crunched over the gravel driveway as she left for the set. I had no idea what my dick had been thinking, but messing around with my new best friend in her bed with the hangover from hell and the worst breath on the planet had not been my most suave move. But for fuck's sake, her skin was the smoothest and softest that I had ever touched. Every one of her curves had fit seamlessly against the harder edges of my own body.

I wrapped my hand around my cock and stroked myself idly, getting harder and harder, imagining a whole scenario where morning sex was an actual option. If we could actually be together. How she would look beneath me, my hands holding her wrists above her head, begging her to open her eyes and watch me, watch us... So lost in this erotic vision, I wasn't ready when I started to come uncontrollably hard, her face fading from my mind's eye and into oblivion.

I threw off the covers and shook myself like a dog getting out of a lake. *What the fuck am I doing?* Without dressing, I strode into the bathroom to shower. As the water heated, I considered whether I was still drunk or delusional, fantasizing about Alina when I had ten times the usual amount of pressure on me. I'd only recently been dumped, that wound still smarted, and my ex was possibly stalking me. I was persona non grata in my industry and relying on a tiny role on a failing TV show to re-up my image.

My attraction to her was easy to explain — she was beautiful, smart, tenacious and hilarious. But I wasn't sure I was ready for anything serious. Plus, other than this morning, she hadn't seemed interested in acting on any attraction she might have felt, and I couldn't ever see her wanting to try something with me — an actor on her show. I had a feeling she wasn't into the whole workplace romance thing. *Romance? Shit.*

The steam billowed into the bathroom when I opened the stall door to step in. The tiny fan worked overtime above the sink, attempting to dispel it. Alina's shower had a window facing the beach, and I watched little groups of people wander around the water's edge as I cleaned myself up. Getting out, I wrapped a towel around my waist and grabbed my jeans. The smell of stale smoke and cheap booze emanating off my clothes made me want to vomit, so I brought them down to the laundry room, threw them into the wash with the bedding and started a cycle.

I glanced at the clock on the stove and saw that it was still early, before eight o'clock. Time to get caught up with my team. I'd been deliberately dodging everyone but Will, and I'd managed to keep that to one or two calls. Pretending things were normal. Super healthy. A conference call would be easier, so I shot Will, Roger and Claire—my manager, lawyer and P.R. rep, respectively—a group text scheduling a call in the next hour. We needed to make final plans for announcing the break-up with Kate and managing any fallout. The initial messaging we'd put out about us being on the rocks had gone smoothly, but it turned out that breaking up with one of America's Sweethearts was complicated.

As I curiously rifled through Alina's pantry to scavenge for breakfast, I smiled when I hit jackpot and discovered the four varieties of kids' cereal hidden away at the back of the very top shelf. I tried to eat healthy, but sugary cereal was my Achilles' heel. We simply hadn't had that kind of thing when I was growing up in Germany, and eating it made me feel like I was getting away with some sort of crime.

After eating, I put my dish in the sink, moved the laundry to the dryer then got on the phone with my team. Claire promised a full media plan, which was ridiculous since our break-up was really no one's business but mine and Kate's. Will gave me shit for not talking to Michael yet about making my role more permanent and Roger received the green light to start assembling the legal documentation to supplement the potential new contract.

After we all had our marching orders, we signed off the call. I took a last look around Alina's house before leaving, touching the homey little objects she'd picked up for no other reason than they had meaning to her— a collection of geodes and crystals on her desk, the

1970s-style chunky weavings in blues and greens on her wall. I scribbled a fast thank-you note and headed out to track down my car.

\* \* \* \*

The lot was humming as I drove in, parked and headed to the set with an eye and ear out for both Michael and Alina, hoping to corner him with my pitch to make my role permanent and her to back me up. I didn't see either of them immediately and checked in with one of the production assistants before stepping into my trailer, where a semi-familiar makeup artist was waiting.

"Hi, Markus. Let's get you going. You've got kind of a busy afternoon ahead of you."

"I'm sorry. What is your name again?"

"Candace! We've met before? Alina and I were roommates in Savannah. She's the best. You guys are friends — right?"

"Sorry, Candace, I'm terrible with names. Yeah, I remember seeing you at the house briefly after I rescued your friend from that natural disaster of her own making." I smirked at her and she laughed.

"Oh, yeah. Alina is fantastic at crafting her own disasters. Thank god you were there to save her," she joked.

"Hey! What are you two saying about me?" Alina's offended cry preceded her as she made her way over to the vanity where Candace was working on me and leaned up against the edge.

"You know, reviewing your capacity for boneheaded decisions when venturing out into the world. I'm still pissed at you for that rock-climbing stunt. No one knew where you were and you could have been—" She cut herself off as she frantically started rifling through her toolbox, muttering about butterfly brushes.

Alina sighed and reached over to pull a brush out from behind Candace's ear. "Here, I think you're looking for this. Promise it won't happen again. Markus, you're needed in ten on stage three. I've got to run, craft services fucked up big-time and Michael doesn't have his green M&Ms to pacify him. We may have a monster on our hands." She winked at me in the mirror and I watched as she whirled around and bustled away, face already buried back in her ubiquitous clipboard.

Candace nodded decisively and finished dusting me with powder. "Anyways, I'm about done with you too, and then you can throw on the clothes over there and head out to find Michael. Good luck, no green M&Ms are a bad sign."

The door closed as I moved over to the couch where a few things were laid out for me. I quickly sent Alina a text.

*Didn't get to thank you for the Cocoa Puffs this morning. They're my favorite, thanks for the three bowls. Also, I left your house intact and locked up.*

Then I waited for her response, hoping that she'd tracked down those green M&Ms. A few minutes later, I saw the dancing dots of a reply and smiled happily, imagining her staring at the phone, fingers flying over the keyboard.

*THREE BOWLS OF MY CEREAL??? You bastard. Hope you're not as hungover as me.*

I grinned at my phone like an idiot and responded.

*Yeah, do I have time to grab coffee before I need to be on stage three?*

*Yeah, Michael's pushing back the call time by 30 min, was going to text you anyways. I'm in craft services attempting to caffeinate. Come over if you're bored.*

I headed over to the craft services setup, where I found Alina deep in conversation with one of the casting agents.

As I approached, I overheard the agent say to her in a frustrated whisper, "Girl, you've got to get your shit together and pick someone. I know that Michael is giving you hell over this, but I can't keep pulling in talent for one measly scene without breaking the budget here."

"Yes. I'm aware," Alina muttered. "You know who my top three are so far. I'll have a decision made before we leave."

The casting agent spun around and flounced off, her hand going up to tap her headset to make a call.

"Fun times?" I asked in my best Michael impression, then enjoyed watching her jump about three feet in the air. She whipped around, realized it was me then deflated. She leaned toward me, butting her head against my shoulder.

"This has been my morning—nonstop bitching from Michael and Casting trying to find a woman for the dumbest extra role that his royal bitchiness somehow thinks is important," she complained, her voice muffled by my shirt.

I looked around. We were attracting curious glances from everyone in the vicinity, so I stepped away abruptly and jerked my head in the direction of the smoking area. "People were staring, not that I really care, but people talk and the last thing you probably need is to be linked to me."

"Oh! Shit. You don't care? Huh, I mean, I guess I don't either. They're complete idiots if they think you'd be into me." She was trying to be self-deprecating, but I immediately bristled at her put-down.

"They wouldn't be wrong," I muttered as I patted my pockets in search of a lighter. She gaped at me and I rushed to change the subject. "Why the epic quest for an extra?" I tried to joke as I lit a cigarette that I truly had no interest in smoking.

She growled in disgust as she waved off the plume of smoke. "Can you, like, not do that? Gross." I quickly stubbed out my cigarette and swigged some hot tea to replace the nicotine with caffeine, burning my palate in the process. As usual, she rescued me with a water bottle from the holster on her belt and I desperately gulped it down. I needed a chance to save her soon or this was going to be the most lopsided arrangement in history.

"Oh, the extra thing. Michael has it in his head that you need female backup in your big fight scene with Ethan."

"Ah."

"Yes, that. Gender equity. Which is a great thing for him to finally be considering with casting choices, but I also think maybe you — or we — should take this as an opportunity to revisit the whole fight scene with

Michael. We can't kill you off if you're hoping to stick around. I found his Precious, let's go track him down," she said as she impatiently shook a plastic container containing only green M&Ms like a maraca.

"C'mon, do you want this or not?" she asked when I didn't immediately take a step toward Michael. "You told me you need the job, and we really could use you given the network's waffling about renewing us. We'll sedate him with his favorite candy and drop the news. You in?" Her hands were raised in the air like Rocky Balboa as she finished her pep talk, the candy threatening to fly away with the emphatic gestures she'd used to punctuate her words. I couldn't help but laugh—she was too adorable.

"Sorry, distracted and hungover. You're right, let's do this." I pulled her in for a hug and she squeezed me back. We were getting incredibly comfortable with each other. Possibly too comfortable, as I noticed a bunch of avid looks directed our way. *Dangerous*. The last thing Alina needed in this sexist industry was a reputation as a star-fucker. She was the furthest thing from it but I didn't think I could stand being responsible for her getting knocked off the ladder.

# Chapter Nine

*Alina*

"Michael, do you have a second? I've got your green M&Ms and Markus needs a word." I watched as Michael's face contorted from, "I will set you on fire if you come at me with something stupid," to "My Precious," then somewhere halfway between with "Oh, yes. My super important guest star who I love like a brother and would like to please if at all possible."

He snatched the container from my hands and shoved a handful directly into his mouth. "Sure, shoot," he said through the crunchy green-and-brown goo.

I looked at Markus in encouragement and he stood there, staring at Michael's open-mouthed chewing in absolute revulsion. I nudged him, hard, in the arm and he jumped a foot in the air.

He began with flattery, an excellent choice. "Um, yes. Michael. Have I mentioned that I've really enjoyed being a part of the cast even for this short time?"

Michael shoved another handful of candy into his mouth and nodded genially.

"Anyways, I was thinking that the plot could use another villain, no? Keeping on a member of the enemy faction could be a really interesting juxtaposition, a subtle play on American politics, the fox in the henhouse —"

I snorted and cut him off. "What he means is that he'd be down to stick around for next season if you want him to," I said, while Markus glowered at me for interrupting his flow.

Michael looked back and forth between us, fascinated, his face smeared with chocolate around his mouth and in his patchy facial hair. "Seriously? Shellenberg, is she kidding?"

Markus hemmed and hawed for a moment before finally saying, "No, she's not. I'd like to stay on. That is, if there's room for me in the next season's arc."

Michael was stunned. "Really? This might be the best news I've heard since I found out that the McDonald's down in Los Feliz was going to keep the McRib around through March. Fuck yeah, I'd like to have you. I'd *love* to have you!"

I smiled, mission accomplished. "Okay, Michael, Markus. How do we do this? Make it happen?"

Michael spun in a circle and threw the remainder of his container of candy in the air, and I cursed silently — those were the only M&Ms I'd been able to track down after sending three assistants on a wild goose chase around Studio City. "Oh yeah, this is going to be great. Network's gonna shit their pants. Listen, I'll get on the horn with them and we'll set up a meeting for…" He looked at me, his human calendar.

"Tomorrow should work," I helpfully supplied.

"Tomorrow. Alina, set it up." I nodded and he continued, "This is going to be amazing!" He started doing his version of a happy dance, wiggling his ass with his hands in the air as he jumped up and down. "Oh my god, I cannot wait for this meeting! Shellenberg, I could kiss you right now!"

"That won't be necessary, just a contract please. And it doesn't need to be a big role, whatever you'd like me to do is fine." Markus grinned at Michael.

"Well, when you put it that—" Michael started to respond, and the sparkle in his eye warned me that whatever he was about to say was going to be highly unprofessional and probably sexual in nature.

I interrupted, "Okay, we're settled? Great, let's get back to filming. Michael, where did you need Markus for the afternoon?"

"Stage three, my lovelies, stage three. Alina, get that meeting scheduled and call the writers. They've got work to do."

"You got it, boss. Markus, see you later." It came out like a half-question. I had no plans for later, but I suddenly felt like celebrating—with my new best friend who I had increasingly inappropriate feelings for. *Shit. I need to get my head back in the game and focus on work. Not fucking around with an actor.*

"Of course. Later." He bowed and winked at me.

Michael raised his eyebrows at both of us and I ran before my stupidly pale skin could give anything else away.

\* \* \* \*

"Alina, girl, get your ass over here," Candace sang in that voice that friends only employ when they think they've caught you out in an enormous lie. She was vibrating with excitement. "You, my friend," she whisper-shouted, "have been keeping a big German secret, have you not?"

"What the hell are you even talking about? And do you think you could keep your voice down a little?" The last thing I needed was gossip about Markus attaching to me. The absolute last thing. Squashing rumors about Michael and me was bad enough.

"You know exactly what I'm talking about. Markus. Shellenberg. Rory and I saw you hanging out this morning. Lots of touchy-feels. Anything you'd like to share?" Her voice still remained in the too-loud-for-this-chat category, but shushing her further was going to be impossible, given her level of excitement.

I managed to pull her off to the side of a trailer, but she wasn't even letting me respond and her super high-pitched voice was getting louder. "I mean, the news broke this morning that he and Kate broke up, the usual publicity crap—but her team is spreading the rumor that he ended things because he was cheating on her. With someone from this show. Any chance that could be you? Also, I thought you said they broke up a while ago?"

"They did, but both sides wanted to keep it quiet till Markus was done with the Sellers film. I have no idea why—nor do I have a clue why her team is starting that rumor. There's nothing going on between us," I said.

The problem was, Candace was my only friend in L.A. I didn't want to lie to her, but really, bar our exceptionally friendly wake-up call that morning, nothing had happened with Markus. And nothing ever would. Not that she needed to know about any of that nothing-ness.

"Look, Candace. I know you want to see something that's not there, but we're not involved. Just friends. I really can't say anything else, okay?" I waited for her reluctant nod before continuing. "Now, let it go. Seriously. Let's not feed the rumor mill."

She sighed dramatically and bowed her head in pretend shame, then peeked out through the tight curls that hid her face. "Of course, lady. But if something does happen, I get to be the first to know, right?" I nodded and she hugged me tightly. "I'm sorry. I got a little carried away imagining double dates."

I hugged her back and laughed a little. "It's fine. Let's drop it, okay?"

She agreed, and I walked off to find Michael and let him know that the execs were good for meeting with him and Markus the next day. Looking wasn't really necessary, as it turned out, because Michael strolled around the corner of a trailer almost simultaneously with my last words to Candace.

"Alina! There you are. We finished one of Markus' last scenes for the last day and I wanted to make sure that you'd had a chance to send that email. I can't even believe this, did you know anything?" He was practically violent in his paroxysms of delight as he attempted to hug and pat me on the back at the same time.

I ducked away and hedged, "I did, a little. I mean, we're kind of friends and we run lines together sometimes. He sounded me out about it, at least."

"You run lines together?" he asked incredulously.

"Yeah, sometimes. When he asks. It's fun and he's really an amazing actor," I answered, gushing perhaps a little too much about how great and wonderful Markus was at pretty much everything.

"Hmm. I didn't realize you were into that. Well, whatever you did worked, and he was even better today than usual. So, are the execs good to meet with us?"

"Yes, they're excited. I have the two of you meeting them at Nobu at eight-thirty for dinner and drinks. Will that work? It was open on your calendar so I took a chance — they didn't give me many options."

He threw his arms around me and picked me up, twirling me in a circle. "It's perfect," he crowed. "Alina, we're saved, the show is saved! And you're coming with us tomorrow. They need to get to know you, the woman who saved the show," he enthused as he dropped me like a sack of potatoes. His little arms were not made to hold up an almost six-foot woman who'd very much enjoyed Georgia's foodie scene.

I cleared my throat and asked, "So, not sure how this affects the fight scene, but we need to figure out a way to make it ambiguous so he can come back from it. What are we doing with this extra? Do we really need her?"

"Yeah, I think we do. It might be interesting for him to have a love interest if he's sticking around, but I don't know if this girl will be the one. So we've got to hint at his sexuality and create that atmosphere, but she doesn't have to be endgame. Got it?"

I nodded, loving how far ahead Michael's brain was working, how many different scenarios he was planning.

"For what it's worth, you're really doing well with production work, and I'm excited to see how you take on directing next season. I know that's your goal. Do you think you'd like to do more, though, than just production and direction?" Michael asked, seemingly genuinely curious.

"Are you seriously handing out compliments and asking questions about my personal goals? Before noon and without a drink in your hand?" I was skeptical. Michael's mentoring had been more or less of the tough-love variety. "Uh, well, cinematography and maybe editing are also things I think I'd be interested in — but that's more craft to support my ultimate goal of directing."

"Hm," he hummed, looking at me strangely. "You've never thought about acting? I feel like there's a natural ability in you."

"Hard pass. I prefer being back here, behind the camera."

"Well, if you ever change your mind, I might have the perfect role for you."

I laughed. "Will do, boss. Will do."

"Great, now go herd some cats. Quickly. We'll be rolling shortly, and I need your inspiration with me today. I'm feeling depleted."

I walked away, rolling my eyes. Michael's ridiculousness had reached critical levels.

# Chapter Ten

*Markus*

"Alina, hey!" I poked my head out of the door and whisper-shouted as I saw her messy pony-tailed shadow walk past my trailer.

She slowed and came to a halt, turning back. "Yeah?"

"Yeah, so, you said something about seeing me later?" I took a deep breath to try to slow down my heart rate, catching a whiff of her sandalwood and gardenia shampoo in the process.

"Oh. Totally, um, I don't really have any plans. You?" She looked a little surprised as she hugged her clipboard to her chest.

"No, I was actually wondering if you might want to hang out. I'm not feeling like going home. We could grab a drink? I could call my security team, have them meet us somewhere to keep the looks down."

"Security? Is that necessary? You were out the other night without anyone." She seemed confused but, then again, she had never traveled in the circles that I usually did and I seriously still had no idea how we hadn't been spotted the other night.

"Yeah, we got lucky. I don't usually do that. But it's not a problem to call them. Where do you want to go?"

"Honestly? It's been a long day and I feel gross and want to go home. You're welcome to come over, I guess, but I'm not going out looking like this." She gestured up and down her body, drawing my attention to the way her shirt pulled tightly across her chest — never mind the sweat stains around her collar.

I grinned at her. "Sure. I can do that. Do you want to meet there? David isn't here yet. I could come with you?"

"Whoa. I mean, okay? Aren't you worried about someone seeing us and talking shit?" she asked nervously.

I shrugged. "Haven't most people left already?"

She looked thoughtful, like she was weighing the pros and cons of being seen with me by anyone else on the set, especially with the news about me joining the show for the next season not being out yet . "I guess, but I still don't want people getting the wrong idea. Like we're together or something."

I leaned against the doorway. "Would that be so bad? I mean, what would happen?"

Her eyeroll was so extreme it looked like she was in danger of giving herself brain damage. "Stop playing dumb. Nothing would happen to you, but I'd get a rep and I don't need that. I'm trying to climb the ladder, not hump my way to the top, and I don't want any questions about that when I've already moved up pretty quickly."

I raised my hands and backed off. "Sorry, yeah, totally get it. I'll call David and have him drop me at your place, good?"

She sighed deeply. "Thanks, I'm heading out now. I'll leave the door open for you in case I'm in the shower and don't answer the door when you arrive."

"Cool, I'll see you in a bit." We both hesitated for a second, but then I leaned in and kissed her cheek, smoothing her hair away from her face, and booped her nose. "Drive safe."

\* \* \* \*

*Alina*

I was running a brush through my wet hair when the doorbell rang. My stomach immediately lit up with nerves as I ran to open the door. Markus was leaning against the frame, grinning at me like he knew the sinful secret to a perfect sex life. I immediately transposed that first glimpse of him to a life size poster that I wanted to permanently paste to my ceiling like a lovesick teenager with her favorite *Tiger Beat* photos.

"Sorry it took me a while, had to run home first to grab something for you," he said as he waved a wine bottle in my direction like I was a skittish dog he had to treat to get within touching distance.

I snatched it from his waggling fingers and examined the label. "Oh, nice! Hey, is this from your family's winery?"

"Yeah, my brother sent me a case of it. It's supposed to be good."

I was tracing the letters of his family's name on the label as he followed me into my tiny kitchen, where I pulled out a wine key and pointed him at some stemless glasses on one of the floating shelves. "Grab those and we'll head outside. Are you hungry? I can order something for you — I ate back at the studio."

"No, I'm good. Just the wine, then. And the company. Quite the celebration for my new job." His smile broke through again and it was blinding. I couldn't help but return it.

"It's very exciting, and I'm selfishly glad you'll be sticking around. What are you going to do between now and when filming for next season starts?" I asked as he sliced off the wrapper over the cork.

"I'm going back to Germany for a bit. It's been too long since I've spent time with my family. So I'll do that, but only for a couple of days rather than the few weeks I'd planned." He opened the bottle with a flourish, passed the cork over for me to sniff and poured us each a glass. We toasted wordlessly and stared out at the beach beyond my back gate. The silence was peaceful as we lounged, but Markus seemed a little antsy. He motioned toward the beach. "Do you want to go for a walk?"

"No, it's late and I'm physically exhausted, but my brain won't turn off. Want to watch a movie?"

"Oh, sure. Your choice. I'm only here for the celebration," he joked.

I smiled and my nerves finally started to calm. "Ah, perfect. Can we watch shitty nineties teen rom-coms?"

He groaned a little then surprised me with his accepting nod. "Heath Ledger is my idol. Always wished I could have worked with him," he said as he held out a hand to pull me up. The minute our palms connected, a mini electric charge pulsed outward and up my arm, leaving a trail of goosebumps in its wake.

Reflexively, he yanked me toward him and I stumbled into him, grabbing his bicep to keep from falling over completely. He steadied me carefully with one hand curled loosely around my waist, trapping me against his chest.

We were too close. I could smell the wine on his breath—the bouquet had expanded and threatened to overwhelm me with its heady scent. His heart rate pounded faster against the back of my hand and I watched in amazement as tiny gold flecks started to pop from his usually solid navy irises. His pupils dilated and he swallowed hard, his eyes dropping to my mouth, then drifting lower to the gaping V of my shirt's neckline.

The heat he was giving off as our bodies came into contact was frightening in its intensity. His head moved inexorably down toward mine and his full lips grazed my jawline. "Do you feel this too, when we're together?" he whispered.

All I could do was nod, swaying forward even farther to erase all space between us. One glass of wine deep and I was more than okay with climbing this guy like a tree. I felt like I had been suppressing every filthy daydream about him since waking up together hungover in my bed. *Finally.*

My fingernails dragged a shiver out of him as they moved up his chest to tangle in his hair. I tugged gently and he reached out and traced over my eyebrows and cheekbones with a feather-light touch, as if he were afraid he might break me.

My head fell back and he began to nip at my earlobe and down my neck to my exposed collarbone. I felt his groan in a bone-deep vibration that woke up every sensitive synapse along my body. It felt like lightning was crackling between us.

"We need to stop. I don't think we're ready for what could come next," he ground out.

From a very remote space, some part of me agreed with him—we'd never even talked about the other morning—and I managed to push him back the requested few paces. The rest of me practically wept at the loss of his physical presence.

He bent over at the waist, hands on his knees, gasping like he had run a marathon. Shakily, I tried to downplay our mutual reaction to each other. "We've got to knock this shit off, or every time we hang out is going to be an exercise in denial."

His eyes blazed up at me as he suppressed his desire, hands clenched on his thighs. He breathed out heavily, shook his head hard and gestured to the sliding door. "After you. I believe we have a date with a shitty nineties rom-com?"

"Teen rom-com," I corrected him self-importantly, while I tried to control my own shaking hands and play it cool. We really needed to have that talk about what the actual fuck we were doing with each other. Whether or not it meant anything. Denial was more than the name of a river in Egypt.

In the living room, Markus refilled my glass and gestured for me to sit down on the couch. I slumped down, still a little stunned, and grabbed the remote. After scrolling through our options, I clicked on *10 Things I Hate About You*. "Work for you? Since Heath Ledger turns your crank and all."

"Sure. Your house, your choice," he answered easily and sat down on the opposite end. "Holy shit, your couch is outrageously comfortable!"

It was. It really, really was. Soft and squishy, it basically ate everyone the minute they sat down. I threw a blanket toward him. He nodded gratefully and stretched out his legs on the couch while I tucked mine up. Our feet entangled almost immediately as the familiar opening scenes started to play.

Predictably, I woke up an hour later to run to the bathroom and drink some water to ward off the pounding headache that had hit after we'd finished the bottle of red wine. Markus had turned over and his face was buried in the back of the couch, and my heart ached with how badly I wanted him. After that life-altering kiss, I couldn't lie to myself about how much he was coming to mean to me, but the depth of my feelings was confusing. I didn't know if I could trust myself—or him, for that matter. Did he want me? Was I simply convenient?

I sighed and lay down behind him, my body curling around his, taking comfort from his warmth and proximity. *What's one more night of cuddles among friends?* As I drifted off, he sighed and muttered something in German. Then he grabbed the hand that I'd tentatively placed on his side and pulled my arm over him, tugging me closer until our bodies were plastered against each other and one of my legs slid between his. The reassuring beat of his heart echoed against the cheek I had pressed against his back.

\* \* \* \*

Waking up to Markus doing his very best impression of a boa constrictor for the second day in a row was oddly comfortable. There wasn't an inch of air between us from nose to toes, and we were clutching each other as though we feared someone would try to drag us apart, never to see the other again.

My television was still on in screen saver mode, and the flickering fireworks battled the early morning light as I shifted slightly away from him, trying to reach for my phone to check the time. The hand that was tangled in my hair, holding my face against his chest, slid down to cup my ass, a fingertip skating beneath the hem of my shorts to tease the soft skin on the back of my thighs. I gave up the search for my phone, instead letting my fingers dance across the smooth, hard-stacked abdominal muscles beneath his shirt while brushing my lips against his chest. The temperature of his body seemed to rise as our touches became bolder, more sure of their reception.

He growled into the top of my head and his wandering hands tickled my ribs as they skirted back up to stroke the sides of my breasts. As his thumb circled around to flick my nipple, I moaned and craned my neck up so I could reach his mouth. I bit down hard — harder than I'd intended — onto his full lower lip, and he effortlessly flipped us over to cage me in beneath his body.

"You bit the shit out of my lip..." He trailed off as he dropped his mouth to mine in a bruising kiss that left me tasting blood. The urge to consume each other took over our half-awake bodies as we kissed in a hot, messy tangle of lips, teeth and tongues.

My phone started ringing as he toyed with the hem of my shirt, and I groped blindly to silence it. He pulled back abruptly, almost leaping to the other side of the couch, and scrubbed his hands through his hair. We sat there panting, me clutching my phone as an ineffectual barrier. He gestured roughly between us. "Forgive me. I have no idea what's going on with me, with this. I feel like I'm on fire when I'm with you, like touching you is the cool water bringing relief."

"Markus, stop. I feel the same way." I gulped, deciding to be brave about the feelings I was only now starting to admit to. "But maybe it could be more, right? Do you feel that too?"

"Maybe? No. We're friends, right? I mean, if you wanted to try friends with benefits I'd be into that. But 'more'?" He shook his head, and his concerned look pierced right through my happy bubble of endorphins.

*Oh.*

He hastened to add, "I mean, I'm really fucking attracted to you, and I like you a lot. But I'm coming off of a terrible relationship, amongst other shit. 'More' shouldn't even be a possibility, given the mess I'm finding my way out of. Right? Why would you even want me?"

*Ouch.* It wasn't as if I hadn't considered the fact that I was a convenient rebound. That didn't stop his rejection from hurting like a bitch.

I rolled out from under him and adjusted my clothes. "I've got to check who called, might have been Michael. Be ready for that network meeting tonight, it's at eight-thirty."

He nodded and hesitated with a hand halfway outstretched toward me. I recoiled and he finally picked himself up and attempted to flatten out the sleepy cowlicks that had formed in his wild bedhead. We sat there in awkward silence, me huddled into a corner of the couch fiddling with my phone and trying to look as if I was completely absorbed in typing out some stupid text to Michael, him waiting to see if I was going to call him on his bullshit.

"I'm sorry," he said softly. He stood and jammed his feet into the shoes he'd lined up neatly at the foot of the couch. I didn't reply, didn't even look up. Ten seconds later, he was gone, like a shimmering mirage that had falsely promised safety in the middle of the desert. I blinked back the sudden moisture in my eyes, hard. Falling for broken people was a terrible idea and working with them even worse. I didn't know how I'd pretend to be fine the next time I saw him, but I couldn't afford to let anything affect my job.

# Chapter Eleven

*Markus*

It was official. I was losing it. Since I'd left her home that morning after stupidly denying any feelings on my part, I had done nothing but think about Alina and what a relationship with her would be like. Run a scene. Imagine skiing in the Alps with her. Get coffee and try to chat with coworkers. Imagine her laughing while my brothers did dumb impressions of my movie characters. Have Candace touch up my makeup to cover the permanent blush from imagining her unruly chocolate waves spread out across my pillows.

That was pretty much where my head was at all fucking day. And I had messed everything up by pushing her away, telling her that we weren't anything. The regret was eating me alive. I could have come clean, told her I felt the same but that I wasn't ready for anything serious. But no. Instead I had panicked and shot her down in the most condescending way possible.

To cap it all off, Michael seemed to have come unglued and kept unexpectedly switching up the order for the day's shoot before the summit the three of us were supposed to attend with the network execs later in the evening. The production staff was pulling their hair out trying to keep up with him and Alina was nowhere to be found. By lunchtime, Candace was blotting my face — yet again — and I took a chance, asking if her friend was going to be on set soon.

She blinked at me and said slyly, "Wouldn't you like to know?"

I'd never had the patience for dealing with coy women. "Well, yes. That's why I'm asking. I kind of owe her an apology. Is she sick? Michael seems to be losing his mind without his muse in place."

"You like her," she said smugly.

"I do. She's a very nice person who's becoming a good friend, which I'm apparently in dire need of, given the way everyone who I thought was my friend seems to have gone running straight for Kate or the press to take her side in our break-up."

"I know. But you *like* like her, don't you?" She grinned at me, not at all offended.

"Are we in primary school again? *Like* like her? Of course I like her. She's incredibly kind. She likes sugary cereal. And her shampoo smells amazing. Plus she looks fantastic in just a T-shirt — "

Alina's verbal diarrhea seemed to have become contagious. And Candace was staring over my shoulder at someone. Her eyes bugged out as they slid back to me. I was completely lost. "Candace? Is she here or not? If she's sick, maybe I should stop by her place and check on her."

"I knew it!"

I turned slowly away from Candace to face Michael. "Knew what? I was only asking—"

"Oh, I get it. I know what you were asking. Her shampoo smells amazing and she looks fantastic in just a T-shirt? How long has this been going on?" He continued, gloating, "I knew something was happening with you two."

"No, n-n-no. We've hung out a couple of times outside of work, but that's it. Nothing going on."

They both stared at me, disbelieving, and I jammed both hands into my hair, tugging on the ends. I wasn't fooling either of them.

"Yeah, I knew it. You two have stupid googly eyes around each other," Michael said, while Candace nodded wildly. "But whatever, it's your business. I need to head back. We're shifting scenes again. Total pain in the ass, I know, but we'll do that final battle scene sometime this evening." He started walking away shaking his head, muttering, "I fucking knew it!"

I wanted to bash my head into the nearest wall.

As he narrowly avoided crashing into an intern, he turned and shouted, "Oh, and she's out running errands for me today. Should be on set any second. Now keep it together, we've got two more scenes to shoot before that network meeting."

Candace was still staring at me with wide, apologetic eyes. "Hey, sorry, I didn't mean for Michael to hear any of that. Alina is going to murder me." She turned tail and fled.

I dropped my head to the table. It was going to be a toss-up to see which one of us—Candace or me—Alina decided to kill first.

\* \* \* \*

Michael was mid-rant with a hapless production assistant over the temperature of his coffee, of all things, when Alina's voice crackled over his headset. "Boss? I'm back. Heard you need me on Stage Two?"

"Get your ass over here. We're down to the last scenes of this entire godforsaken season and I need an extra hand," he growled.

The production assistant with the coffee calamity had taken advantage of the interruption to disappear — smart girl — but now Michael was pacing in tight circles, yelling out random commands as he waited for Alina to show.

I sidled up to Rory and a few other cast members and asked in a voice that was hopefully too low to be overheard, "Has he been like this the entire time you've been shooting?"

"Totally," Rory answered cheerfully. "Sometimes it's entertaining, but I think we're all a little over it at this point."

Alina came around the corner of the set and beelined toward Michael. "What's up? I tracked down your dry cleaning, got some more green M&Ms, and your wife is now booked for the ladies' spa weekend of her dreams." Her face was red and a light gleam of sweat covered her forehead, a single drop tangled in her eyelashes. She looked run off her feet.

He swung her into a bear hug. "Alina, have I mentioned how much I fucking love you?"

She squirmed out of his arms and rolled her eyes. "Yes, a few times. Back it up, personal space here. What do you need?"

"We're on the last scene — the battle between Markus and Ethan — and I have to work out a few technical details. The extra you called in is still in makeup and we've got that meeting in an hour and a half, so I need you to stand in for her. We'll get everything blocked out around the three of you, okay?"

She frowned at him and asked, "Stand in?"

He impatiently grabbed her by the arm and pushed her toward me, Rory, Ethan and the scene choreographers. "Yeah, run the lines together and hit the marks so we can work out lighting and sound."

She shrugged. "Sure, I can do that."

"Great, places, everyone!"

The choreographer rushed up to our group and ran us through the action. Alina still looked a little bemused and out of place in her street clothes, while the rest of us were all in some badass fighting gear.

I sidled up to her. "You sure you're okay with this?"

She shrugged a little stiffly and wouldn't make eye contact with me. "Yeah, I've done this before when our visionary captain decided to do some last-minute changes to characters' wardrobe and makeup, no big deal. I'm only a body, you know? Plus, we *have* to make that meeting or we're fucked for next season."

I tugged her sleeve and she swung around, her hair wafting that faint floral scent my way. "Listen, I wanted to apologize for what happened this morning. I didn't explain myself well and I hurt your feelings. I really want to talk—"

Her eyes narrowed as she waved me off and mouthed, "Later."

"Okay, everyone. Let's walk it through, action!" shouted the assistant director while Michael continued to buzz around making minute changes.

Someone thrust a script into Alina's hands and we kicked off, walking side-by-side over to Rory and Ethan. The scene unfurled and Alina's and my scripted banter was actually a lot of fun as we taunted Ethan's character. We vibed off each other so well—maybe too well.

Finally, Ethan threw the first punch at me. Next to me, Alina growled and I bit my lip to keep from laughing. I dodged and faked my own first punch, then pulled out a futuristic fake sword. The half-battle commenced and Alina followed me from place to place. The actual actor would be heavily involved, but she had no idea about the choreography and there wasn't time for her to learn.

Finally it came to a climax as Ethan and Rory cornered Alina and me against a wall, swords at our throats. It was my cue to surrender and I said my idiotic line. Ethan and Rory melted away, leaving Alina and me alone, still pressed against the wall.

I turned to her and she was frowning down at the script as she said her line, "Well, that could have gone better." Her delivery was well-paced, a little out of breath, as if she had been fighting too, but I knew what was coming next. The role she was standing in for was a love interest as well as my partner and the screenplay called for us to have an emotionally charged kiss next— although exactly why this was supposed to happen was beyond me. *Ridiculous show.*

She frowned again and looked up, rolled her eyes at me and sighed. She went up on her tiptoes and leaned into me. We mis-timed the entire thing. I was going for the perfunctory cheek kiss, as was she, only our lips met in the middle as we both went for the same cheek.

My eyes were open, but hers weren't. Until our lips met, and they went wide in surprise. It was a gentle press of our mouths, but the sheer electricity that traveled down my spine was as brilliant as more than half of the full-on sexual encounters in my life. We stayed frozen in that pose and stared at each other. My arms went around her reflexively as she swayed on her toes and I lifted my head from hers. She was frowning at me. "Dammit, every time. Are you okay?"

The room seemed to have disappeared. "Yeah," I whispered. "Are you?"

She sighed and my arms tightened around her. "I'm fine. Also, yes, you hurt my feelings, but I'm trying to forget about that for the moment. Can we talk after the meeting?"

Our lips hovered within inches of each other and I longed to close that gap. "Yes, after the meeting. Again, I'm sorry."

"Whoa, cut!" Michael's incredulous command broke us apart. "Well, you two. That escalated quickly. Alina, thank *you* for your willingness to assist. Great job with the lines. Can you get everyone ready to break down the rest of the set and clear out while we film this?"

She stepped away from my arms, her face bright red. "Sure, Michael," she said briskly, trying to recover her equanimity. "I've got this."

I watched her walk away and Michael strolled up to me, hands in pocket, shit-eating grin on his face. "Mmhmm, you just *like* her, eh?" he said sotto voce, then clapped his hands. "Everyone ready? Places. Last run-through, this one at full speed with fighting choreography."

A short-haired blonde stepped next to me and smiled. "Nice to meet you. That was super-hot with the stand-in. Do you think she's into women? Can I get her number?"

I shook my head in confusion.

"Action!" Michael shouted.

I totally *like* liked her and I needed to stop lying about it.

# Chapter Twelve

*Alina*

While they rehearsed and finally ran the scene, I got the crew ready to wrap. People clapped as I closed the door to the stage where the action was happening and I took several awkward bows. I issued Michael's orders to break down the remainder of the small sets so there would only be the one they were presently using to take care of when filming finally wrapped for the day.

There was a lot of catcalling about making out with the hottest man in the world, and more than a few speculative looks, but it was relatively good-natured, as if no one would ever think that we'd *really* be together. And that was both reassuring that I wouldn't get caught up in gossip, but also a little bit of a kick in the teeth of my insecurity.

Everyone was chattering and gossiping about the karaoke battle planned for the informal cast and crew party that night and, luckily, we were almost immediately forgotten in the excitement. I had hoped to drop into the party after the meeting, but now I had promised Markus time to talk. I steeled my spine as I thought about exactly what he might have to say.

* * * *

Candace took one look at me in my sad clown makeup and still-wrinkled little black emergency dress and practically tore it off my body. She threw it at a passing wardrobe assistant to iron, shoved a robe at me and marched me to a vanity for quick makeup and hair.

"Girl, you're going to look great. Where are you going again?"

"Nobu. It's only dinner with the execs, but we're selling them on Markus joining the show and it's a huge opportunity for me to network," I nervously confessed.

She stopped working, the brush still held against my face, tickling me. "He's joining the show? And you two? What's going on there?"

"Yes, shit, I wasn't supposed to say anything! You can't tell anyone about him joining the show. If it happens, it will be announced at the Premiere." I batted her hand away from my face as I sneezed. "Nothing's going on with us. We're friends, okay?"

Candace started working again and hummed in agreement. "You better believe you're going to spill the details later, girl." Her words were vaguely threatening.

"Of course, promise." I trusted her, but couldn't deal with the third degree on the full Markus-Alina saga. Not when his rejection was so raw.

Michael burst in as I was sliding into my heels. He whistled as he looked me up and down. "Very nice, m'dear. Are you ready? Our chariot awaits. How do I look?" He had changed into a new Hawaiian shirt over his usual jeans and Birkenstock sandals, and looked like the aging hippie artist he was.

I stifled a laugh and said, "Lovely, boss. Let's roll. Are we waiting on Markus?"

"No, he'll meet us there. He needs to shower and change, get rid of that makeup. Besides, I want you to have time to impress the suits before he shows up. You deserve that, at the minimum, for getting him onboard."

I protested that I'd had nothing to do with it, but he wasn't listening as we ducked into the waiting car. He instructed the driver where to take us and turned to me. "Alina, I have something I want to ask you. A proposal, if you will."

I dropped my phone into my bag and glanced over at his uncharacteristically serious face. "Sure, what's up?"

His face was so innocent, his eyes huge like a baby deer's. "Well, it's like this. Remember when I asked if there was anything else you wanted to do besides produce and direct?"

I nodded, wondering where this was going.

"And then I asked if you'd ever thought about acting?"

"And I said, very clearly, 'no'?" I answered carefully.

"You did, but I'm wondering if you'd reconsider."

Shockwaves emanated through me. This was not part of my Plan.

He took my silence for permission to continue. "Having Markus is great and it will totally sway the network into renewing us for at least the next season.

But what if his love interest storyline went deeper? With someone he really had chemistry with? It wouldn't have to be the main arc in the story, but a few steamy scenes would make ratings go gangbusters and the viewers would eat that shit up with a spoon and lick the bowl." He looked at me hopefully.

"Yes, I can see why that would be an attractive addition to the season. Are you running this by me to see if I think the idea is a good one, or for some other reason?" I was so, so hopeful that he wasn't about to ask what I was pretty sure he wanted to ask.

"No, not exactly. I'm wondering if you'd be willing, on behalf of the show, to step in for a small-ish role as Markus' character's love interest. I promise that it would be a very little part and that I'd totally make it worth your while."

I exploded. "No, Michael! I did not sign up to be in front of the camera. I do not want to be known for this. No."

"Alina, I know, I know," he soothed. "This is very sudden, but hear me out. If you were to do this, and if Markus is amenable too, we could even spin a whole 'real' relationship arc. Play it off as if you were this starstruck couple from different sides of the industry track. It would be huge publicity for the show. Life imitating art."

I looked at him in disbelief. We were almost to the restaurant and a dull hum seemed to block out everything but Michael's voice.

"And we'd make sure you got paid very well for your part. I'd also include an offer to be my assistant director on an upcoming film project—your choice which one. Plus introductions and references for any of my contacts. If we can get through this next season, you, me and Markus can walk away with our heads high and reputations very well enhanced."

"You're not kidding?" I asked, still wondering when the "April Fool's!" was coming, even though it was August.

"Nope, I'm not. Seriously, you two have en fuego chemistry and that will make it easier if we script in a love interest at the last minute. I loved watching you run lines together during the walk-through. Markus hasn't come alive like that since he joined us and it's been like pulling teeth. I mean, he's a consummate professional and way better than anyone else," he said carelessly.

"Ouch," I muttered.

"*Psh*, you know it's true. He's incredible, but today was the first day that I actually saw his full range again. Haven't seen that since we worked together a few years ago," he reminisced.

"Hmmm," I murmured, wondering if he'd finally get back to his point.

"Anyways, added bonus if you join, the network heads would go bonkers if we could at least hint that the on-screen romance might be turning slightly real."

"Let me get this straight. You think that me taking on a small role will make Markus even better. I'll have a couple of steamy scenes with Markus Fucking Shellenberg. And somehow this combination will save the show?" I asked incredulously.

"Yep. Definitely. Having him on is the big deal, but you'll help get the most out of him. Your chemistry, the trust he has in you, it's all going to make him more effective." Michael sounded positive and, worse yet, he was starting to convince me.

"So, what's in it for me?" I asked. "You're serious that, if I do this and the show is 'saved', you're promising me an assistant director cred on the upcoming film project of my choice? Plus access to your Rolodex."

"Uh-huh. Cast salaries are a lot higher than crew, too. If the network sees the value in Markus joining as a regular, they're going to be prepared to open the purse strings. Opening them a little further for you shouldn't be an issue if they buy this."

"Can I think about it?" I asked, desperately hoping to put this off. "Also, shouldn't we ask Markus how he feels?"

"Nope, he's an actor. The script is the script. You're different, though, and we need to be on the same page. Ideally, I'd like to propose this tonight, and we're going to be at the restaurant in — " He looked out the window, craning his head to see through the tinted glass. " — five minutes."

I dropped my head to my hands and started massaging my temples. This was a bananas offer. A little bit of bribery, to be sure, but an incredible opportunity. The contacts alone would be worth it. And kissing Markus here and there wasn't exactly a hardship either. My thoughts raced as I considered all the ramifications of saying yes. This would derail my steady rise for a year while I acted and it was possible that there would be a lot of gossip about me being linked with Markus that could invade my privacy, but the payoffs…were too good to pass up.

"Michael, I'll do it. Under two very important conditions."

"Shut the fuck up, really?" he crowed.

"Condition one—it is a small part. I'm an addition to the storyline, this isn't a leading role and the current characters remain in the forefront. Condition two—we are absolutely not pretending to be together for the press or publicity."

"No real-fake relationship? C'mon, Alina, that's half the fun of this idea." He pouted.

"Absolutely not. If you want to propose it to Markus and me, together, later, fine. But I'm not doing it unless Markus and I discuss it first. Away from you." I was adamant on the last one. I'd do almost anything for access to Michael's contacts and that A.D. cred, but not fake a relationship with someone I didn't want to admit I had real feelings for.

Michael's piercing gray eyes speared through me as he weighed my sincerity. "Fine. I accept your conditions, but we are definitely going to bring it to Markus for discussion at a later date. Can I tell the execs about this August surprise?"

I nodded, wondering what Markus would think. "Yeah, but I want a contract ready at the same time Markus' is. And you better believe I'm going to be going over it with a fine-tooth comb."

We walked through the usual camera-happy crowd lined up in front of Nobu and into the restaurant. Right away, I noticed the group of two men and two women in suits at the bar, the smell of money, power and prestige washing off them and pulling looks from tables nearby. While not well-known figures, they had that stance—impeccably lazy posture, open body language but narrowed eyes—that let people know they were important, not to be fucked with.

In his trademark loud Hawaiian shirt, Michael led the way as we cut through the crowd. People attempted to stop and chat almost every step he took, but he waved them off, eyes on the prize. I trailed behind like a duckling, murmuring my "Excuse me"s like the polite Midwesterner I was. Finally, we reached the suits.

"Barry, Christopher, Susan, Frances, how are you all on this fine, fine evening?" Michael had his jovial, working-the-room voice in full effect as he went through the handshake-air-kiss routine with each of the execs. "This is Alina. She's one of our assistant producers and the reason we're all here tonight."

They looked at me curiously and nodded, but no one held out their hand for a handshake or stepped up for the cheek kiss. I nodded and faded away into the background as the Michael Show took off.

"Have you ordered drinks yet?" he asked.

"Yes," one of the women—Susan, I think—answered. "And our table should be ready shortly."

Michael waved down the bartender—probably a struggling actor—who immediately walked away from another patron. "Sir, can I get you anything?"

"I'll have a vodka gimlet with a lemon. Alina?" he asked as he nudged me.

The bartender didn't look in my direction as I asked for a glass of white wine. He knew where the sources of power and influence were in the room. He returned with our drinks in record time as Michael made small talk with Barry and Frances, who, it turned out, were married and had attended Michael's most recent wedding.

"Sir? Your drinks. Can I say that I really enjoyed this last season of *Southern Gods*. I love the show. Are you doing any open casting?" gushed the bartender.

Normally Michael would have brushed the guy off. In this case, though, he had something to prove.

Michael handed me my drink and looked at the execs, smirked at them, and replied, "Oh, it's possible. Keep an eye on the message boards. You may see something soon, very soon."

Frances and Susan looked at each other with raised eyebrows, and it looked like Susan was about to ask Michael what he was talking about when the host came over to seat us. We were put at a corner table with plenty of space for privacy, as I'd requested, and I felt a momentary relief that my efforts hadn't been in vain. As soon as we were seated Susan leaned over to me and asked confidentially, "I'm sure you know what this is about. Could you give us a hint?"

I smiled at her and tried to defer. "Oh, you know Michael. When he's this excited, do you think he's going to keep it a secret much longer?"

She hummed in agreement and turned to Michael. Her voice and demeanor hardened. "Michael. What's this about? You wanted to meet with us. You know where we stand on renewing the show. What on earth do you think might change our minds?"

I liked how she took charge of the conversation and that the men sat back while she did so. I didn't know much about Susan from the network, but I kinda wanted to be her when I grew up. Immediately, I started cataloging her body language and vocal delivery.

"Susan, please. I would *never* think to try to sway you one way or another," Michael said. Barry and Frances looked incredulous, Christopher actually snorted, but Susan never changed expression.

"Oh, all right, fine. The thing is, Alina here is friends with our guest star, Markus Shellenberg. You know he did this short stint as a favor to me, but he recently came to me with an idea for his character to be made permanent. Actually, Alina suggested it when he told her that he was enjoying himself with the show, then they brought it to me." Michael's self-satisfied proclamation landed like a grenade on our table.

The four suits looked at one another and seemed to have an entire nonverbal conversation. Then Susan picked up point again. "Why is that an attractive proposition for us? We've all heard the rumors about him, that he's unreliable and something of a loose cannon on sets. Sure, he's a truly great talent, but I don't know if hiring him is a such an advantage."

That was how Susan lost credibility with me, and my stomach started to churn, my hackles went up and I was *this* close to interrupting her and demanding a retraction when Michael smoothly stepped in. "Susie, Susie, please. You know that's a big pile of horseshit. George Sellers put together a terrible movie and is blaming it on everyone, especially Markus. Sellers can't own up to the fact that he's lost his vision and touch. He's done."

I'd had no idea, and filed that away for future consideration when I looked at jobs.

"Markus is rock solid and incredibly bankable. I've had zero issues with him during this shoot and he's fit right in with our little family, right, Alina?"

I nodded, and the Michael train barreled on, "You know he's good, so stop trying to stonewall me. There's an added benny too. Alina here has agreed to take on a tiny role as Markus' character's love interest."

Everyone's attention immediately shifted to me and sharpened. I felt incredibly exposed in the predatory gazes of the four executives. Frances chose to speak first. "Why is that a good thing?"

"Oh, come on, Franny. You *know* it's a good thing. Markus gets a love interest and runs some sexy scenes — excuse me, his *character* gets a love interest and the press will eat that shit up. I mean, Alina stood in for a scene with him while we were waiting for the actress to get through Wardrobe and their chemistry is incredible. The press will probably manufacture an entire relationship for the two of them and the publicity will be unbelievable."

My misgivings about agreeing to this idea were mounting as all of the suits transferred their focus back to me and nodded decisively.

Christopher tossed Susan a 'back-off' look and took over point. "Michael, I love it. Any publicity is good publicity, and we know that for a fact. Having him on will definitely be publicity-worthy." He sounded so smug as he raised his glass to his lips and took a sip, then set it down with a loud thunk. "Alina, congrats. You've single-handedly saved the show."

But I was still watching Susan and Frances, who were skewering me with their eyeballs. Susan angled her head away and stood abruptly. "Excuse me for a moment, I need to take a call." She looked at me meaningfully and turned and headed back to the crowded bar. After a moment, I stood as well and muttered something about the bathroom, but no one was paying attention to me anymore after toasting the next season.

"Alina." Susan appeared next to me at the corner of the bar. Her Botoxed brow managed to crease in concern. "I want to make sure that this is something that you're comfortable with. The press attention, publicity, it's going to be a lot for a newbie. The scenes as well. I need to hear it from you that you're truly okay with what amounts to a massive life change." She looked wistful for a moment as she said, "I was you once and I would hate to see a promising career get waylaid by ugly gossip."

"Susan, thank you for asking and your concern. I can't tell you how much I appreciate it," I began. "But I'm fine with this. Completely comfortable. Markus and I are good friends, nothing is going to affect that and, I think, with the right legal documentation, I'll be largely safe. I also trust Michael."

She shook her head ruefully at me. "I'd be careful about who you trust in this town, but it sounds like you've got it all figured out. Here, take my card. If anything comes up during filming, feel free to reach out to me. Anytime."

I took the card she pressed into my hand and nodded. She squeezed my shoulder in an unexpected moment of solidarity and walked back to our table, the clicking of her skyscraper, ass-kicking heels muted by the clashing conversations of the diners and bar patrons. I read over the words on her card—her title, cell, email—as I tried to give enough space between the two of us returning to hide our private discussion.

The heavy weight of an arm wrapping around my waist and the nudge of a chin on my shoulder had me whirling around, ready to give someone a major lecture on personal space. My pointer finger poked into a hard chest covered in soft oxford cloth, and a familiar laugh tickled the hair on my neck. *Markus*.

"Oh, it's you," I said stupidly.

"Hey, I'm sorry I startled you. It's crowded in here and I haven't been able to find anyone." He looked around as if he could make Michael materialize before our eyes.

"Ah, no. I mean, it's okay. I'm fine. Actually, I'm glad you found me out here before getting to the table."

He stepped back and raised an eyebrow at me. "Oh?"

I nudged him with my elbow. "Yes, oh. I'll make it quick and then we should get over there. I think they're anxious to meet you in person." I took a deep breath. "Okay, here it goes. On the way here, Michael offered me a role on the show too. As your love interest. Not that that's really super important, but he offered it to me with a couple of huge benefits — along with making a lot more money than I am now — and I said yes."

Markus's face went through a gamut of emotions — surprise, excitement, before landing on furious. "You're joking, please tell me you're joking."

"No? Why? What's your problem with this?"

"My problem, Alina, is that's coercion, bribery, extortion."

Now I was starting to get mad. "Markus, I laid down conditions. I'm fine with this. You don't get to make these decisions for me."

"You're sure about this? He could try to manipulate the situation badly," he muttered.

"I'm one hundred percent sure," I said firmly as I took his hand in mine and pulled, bringing him down to my level. "It's going to be fine."

He stepped back but maintained a hold of my hand and nodded reluctantly. "Okay, it's your decision. Show me to our table?"

I pulled him along behind me and could feel his eyes hot on my backside, roving up and down my exposed neck to my heels. He pulled closer and whispered, "You look gorgeous in that dress. Can we still talk later?"

By that point we were at the table and I nodded, working my hand out of his grasp, and sank into the chair he pulled out for me. He took the empty chair to my left and nodded at Michael and the suits. "Hi, I'm Markus. Sorry I'm late, took a little longer to get here from the set than anticipated."

Barry jumped in first. "No problem, Markus, we're glad you're here."

"Yes, it's really lovely to meet you. I'm a big fan of your work," chimed in Frances.

"Indeed, and we hear that you'd like to join our little show?" asked Christopher.

Susan remained quiet, stone-faced but watching Markus closely. Every one of his twitches and facial expressions was under her microscope. I reached out without thinking and placed a hand on his leg, which had gently started to shake.

"Well, yes, I'd love to, actually. I've really enjoyed my time on the show. It's been fun to work on a series as opposed to a film, and I have a great relationship with Michael. This has almost felt like a vacation!" he joked.

"And Alina," muttered Michael helpfully as he reached for the appetizers they'd ordered while I'd been speaking with Susan.

"Yes, and Alina. She's fantastic, great producer." He smiled at me and I looked down at the table. I wanted, badly, to go back to being a fly on the wall.

"Thanks," I murmured.

"Markus." Susan joined the conversation. "What do you think about this idea to have Alina join the cast as a love interest for you? She's not a professional actor and I'm concerned this will affect the storyline and shooting timeline adversely if we lose one of the top producers."

"Michael, I'll leave the production point to you, but I'm fine with it if it's what she decides that she wants to do. I'm sure she'll be perfect given the opportunity to learn. I've read lines with her and she's honestly a natural." Markus played the diplomat so well.

"She's gonna be great. Got a coach already lined up—or I will, shortly. No worries here," garbled Michael through a mouth full of sushi.

"Hmm. Well, if everyone is on the same page, then I suppose congratulations are in order?" Susan asked.

Barry, Frances and Christopher obligingly raised their glasses. Markus, Michael and I were a beat behind them.

"To *Southern Gods*," toasted Michael.

"To *Southern Gods*," we chorused.

After dinner, Michael herded the execs over to the bar and nodded at us to get the hell out. Markus and I said our goodbyes. This time I was the recipient of handshakes and air kisses too, and we headed for a discreet back door and a cab stand.

"Alina, are you going home? We still need to talk," Markus said in a concerned tone.

"No, I'm not going home. Sorry, yes, we do need to talk, but I'm supposed to meet up with Candace and the rest of them at that party. Would you like to come? Or we could get a car together, talk on the way and you could drop me off at the club?" I offered.

"Is the party secure?" he asked nervously.

"Um, I think so?"

"Hmm. I'm going to assume that means no. I'll come, but I'm going to call some people and tell them to meet us there. They'll be unobtrusive, promise."

"Okay," I said slowly, not liking the reminder of the differences between us.

"I know, I know. But still. It's important, okay? I had David wait. He should be already outside. He can take us. Will that work for you?"

"No need for a stinky shared car? Hell yeah, I'll take the free ride, let's go!"

Markus laughed, took me by the hand and pulled me out of the door and into the waiting SUV for our Talk, and this time I was determined to get the last word.

# Chapter Thirteen

*Markus*

I slid into the car after helping Alina up, and settled in with a probably dark look on my face. While I didn't think Alina and Michael were trying to pull one over on me, I was a little peeved that they hadn't conferred with me about her joining the show. I was pretty sure that was wounded pride over her making such a big decision that affected the both of us, without confiding in me. And maybe that was something I needed to work on, but I felt extraordinarily protective of her — her reputation, as well as her, personally. The film industry, and Hollywood specifically, could be very cruel to newcomers and I wanted to help her navigate it.

"So, do you want to tell me the long version about what happened this evening?" I asked.

"Um, it depends, I guess," she said.

"On…what, exactly?" I tried to keep my impatience in check, but I'd always hated feeling left out, not knowing the motivations of everyone around.

"On whether or not you're pissed at me. Because it kinda looks like you are, and that makes me a little mad. It's my career, my life. We're *friends*, but that doesn't give you leverage over me," she said emphatically with her fingers at her temples, massaging the pressure points. "I mean, I'm excited about the doors that this will open for me and you're shitting all over my parade."

"I'm sorry, I don't mean to. I'm worried about this — not you or your decision making — about the magnitude of work you're about to take on. Plus the potential for the network and Michael to try to push us into some sort of publicity stunt. I don't want you to get caught up in any of that."

"That's fine, Markus, and I appreciate it, but it's not your job to protect me. We'll take it one day at a time and, for now, let's be excited about what comes after this for me — an A.D. credit on an upcoming film? Access to Michael's contacts? Fuck yeah." She crowed and held out a hand for a high five.

"Besides," she said, "the screenwriters are going to have to work overtime to even create small roles for us. There's simply not enough time between now and when we're supposed to start rehearsals. We'll see when they get the contracts and story capsules to us, I guess."

I rubbed my chin and jaw, feeling the scrape of stubble I should have shaved before leaving the set. "You're right. Hadn't thought about it that way. What are you going to do about the contract negotiations? My team is available if you'd like to use them."

She looked a little embarrassed as she muttered, "I might have already told Michael he could send the contract directly to them with yours."

I burst out laughing. "Not presumptuous at all. Perfect, saves me the trouble of doing anything but texting them." I pulled out my phone and sent the team a quick note that they'd be handling negotiations for two people. The car rolled to a stop before I could finish.

"We're here, Markus. If you want to talk to me about our penchant for inappropriate wake-up calls, it's going to have to be inside." She pushed me toward the door.

"Already? Security isn't here yet. I'd kind of like to wait." I wanted to keep driving around. Talk out what was happening with us privately and not in a huge group of all-seeing eyes.

She shrugged. "If you want to wait for security, you do you. I want to get in and get a drink. Do you think I can tell people?"

"You can tell Candace, which means Rory and Ethan too, I guess. I only know a few people on this set, but I can guarantee not everyone is going to be pleased. Many will feel threatened. So maybe we wait till Michael makes the announcement and we have a messaging plan in place to control the narrative." This reminded me, uncomfortably, of my relationship with Kate, how every movement, word and gesture of affection had been choreographed and examined so closely that they were eventually stripped of all meaning.

"Whatever, you're probably right," she said, and the excitement in her eyes died a little. She rolled her shoulders back and opened the door a crack. "Sure you're not coming?"

"I'll be in within ten minutes."

She nodded, reached out and tapped my hand. "See you inside."

My hand burned from that slight touch as she hopped out and slammed the door closed.

From the front of the car came a low whistle, and I looked up at David's grinning face in the rear-view mirror. "Oh, man. You're in trouble. Can't wait to see how this unfolds!" he said gleefully.

I glared at him and spun my phone on my thigh, wondering why it was taking so long for security to arrive. "David, come on. It's not like that, or it shouldn't be, you know? All that shit with Kate, I'm not doing it again."

"Markus, if no one else is going to tell you this, then I will. That woman is *not* Kate Williams. I've only met her twice and can already tell that she's the furthest thing from it. She's real and smart and determined. Not an ambitious climber or manipulative actress trying to keep you under her thumb."

I gaped at him, wondering why on earth no one had bothered to say anything to me before. David seemed to understand my silence and he said, in a more comforting voice, "I'm sorry I didn't say anything earlier. She had her claws in you deep and I was worried I'd lose my job. Alina is not like that, Markus, so be careful with her. Stop looking for ulterior motives."

*Ping!* A chime from my phone alerted me that security was in place, and I tried to smile at David. "Thanks, I understand. Can you circle around for a while? I'm not sure how long we — *I* — will be here and I might need a quick getaway."

"No problem, Markus. I'll be here."

Walking into the club, I saw the place was packed. Talent, crew and a few hangers-on — everyone was there and I couldn't see Alina anywhere. I headed for the bar and ordered a vodka soda.

"My man!" A voice cut through the crowd as Rory strolled up with Ethan close behind him.

"Guys, hey," I responded as I tried to see through the crush of people.

"She's around somewhere, saw her at the bar with Candace," Ethan offered while Rory smirked next to him.

"Hmm? Who?" I asked, now up on my toes and using my full six feet three inches to my advantage.

Rory punched my arm and yanked me down. "Damn, dude, be cool. Alina, man. She's with Candace right now. I'm sure we'll see her in a few. Now talk to us. A little bird in Michael's office had some interesting things to say about you, our favorite assistant producer and next season."

"What?" I asked, stunned that the news was out already. The gossip red flags from day one started to wave in front of my eyes.

"One of Michael's assistants overheard him on the phone with the screenwriters after our last scene. He asked them how they were coming along with your new part and then ordered them to factor in a love interest for you that would be played by a new actor who's already involved with the show. Assuming that's Alina," Ethan explained patiently, while Rory's grin and wiggling eyebrows had me gearing up for a fight.

"Oh, shit," I muttered. Then, in a louder, stronger voice, "Please keep this to yourselves. Officially, contracts haven't been signed, so we're not talking about it."

"What's all this? Hot guy convention?" Candace asked with a flirty smile as she strolled up and kissed Ethan and Rory on the cheeks, Alina trailing behind her with two glasses of what looked like vodka sodas. She wordlessly handed one of them to me.

"Oh, no. Markus was about to confirm something for us." Rory smirked.

"This is all I'm saying, and this does not leave our little circle here, okay?" Everyone nodded earnestly. "I wanted to join the cast if Michael had room for a supporting role. He said yes. Then, today, he asked Alina if she wanted to add some 'dimension' to my character by taking on an even smaller role as my love interest."

"And I said yes, because he also offered me some sweet, sweet bennies," interjected Alina. "That's it, guys, no other news. It's very much a not big deal."

Rory, Ethan and Candace all looked at one another and, in concert, snorted. Candace recovered first. "Oh, my sweet summer child. If you believe that, I've got a bridge in Alaska to sell you. It's going to be a huge deal, but you should enjoy it before news gets out." She pulled Alina in for a suffocating hug. "You're happy?"

Alina nodded.

"Then I'm happy for you. Come on, boys, let's go hit the karaoke." She pulled Ethan and Rory after her. Rory turned back to wink and make kissy faces until Ethan grabbed his chin and turned him to follow Candace's swaying hips through the crowd. The look of affection on Rory's face as he glanced at both of them was undeniably sweet.

Left alone, Alina and I stared at each other, a little island in the sea of people. Her eyes dropped to her drink and she stirred it up with the straw, making the ice cubes clink musically.

"It's going to be a big deal, isn't it." It wasn't so much a question as a statement and she let loose a massive sigh, her shoulders slumped in disappointment.

"Yeah, it is, but we can ride it out together. Should we go watch the karaoke?"

"Yes, let's do it, maybe we should sing? *I Think We're Alone Now* is always a huge hit," she said with a smile so bright it practically blinded me.

I frowned at her and she elbowed me in the ribs. "Kidding, jeez. You know I can't sing unless wasted, and I'm at least four drinks out from that."

"Probably for the best." I laughed, but she'd touched a nerve. That reminder of how she'd stood by me when I was on such unstable footing after joining the show, her smile that never failed to reach me, the high of being with her — and having a guarantee that we'd be together, even for work, for a while — flipped a switch inside me. I suddenly wanted — no, ached — for *more*.

"Nah, I want to watch tonight, and we still need to talk." It came out flirtatious, and I was glad, because suddenly I had the balls to propose something that was borderline stupid.

# Chapter Fourteen

*Markus*

We settled into a couch in a quiet-ish corner of the karaoke lounge and I slung an arm over the back of the loveseat. My security team had unobtrusively followed us in and were stationed at a table near our couch, chatting over two glasses of what was definitely water. Alina leaned in to whisper something in my ear as I turned to ask her if she wanted another drink. The timing was perfect and our noses bumped as our lips met with a static shock.

She pulled back abruptly and brought her fingers to her mouth as she shook her head. "Dammit, Markus. What are we doing here? What do you want from me?"

"I'm sorry," I rushed to say. We sat for a moment, eyes locked on each other, and the room seemed to fall away. Watching her own her future tonight, I wanted to be part of that—somehow. The thing was, I didn't think I was boyfriend material at the moment, and who knew if I ever would be again? And 'boyfriend' was such a foolish word for what I wanted to be to her. I took a deep breath.

"I'm sorry about what I said to you at your house this morning. You were brave and I was a coward. You were right, this thing between us is more than attraction and, maybe, it could be more, period. But I disregarded what you were saying and attempted to ignore how I was feeling. I've got some groveling to do, so I'll do it if you'll let me."

"Continue," she said with a raised eyebrow.

"Here's the thing. I feel like I just woke up from a five-year nightmare. I'm not the person I thought I was, and I'm trying to figure that out, you know? Meeting you, our friendship, it's been a huge part of that process. Every time we talk, things fall more into perspective. Every time I'm with you, I feel like I get a new piece of myself back."

I attempted a smile, but her poker face was rock solid. "I don't know if I can be in a relationship right now. I got lost in my last one and don't really trust myself. When you asked me the other morning about the potential for *more*, I kind of freaked out. It's not that I don't feel the same, but I guess I worry that I'd hurt you, or that you'd hurt me, and I'd end up losing you altogether."

She looked down at her drink and swirled the last of the melting ice cubes around. "I don't know what you want me to say."

My voice came out strained and unnatural. "Nothing! There's nothing I want you to say, except maybe that you understand."

Alina finally looked up at me, her eyes suddenly shadowed and weary. "I get it. You're a little broken.

For some reason, I make things better, and you'll use me in whatever way I'm willing to be used in order to knit yourself back together. But I shouldn't have any hope that you'd actually want to be with me. That about it?"

"No!" I reeled back. *I'm fucking this up.* "More like you'll run for the hills once you actually spend time with me. I can be a selfish asshole."

Her half-smile gave me hope. "You're not a selfish asshole. You're an overprotective, moody, codependent asshole. Who isn't always honest with himself or others," she corrected.

She'd called me out brutally there. I gritted my teeth and looked around. Candace, Rory and Ethan were belting out an ABBA song and everyone was focused on them. "I'm sorry. Really, I sent a lot of mixed messages between the kisses, the touching then pulling back. Acting like it didn't matter."

She snorted. "You sure did."

"Look, all I do know—literally the only facts that I know for sure in my life right now are these. One— somehow you've become my closest friend. Two—I have never been as attracted to someone as I am to you. And three—I'm not ready for anything serious right now, but there's something here between us that I want to explore. I don't know what to call it, dating, casual, whatever. It's more than friends and it's definitely exclusive, but—"

I came to a stop and dropped my head into my palms. I had no idea if I'd made sense or if what I could offer was something she'd be remotely interested in. Her face had gone completely still, and only the motion of her throat as she swallowed hard gave the smallest hint that my words had affected her.

She brushed her fingers through my hair and tugged a little so I would look up and meet her eyes. "Markus, I feel pretty much the same about you. This whole thing with us is confusing and scary. I don't fuck around with actors — especially ones on my set. I'm worried that you could ruin me completely."

I was more than a little relieved to hear her say that she felt somewhat the same, but her reservations were legitimate and I had no guarantees for how things would play out. Her hands were lying folded in her lap and I reached out and clasped one of them, my thumb brushing slowly over her knuckles. We watched one of the lighting guys ham it up to Bon Jovi for a while, and all the thoughts of what to do next were whirring through my brain. Finally they settled like a slot machine on a hopefully winning combination.

"Alina, can we try something?"

She looked at me like I was a potentially venomous snake. "What?"

"Can I kiss you?"

She was momentarily stunned, but then she shocked the hell out of me as she pulled me up and led me out into the empty hallway outside the private lounge. Her determined strides squelched on the sticky floor. She came to a halt and turned me around by the shoulders so I was pressed up against the wall with only a few inches between us, and pulled me down to her for a soft kiss. The barely there press of her lips rocked me to my core.

"And now?" she asked softly as she settled back to her heels.

I caught my breath slowly and let it back out. "Now I ask if you felt something there too. Because I did — even though that was the kind of bullshit kiss you give your grandma. I felt that kiss lighting up parts of me that I thought were completely dead. I don't know what to do with it all, but I want *more* with you. More than being your friend. Can we try this dating thing? See where it goes?"

Her eyes darted back and forth. "'See where things go'? Yeah, I don't know — casual isn't my usual mode."

We kept up our staring contest until she clapped a hand over her eyes and groaned. "Ugh, fine, yes, I felt that same thing too. I do every time we're near each other."

I reached out for her hand and twined her fingers in mine. We both looked down at our joined hands.

"It's a lot, yeah? Can we, though? Try?" I tugged her closer and she leaned into me, sighing as I kissed the top of her head.

She stepped back abruptly and poked me in the chest. "I want one more apology. You're such a fucking tease."

"Me? Yeah, probably, I'm sorry." Her glare was accusatory, but I swear there was a slight twinkle in her eyes as I grinned at her. "But you know you still want me, and besides, it takes one to know one."

"So, what does *more* even mean? Are we dating? Like, we hang out a bunch, go out in public maybe, hook up?" she asked a little sarcastically as she flattened her hands on my chest.

"You make it sounds so sterile," I complained. "I want to take you out, to the Premier for last season, which is coming up in a few days, for one thing. Spend time at each other's houses, talk about childhood nonsense, I don't know. And, yeah, of course I want to do other, very grown-up things with you. I've never been this drawn to someone. You're burned into me."

Something—I had no idea what—passed between us in that moment. A very tiny part of me seemed to wake up and flare to life, eager to be handed over to her without reservation. It was surreal and I wondered if she felt the same—as if we needed to trade these little fragments of ourselves to remain whole.

She pulled back and looked up at me as she cupped my jaw in her hands. I wasn't quite sure what she saw in my eyes as she stared at me, searching for the truth behind my words. Finally she nodded to herself and stepped back so only my fingertips dragged across her forearms. "All right, Markus. You're on. We can 'try'."

My breath gusted out in a relieved sigh and I smiled at her. "Trust me, you won't regret this."

She wasn't smiling, though, as she said, "Oh, trust *me*, I'm going to hold you to that. Now if you'll excuse me, I need to run to the restroom."

"Okay, I'll meet you back in there?" I jerked my chin in the direction of the lounge.

"Sure, be right back," she assured me and hesitated slightly.

Then she rose up on her tiptoes and kissed me, soft and quick as a butterfly landing on a flower, and was gone. I walked back into the lounge in a daze, nodded at the security team, who looked curiously at me, and headed over to the private bar in the corner. I was perusing my options when Rory approached again, this time on his own.

"So," he said with only the barest slur to indicate his inebriation. "Alina and you, huh?"

"Rory, please don't take this the wrong way, but I'm not ready to talk about it," I said distractedly, looking over my shoulder toward the door.

"Hmm. Whyever not?" he asked sarcastically.

"Okay, fine. I like her. A lot, but we're friends more than anything. I was with Kate for a long time and I don't think I'm ready for anything more than what we have going on right now." I sidestepped the fact that we'd literally decided to take things further five seconds ago.

"Be careful with her," he cautioned, suddenly serious. "From what I understand, she's been through a lot and plenty of people on set are jealous of her. She climbed the ranks very quickly and even though it's pretty obviously not the case, there's always been talk that she slept her way up. Michael, Terrance—"

"That's ridiculous," I interrupted. "You've seen her, worked with her. She's fucking great at her job."

"You and I know it, others do too, but the gossip on the set is high. She deals with it really well, but I worry that this is going to be too much," he confessed.

"Thanks for letting me know. You're right. We both need to be careful."

He nodded solemnly. "Ethan and me have your back and we'll let you know if we hear anything. Candace too."

"Thanks, Rory." I hadn't been expecting him to take something so seriously and appreciated that it was on Alina's behalf.

"You've got it. How's tonight going?"

"Fine, fine," I said, distracted while continuing to search the crowd for Alina. "Thanks for the talk, but I'm going to head out and look for Alina."

"Sounds like a plan. Be good to her." He smirked and strolled off, teetering a little as he navigated the lounge in search of his people.

I gave my security team a signal that I was heading out and that they should clear a path to the car and sent

David a text to let them know that I was ready to go and asked him to keep an eye out for Alina. I circled through the main bar area again before worming my way out to the patio. She was there, held hostage up against a towering planter. Her eyes were shiny, darting back and forth as she if she were seeking an escape route while Vanessa stood in her face, bony index finger poking her in the chest.

I moved closer until I could hear her. "I don't know who the fuck you think you are, but if you think you can waltz around, sleeping with anyone who will give you a bigger piece of this show, you can fuck right off."

Alina tried to placate her. "I don't know what you've heard, but I would never —"

"I haven't forgotten how you tried to break up my marriage, and if you thought I didn't know about that you're even stupider than I thought. And now you think you're going to take over my show? I don't think so, sweetheart."

I pulled out my phone and sent Alina a text.

*I'm right here. Team is making a path to the car. Get to the front and I'll get you home.*

I waited till I saw her glance down at her phone before I started moving toward the entrance to the club. When David pulled up I jumped in and he drove down the block a bit from the club entrance, to where Alina was up on her tiptoes, looking above the crowd for her getaway ride. Security was standing between her and the milling crowd outside. I slid down in the seat as far as I could and switched off the dome lights so they wouldn't announce my presence to Vanessa, who I could vaguely see had been stopped by security.

She got in, looked at me, dropped her head to her hands and started laughing hysterically. "Thanks for the rescue, my knight in semi-tarnished armor."

"I'm so fucking sorry. Should I have intervened directly? I was worried you'd be pissed at me for fighting your battles."

She sighed, hiccupping adorably. "No, that's okay."

"Do you want someone to stay with you tonight? I can, or if you want me to run back in and track down Candace—"

"Stop, no, it's okay. I appreciate it, but I think I need some space. I should have realized, but I didn't think it all the way through. It's a lot with the show, you and now this shit with Vanessa. I take it you overheard her?"

"If you need space, take it. And yes, I did hear some of what she said. Do you want to talk about it?"

"No, our disagreement goes way back, and it's... complicated," she said, sounding a little uncomfortable.

"Well, if you want to talk, you know I'm here for you." I squeezed her hand.

She nodded and laid her head on my shoulder. I held her tightly the rest of the way to her house. We arrived, and she gave me a quick kiss on the cheek and crawled out of the car.

"I'll talk to you tomorrow. Maybe we can hang out."

"I'd like that. Text me whenever." I smiled at her as she walked backward up the path for two steps, waving at me before turning around. David stayed where he was until we saw her enter the house and close the door behind her. The lights flickered on and we watched her close the blinds to the big picture window in the front, giving one last wave to the car.

I sighed deeply, and David laughed. "Glad that worked out for you, Markus. She's one of the good ones."

# Chapter Fifteen

*Alina*

"Oh, fuck, Markus. Yes!" My fingers clenched in his hair, pulling him tighter against me as he slowly teased me with his tongue and fingers. Waking up to kisses and love bites on my inner thighs as his scruff scratched the thin skin was the most persuasive alarm clock I'd ever owned.

As he knelt between my legs, he looked like a Viking ready to pillage my body. His choppy blond hair was a tangled mess from my fingers, and light scratches from my fingernails marked his shoulders and biceps. Electric-blue eyes shooting sparks, he hovered over me and grinned a dirty smile that told me how much he liked me naked and submissive, begging him for relief.

"Watch, Alina," he hissed as he slid home. The swollen walls of my core stretched to accommodate him, the slickness of my overstimulated body making it a smooth glide till he bottomed out inside me.

As Markus started to increase his speed, alternating long drives with sharp snaps of his hips, he reached between us to circle my clit. He murmured, keeping his speed steady, "I want to feel you milking my cock, Alina. Come for me. Right. N—"

*Beep. Beep. Beep. Beep.*

*Motherfucking alarms. I was* right there. *So bloody close.* Between the emotional highs of joining a show and getting access to Michael's contacts and the lows of Vanessa's unexpected attack, I was a mess, and Markus was the common theme through it all. Down to the supreme edge he managed to deliver to me in my dreams.

I rolled out of bed with a heaviness between my legs and skin that was so oversensitive that I almost came from the sensation of the salty breeze blowing through the open window across my naked body. The shower was turned up as hot as it could go and the water scalded me as I scrubbed away the remnants of the dream.

My heart and brain fought it out as I castigated myself for jumping into things without thinking them through. Letting my feelings lead me into a career move that held such a significant amount of risk to my personal life and following my heart into a tentative relationship with Markus, someone whose level of celebrity was sure to turn my world inside out. Not that I didn't want it to, but it wasn't a sure thing and uncertainty made me antsy.

While drinking my coffee at the bar in my kitchen, I scanned through the notifications on my phone. Nothing about *Southern Gods*. I flipped to the non-industry news, nothing good to see there — global crisis after crisis that made me ashamed of my very first-world problems.

The chime of a text notification, followed quickly by a second, interrupted my musing. Markus, then Candace. I glanced at Candace's text first.

*You doing anything today? Want to get brunch or something and catch up?*

*Hmm.* Yes, I did want to hang out, but I'd promised Markus I could get together as well. I swiped over to his message, a long one. He clearly wasn't a big texter.

*Hey, I hope you slept well, I know we said we'd try to do something today, but I've got a bunch of Sellers-related P.R. shit. I don't know when I'll be free, maybe tonight? PS: I had the most incredible dream last night. You tied me down and sucked my cock for a half hour, stopping every now and then to tickle me. It was weird.*

I smiled as I typed my response, somehow feeling both exasperated with his almost-perfect grammar and texting PSs and aroused by the blatant imagery his text inspired. This was coming to be a common theme in my interactions with him.

*Hey yourself…that's cool, let me know if you're free later. Going to grab brunch with Candace and run a bunch of errands. PS: Slept mostly well except for the fact that you edged me out HARD in my dreams. Didn't realize we both had such serious oral fixations. ;)*

He didn't reply immediately, and I swiped back to Candace.

*Yes, definitely! Need girl time. Hope your night had a happy ending...*

Unlike Markus, Candace had an unhealthy and codependent relationship with her phone. She responded immediately.

*Girl, YES! Meet at Solid Ground? 10:30?*

*Perfect*

\* \* \* \*

Solid Ground was a coffee shop that Candace and I used to frequent when we'd first met and lived in Silver Lake, back when my job with Michael was probationary and I was renting a room in her group house. I hadn't been in a while, but the familiar scent of freshly roasted beans, the whir of the milk steamer and combined chatter of voices as they echoed throughout the space and bounced off the floor-to-ceiling windows felt a little like coming home. I put in an order and snagged a table outside as a very cute hungover couple staggered away, wincing as they threw on their sunglasses.

My iPad was out and humming immediately as I started tallying up the tasks I'd need to accomplish before rehearsals. Since Candace was running late, as usual, I idly started a totally unnecessary, but very special, checklist of things that Markus and I needed to tick off. I was delighted that only eighty-five percent of the items were sexual.

"Alina! Hey!" a rushed voice called out, and a frazzled Candace appeared in my peripheral vision.

"So sorry. Parking was a bitch. I put in an order. Did you want anything?" She plopped a numbered table tent down to let the servers know where to bring her food, then laughed as she saw mine. "Should have known you'd have that covered."

"Yep, don't mess with my brunch feeding. You know I hate this meal, right? Like, what's the point? Why not get breakfast? Or lunch? Why split the difference so you're starving when you arrive and want to pass out at, like, noon when you're done?" My feelings on brunch were well-known to my exasperated friend.

"I'm not even going to start with that shit right now. We're on a strict agree-to-disagree about brunch. Don't fuck with me today. You've got some serious dirt to dish!"

"I know. I'm sorry. Things have been happening so fast, you know?"

Candace nodded, her sunglasses hiding what I was pretty sure was an impatient expression as she leaned into me. "Yeah, and last time we talked, you said that nothing was going on with Markus. Last night though, you two told kind of a different story — we saw you canoodling on that couch during karaoke. And this bombshell about joining the show?" She mimed wiping the sweat off her brow and fanned herself aggressively.

I laughed at my over-the-top friend and cut off as the waiter deposited our food. We both dug in for a few bites before I paused to answer her question. "I know, it's a lot. I said yes to Michael and the show without thinking it all the way through. I saw a shortcut to the endgame of my Plan and got greedy. And Markus, yeah, he's got me tied up in ten kinds of knots. He's just so, argh..."

"Fucking gorgeous? Those the words you're looking for?" She grinned at me.

"Yeah, that, but so much more too. I really like him." I pointed a fork at her, complete with pancake and dripping syrup. "What we're talking about does not leave this table. Got it?"

She flipped me off, scratching between her eyebrows with a raised middle finger. "Duh. Promise."

"Okay. Well, last night things may have gotten a little heated —"

"Oh my god, so hot. Did you two finally get it on?"

She'd totally derailed me. "No! Anyways, we were finally talking about what's going on with us. The crazy attraction, whether there's feelings attached. It was overdue given the fact that our little walk-through scene was like the third time we've gotten carried away with each other."

She looked at me with question marks in her big brown eyes.

"You know, physically. Carried away. First base? Maybe second? Does that still mean anything? You know, never mind."

"*Squeee!*" Her giggles triggered mine, and I almost choked on my pancakes.

"Mmmhmm. Suffice to say that, yeah, we've had a few encounters, and I'm sorry I didn't tell you, but I wanted to keep it a secret since I didn't think anything was going anywhere and really wanted to ignore what was happening."

"And what *was* happening?"

"Stuff! You know!"

She grinned wickedly. "No, I don't know. What is this 'stuff' you speak of?"

"Fuck you, Candace. You know. Feelings, all right? We were friends immediately. I feel like I've known him forever. There's such a strange level of comfort and ease when we're together. There's something about him—about us together—that is so terrifyingly right, and I've never felt that before."

Her jaw had dropped somewhere along the way, and she stared at me with hearts in her eyes. "You love him! *Eeeep!* You. Love. Him!"

I shushed her and looked around to make sure no one had heard her squeals. "No, no! All I know is that we've come close to hooking up a few times, but one of us has always stopped it. Yesterday he finally admitted that he did have feelings, but wasn't sure if he could commit to anything and asked if we could we try casually—but exclusively—dating and see where it goes from there. And then Vanessa cornered me, but he rescued me—and oh my god, my life is a soap opera." I slumped in my seat, ready to hide in the collar of my shirt. This was nuts. I was a producer, the furthest thing from an A-lister in this town.

"So you're together?" Candace cut to the heart of it.

"I don't know. Kind of? It's casual, though. I mean, saying yes to anything with him was such a relief—like, *finally*, I was where I was meant to be. Trying to deny those feelings felt so wrong. He's a magnet, always pulling at me, and when we're together literally nothing else matters."

"Alina, I am holding back my screams right now. Maybe you can't tell." I could tell. Her eyes were huge and deranged. "He may have made it sound like he wants casual, but that guy is *so* into you. He gravitates toward you on set, always looking for you, and the relief on his face when he finds you…"

"So I'm his security blanket?"

"A little, but there's more there too. I think your attraction goes both ways and, like you are, he's surprised by the strength of it. My guess is that Markus feels that sense of relief too — you're both where you're meant to be now. Fighting it so hard must be exhausting, even if the feelings are super confusing." Leaning back, she crossed her arms, dropped her chin and looked at me over her shades. "So, very exciting. Something else is up, though. What is it?"

"This whole show thing. I'm completely freaking out. Did I do the right thing? I feel like I'm taking a shortcut and didn't think it through enough."

"Uh, yeah. You definitely didn't think it through. But I don't think it's a bad thing. This industry is impossible and it never matters how hard you work. I've seen so many talented people stall out. You have to know the right people, work the right angles. And a lot of it is luck."

"That was my instinct too," I murmured, semi-reassured, as I toyed with my napkin. "So do it? Sign the contract?"

"I would, in a heartbeat. It's going to be really hard, not gonna lie, but I believe in you. You can do this. There are a bunch of us who have your back."

"Okay." I took a deep breath. "I think you're right, I'm going to go for it. But please keep this whole Markus-and-me-feelings stuff quiet, cool?" I signaled the waiter for the check. "I've got to get going. I've got a shitload of errands to run today, but I meant to ask if you wanted to get ready for the Premiere together? Markus asked me to go with him as his date."

Candace laughed and pulled me in for a huge hug. "Of course, Alina, I'd love to style you up. Don't worry about the Markus stuff—live in the moment. The way you two are together is so sweet, and it's been hilarious watching y'all fumble your way toward each other. Now, go get your shit taken care of. I've got the check. Give Markus a hand job for me or something." She winked and smiled as she shooed me away from the table.

"Gross. A hand job?" I shook my head and hugged her again before grabbing my bag to go.

"Hey, now," she said as she giggled. "Hand jobs can be very romantic."

As I walked back to my car to get started on my interminable list, I texted Markus again. He'd replied to my last message while we were at brunch.

*Oral fixation? More like fixated on every inch of you.*

We'd have to work on his texting skills. He gave good sext, but this proper grammar shit was annoying.

*Lol can't wait. Good luck with your P.R. song and dance.*

Almost no time passed before I saw the dancing dots of a reply.

*Oh, it's just going to be the most fun. I'll call you about tonight.*

I smirked as I dropped my phone back into my bag and twirled my keys like an Old West gunslinger. *Game on, Markus. Game. On.*

\* \* \* \*

My good mood lasted until I saw the package delivered by courier on my front steps when I got back from brunch and errands. The contract. I grabbed it and eagerly tore it open as I shouldered my way through the door. I quickly fired up my espresso machine and took my doppio out to the table on my patio. As I read through the contract while sipping the rich coffee, my head started to throb with an impending migraine. The legalese spun a deceptive picture, but a careful reading immediately called out the fact that the whole thing was bullshit, a starting point to test whether or not I knew anything about the industry.

My inner Depression-era grandma started noting out all of the clauses that were oppressive, disrespectful and downright cheap. Markus' team was going to tear this shit apart and get me what I deserved.

# Chapter Sixteen

*Markus*

After my sexually fraught texting exchange with Alina, my morning workout was more half-assed than eighty percent of the crap Tarantino slapped his name on. I couldn't concentrate for the life of me. The truth was that my feelings for her scared the shit out of me and I knew a casual thing wouldn't be enough. I worried that she'd bail on me if things got too tricky with media attention. In an attempt to distract myself, I tore open the couriered envelope my housekeeper had dropped on my counter and scanned through the pages of our shiny new contracts

Michael already knew what I would demand and his offer was fair. Alina's, on the other hand, was complete horseshit. My blood pressure started to climb as I flipped the pages on her contract. I grabbed my phone and hit speed dial to Will.

"Have you seen this total bullshit yet?" I seethed.

"Markus, hey, how's things? Yes, it's a lovely day, and yes, all is well in my world."

"Fucking smart-ass. Have you seen these contracts or not?"

He got serious quickly. "Of course. Yours is fine, but I think we can do better. The young woman's, though, is going to take some work."

I could practically hear him cracking his figurative knuckles as he got ready to dig into the contract. The guy was bloodthirsty, and I turned him loose. "Get her the best deal that you can. I guarantee that she'll reject this, as well. Text her to confirm. She's got priority."

"Done and done."

\* \* \* \*

With time to kill before the P.R. blitz, I decided to get some shopping in for my nieces. Stores were crowded, but everything seemed to be going smoothly for once. I had left the house without security and completely alone, something I rarely attempted. Alina's involvement in my life made me curious about whether or not we'd ever be able to live a 'normal' life together, or if being with me would strip that freedom from her.

No one seemed to recognize me in the first shop I visited, which had me feeling optimistic, and I whistled my way down the street. But that optimism went crashing straight into the ground when I saw the photographers waiting for me as I left the second.

"Markus! What's going on with Kate? Tell us about the break-up. Are you going to work things out? Did Sellers fire you?"

The shouts all ran together into one loud, intrusive voice, and before I knew it a small crowd had encircled me with their phones and cameras out, ready to record my tiniest move. I tried to smile and wave them off, but they pressed in closer.

"Markus, how was working with Michael Burch? Is it true that it's your only role? How does it feel to be blacklisted?"

I backed up against the door of a boutique, saying, "No comment, no comment." Things were starting to get frightening with the press and barrage of questions when the door behind me suddenly opened and I tumbled in. A security guard nodded at me and I thanked him.

"No worries, man. I'll clear them out. Call a car and have it come to the back. We'll get you out of here."

Again, I thanked him, texted David quickly and started looking around. The shop, a boutique specializing in vintage high-end Hollywood fashion, was quiet, and a display of jewelry in a case caught my attention. A set of vintage Cartier bangles glimmered in a corner. The small info card noted that they had belonged to, of all people, Barbra Streisand. I stopped to look and a sales associate rushed over.

"Oh, you like these, Mr. Shellenberg?" She blushed faintly.

"Ah. Yes. I do. My, um, sister would like them a lot." I felt trapped by her attention, but also curious as to how Barbra Streisand's jewelry had ended up in this shop.

The woman pulled out the tray and placed it on the case, separating the bracelets for me to look at. "Your sister? Is she a fan? The seller told us that these bracelets were given to Ms. Streisand by Robert Redford during the filming of *The Way We Were*. She had been dealing with a horrendous amount of pressure from the studios and media and was near a breakdown. He had them engraved with some empowering messages and gave them to her for good luck."

The bracelets were nothing special at first glance. They were the traditional Cartier 'Love' design. Everyone and their mother had those bracelets.

"What do you mean 'empowering messages'?" I asked.

She handed one to me and gestured for me to look inside at the engraving.

'Frankly, my dear, I don't give a fuck,' it read. "*Gone with the Wind*?" I asked.

The woman nodded and handed me the other two. I looked at each of them and started to smile. All of them contained some mangled quote from a film that incorporated the word *fuck*. I loved their quirkiness and knew immediately that Alina would too. And I owed her *something* for all of those mixed messages. She needed to know that I supported her — I could be her Redford.

"How much?" I asked, already reaching for my wallet.

\* \* \* \*

Around nine o'clock that night, I heard from Will and Roger that the deals were done. My brain was fried after the run-in with paparazzi and a full afternoon and evening of Sellers-related P.R. nonsense. While I was disappointed that Alina had been unable to get together, it was almost a relief when she texted saying she wasn't feeling well. I opened a bottle of scotch to celebrate the contract signing and paired it with a bowl of cereal. Single adult dinner of champions.

I finished the first glass while reviewing and uploading my contract. The upload confirmation email had a link to the new plot arc summary and scripts, and I wasted no time pouring another while I tore into them. When I finished, I stared blankly at the wall and gulped the remaining whiskey in my glass. Then I scrolled back through the pages to the beginning and read through two more times before tossing my tablet aside.

Seeing it all in black and white made things real, and I started to actually think about the implications of us taking on leading roles. Because that was exactly what the parts were. I wasn't joining the cast as a side character with a girlfriend like I'd been promised. *No, of course not, that would be too easy.*

Michael had somehow gotten the network to greenlight the screenwriters rewriting the season so Alina and I were the main focus, and he'd gotten away with it because we couldn't see the scripts until the contracts were signed. That shark in a goofy artist's clothing. I might not have seen the original scripts, but given the lack of story focusing on anything but our relationship, the entire season had to have been trashed.

The cast was going to lose their shit completely when they found out about all of this, and I really didn't blame them. If it were me, I'd be furious and immediately looking for a way out of my contract. This was not going to make our transition easy—we were both going to have targets on our backs. Forget the 'family atmosphere'. People were going to be pissed.

More alarming, though, than the response of the existing cast—at least from my perspective—was the way that the rumor mill on both traditional and social media was going to react. All of the back and forth about my break-up with Kate was going to gain traction. Alina would be drawn in too as my mysterious co-star and if people found out we were dating, she'd end up cast as the evil other woman. The story had legs now and would take off running. I had to protect her from the coming attacks, but I didn't know how.

I sent Alina a text to ask her if she'd reviewed the contract and see if she wanted to get together to review the scripts and storyline, but she'd gone dark on me after letting me know she had a migraine. With no other options and feeling completely at loose ends, I grabbed the bottle of scotch and headed for my room. If getting or giving head wasn't on the table, solo drinking and binging on bad TV would surely make this nightmare better.

# Chapter Seventeen

*Alina*

When I finally pulled out of my migraine the next day, I got back to work and started to review the scripts over coffee and toast. Almost immediately, my palms started to sweat.

The thing was, the show was more than a little outlandish. Seasons one through three had introduced the audience to a family of immortal demigods who had fled from France to the New World back in the 1500s to avoid the vicious in-fighting within their community of beings. The family eventually settled in what was modern-day Savannah and went underground, content to pass as human.

Sebastian, Markus' character, was the emissary of the shadowy Central organization sent to force the family to ally with the rest of the immortal community. And, according to the original scripts, he had been supposed to die in a battle with another character. The power struggle between the family and the nefarious Central group had been set to be the main arc in the upcoming season.

That plot, according to the pages I'd read, had been tossed completely out the window. The new one pushed all of the other characters to secondary roles, leaving Sebastian and his love interest as the primary protagonists for the season. As the new arc went, Sebastian, who had thrown his lot in with the family during that climactic battle, would meet a woman who would turn his life upside down in the first episode of the season. She would be identical to the love of his existence—a mortal woman who died hundreds of years ago.

Although he'd try to stay away, the woman, played by little old me, would burrow under his skin and he would feel compelled to be near her, to know her. Without a doubt, she is the reincarnation of his lost love and, in a sense, Sebastian would begin to come back to life after a millennium of being alone.

The new arc, despite stretching viewers' credulity to the breaking point and its similarity to some of the old vampire-y shows on the CW and HBO, was miles better than the original. It was poignant and suspenseful. However, its success hinged on me suddenly becoming an actor capable of carrying an entire season on her back.

I grabbed my phone and frantically texted Markus.

*I just read the storyline. Freaking out.*

He responded immediately.

*I know. Do you want to get on a call with Michael later? We need to talk to him about this. It goes against everything he promised.*

I quickly messaged Michael as my unease increased. If Markus was worried too...

*I messaged him requesting a call. What should we do if he doesn't respond?*

Markus didn't reply for a moment, and little black specks started to dance in my peripheral vision.

*It's going to be ok, we can track him down tonight at the premier if he doesn't get back to us. Phone sex?*

If ever I wasn't in the mood...

*What is wrong with you? Now? How am I going to lead this show? People are gonna freak the F out.*

Five agonizing minutes went by before Markus finally responded, trying to reassure me.

*I know, I know. I promise it will be alright. We'll figure this out.*

But I couldn't help feeling that this was definitely not going to be okay and that the Premiere was destined for disaster now that Michael had had his way with us.

\* \* \* \*

Texting back and forth with Markus about our inability to get Michael on the phone was such a wind-up. Especially when he started to integrate such overtly sexual suggestions in an effort to take my mind off of things. I was ready to jump out of my skin from the sheer lust and stress of it all by the time Candace arrived to help me with hair and makeup. She was already done up and looked amazing, her dark skin glowing, natural hair big, bold and gorgeous, and the reddest lip I'd ever seen. I couldn't wait to have her work her magic on me.

"Candace! You look amazing!"

"Girl, you're going to look even better by the time I get done with you. You nervous?"

I sighed with no little amount of regret and we headed to my bathroom, where she plopped me down on the closed toilet to start working on me. "Definitely. I've never done the red-carpet thing and it totally freaks me out. I'm worried about being there with Markus too. I know we're kind of half-assed dating, but it feels uncertain, and you know how I get about uncertain things. On one hand, I don't really give a flying fuck what people think but, on another, ugh…all those eyes on me."

"Mmmhmm," she muttered around a hairpin. "It might get a little hairy, with all of those rumors about Kate and him still flying. I wouldn't worry too much, though. It's *Southern Gods*, not the next MCU movie. Now, deep breaths. Hair is done, on to makeup, give me a second."

"Totally, totally. You're right." I got up and started pacing in circles, rubbing my index fingers against my thumbs. I'd painted my nails that morning and they actually looked good for once, so biting them off was out of the question.

"Come back here. Sit." Candace pushed me back down and gripped my shoulders while she met my eyes in the mirror. She squeezed and rolled them out for me. "You're so stiff, you've got to chill. It's going to be all right. Now, where's your dress? Love your nails, by the way, we need to match them."

"My dress is over there." I gestured at the garment hanging from my shower rod.

She looked over and whistled. "Red is a bold choice. Love it. I've got the perfect lip stain for this."

We chatted about random things while she worked, and she made me laugh at my own nervousness. "Want a shot? I think I've got some airplane bottles of tequila in my kit somewhere," she teased as she started cleaning up her brushes.

"Uh, no. I can hang. You're done already?" She nodded and I turned and looked in the mirror.

Candace had outdone herself. My skin looked flawless, the contouring was amazing and my eye makeup was super dramatic. Hair was gorgeous. I looked like a femme fatale straight out of a Bond movie. "Oh my god, thank you. This is amazing, I look fucking hot."

She handed me a tissue to blot my lips and brushed me off and smiled. "I know. Genius, right? Look, we're going to have a blast tonight, okay? You'll have Markus with you and the two of you can take on Michael. It's going to be fine, keep your head up!"

We hugged and she headed out. I pulled the dress off the hanger and drew it on carefully. The dress was fire-engine red, and the silhouette was pure, silky classic siren with a slit up to my hip and a short train.

It was a halter, tied with a loopy bow at the neck, and the plunging neckline draped in such a way that my cleavage could be classified as 'racy, yet classy'.

I tore through my closet and dug out my shoes — a pair of sky-high gold gladiator sandals that Candace had given me from a previous set. They were going to be super wobbly, but the gold straps that wound up my legs were visible through the slit in my dress and made me feel like a badass superhero about to go knock down the patriarchy.

My doorbell rang and I quickly threw on a pair of gold geometric ear cuffs that straddled the classic yet edgy look Candace had constructed. The walk down the stairs to the door suddenly felt like a death march in my towering heels, but Markus was waiting, and the awestruck, lustful look on his face as he watched me step outside made everything worth it. He opened and closed his mouth a few times like a goldfish before managing a strangled, "Shall we go?"

I smiled smugly at him. "Of course."

He stayed rooted to the spot as he rubbed his chin a few times before finally extending his arm to me. "Mmm, your dress. Are you sure you're comfortable?" He couldn't stop staring as I posed with one hip cocked, his eyes traveling avidly up to my nearly exposed hipbone. I watched in delight as he swallowed hard and licked his lips.

I batted my fake eyelashes at him. Perhaps 'ingenue' would be a good role to try out in preparation for our rehearsals. "Oh, it's fine, maybe a little drafty. Can you help me into the car?"

He struggled for a second, trying to say something, before blowing out a big breath and meeting my eyes as he guided me into the car. "You look absolutely beautiful. I can't wait to see everyone's face when you step onto the carpet."

"Thanks. Candace really should get the credit, though."

"Sure, her work is flawless, but she had exquisite raw material. Here," he said as he handed me a jewelry case. "I saw these in a store yesterday and had to buy them. I think they were meant for you."

I frowned at him but opened the case slowly to find three gleaming gold bangles with a piece of paper set delicately on top. After reading the note about their provenance, I looked up at him. "Are you kidding me? Why is Barbra Streisand giving up her jewelry?"

"Alina, look at the inside. They were meant for you. Regardless of the previous owner, they're perfect."

I turned them over to read the messages and started laughing. "No fucks to give, right? I'll keep it in mind the next time I'm dealing with Michael. Thank you, Markus. These are fantastic. Help me with them?" I handed him the custom screwdriver that came with the bracelets in the case and he carefully loosened them and slid them over my hand one by one.

The heat of his palm holding mine and the weight of the smooth, old gold sliding up my forearm made me shiver as he tightened the screws. God, he was so handsome in his old-school black tux and skinny tie. And the bracelets, the thoughtfulness of the gift, took my breath away. I focused on the other cars traveling beside us to avoid the inevitable, "but what does it all mean?" comment that was burning the tip of my tongue.

\* \* \* \*

Far more reporters than were typically at these types of premieres lined the sidewalk with flashing lights and clamoring voices as we pulled up to the line-up outside the theater a few minutes later.

Markus groaned. "Shit, Michael must have leaked something. I bet word got out that I'm staying on."

I shook my head in disbelief. *Southern Gods* was an established series, sure, but nowhere near the level that resulted in this type of turnout. "How do we do this? Are we going public with our dating now?"

His brow wrinkled in concern as he considered how we should play it. "I'm so sorry, this puts you front and center and we're only getting started. We should have come separately. I'm an idiot." He frowned and his shoulders bunched up beneath his tailored coat. "Two options—one of us goes in first alone, David drives around for a while, then the other goes in separately a bit later. Or we go in together. What do you want to do?"

It wasn't like I'd blissfully convinced myself that dating him would go completely unnoticed by the general public, his adoring fan club, or even the average teenager with a sweet cell phone camera. I'd thought that we'd have more time to ourselves before having to go public like this, though. My fingers pleated the hem of my dress and I tugged nervously on the bow that tied behind my neck, making sure it was secure. I closed my eyes, counted to ten, deep breath in and out, and said, "Let's do this together. If you're okay with it, I'm okay with it."

He beamed at me. "All right, let's do it. Do you want to follow my lead? I think if we do the walk and only talk to one or two reporters, we'll be fine. We'll smile at the cameras and keep moving."

I nodded nervously.

"Ready?" he asked with his hand on the handle as our car pulled up to the front.

I took another deep breath and pasted on my best fake smile. "Let's get this over with."

Without further ado, he opened the door and stepped out, turning back with his hand out to help me as I awkwardly unfolded to the sidewalk in my rented dress and gifted shoes and jewelry. Our eyes met and something ineffable passed between us as I grasped his hand. An affirmation that we were not in this alone.

# Chapter Eighteen

*Markus*

We stepped onto the carpet and were bombarded by camera flashes and reporters yelling at us for a comment. We both smiled — her beatifically, me more grimly — and paused for a photo, ignoring requests for individual shots. Farther down the line, I spotted a journalist I knew from one of the European gossip rags. She respected my reticence and was a genuinely good reporter who wouldn't spin everything that came out of my mouth. As spots from the numerous flashes burned across my vision, I led Alina through the gauntlet to stand in front of her. My palm burned from contact with her bare skin, displayed to such perfection by the open back of her dress.

"Susana, good to see you. You have a question?"

She must heard the 'a' quite clearly, given the cheeky grin she shot my way "No. I have two. Will that work?"

"It will. Hurry, though. We need to get in."

"Fine, fine. Thanks for speaking with me." Other reporters were crowding around her, sticking phones and recorders at us. Susana cleared her throat. "First, about the Premiere. Did you enjoy your stint on the show, and will you be back for upcoming seasons?"

She was far more sneaky than I remembered. Already two questions deep, she would no doubt work in at least one more. I glanced over at Alina, willing her to be ready for what would follow. She simply smiled reassuringly at me, a mysterious beauty who was driving the rest of the media mad. There were more flashes as photographers tried to claim the moment between us.

"Yes, I enjoyed it quite a bit. Michael is a fantastic director and the entire cast and crew were very welcoming to a new addition. In fact, I enjoyed it so much that when Michael asked me to consider returning for future seasons, I accepted."

There, it was out there, and it was enough that she likely wouldn't ask for more details. Her glances at Alina indicated that she was salivating over this unknown woman and why we remained physically attached to one another.

"And who is your lovely companion this evening?" Susana didn't beat around the bush.

"Ah, this is Alina. We met on set and she's quite involved with the show, as well."

I turned away, indicating the interview was over. A chorus of 'boos' from the reporters and frantic follow-up questions about whether we were together, who she was and what our joint appearance might mean for the show followed in our wake. We got to the door and paused. As if we'd choreographed it, we turned toward each other, smiled secretively, then glanced back to wave toward the media with the hands that weren't glued to each other.

Once inside, Alina turned to me and squeezed my hand tightly. She reached up on her tiptoes to whisper in my ear, "Thank you for helping me through this."

I grinned at her. The adrenaline from walking the carpet had me wanting to drag her into a coat closet or bathroom and drop to my knees to worship her with my mouth. I tried to shake it off, but little bursts of energy kept zinging through my body.

Alina continued to press her palm to mine, leaning closer still as if to maintain every possible inch of contact between us. "Should I go grab some drinks? I kind of want to find Candace."

"Sure. I'll go find a table for us."

She nodded and carefully unwound our fingers before disappearing into the crowd, while I headed toward the theater doors. Out of the corner of my eye, I saw Rory and Ethan strolling toward me.

"Markus, congratulations are in order." Rory clapped me on the back so hard that I almost staggered into a server. "Only a bit part, hmm?"

I frowned and my shoulders hunched in embarrassment. "I don't know what to say. Alina and I are trying to talk Michael down from this. It's not fair to anyone and it's going to mess up every dynamic with the cast."

Ethan raised his eyebrows and said, "Dude, it's cool. I still get paid the same amount, regardless of the size of my part, and I'm grateful I get to stay on. I totally thought Michael would drop me when I heard about you."

Rory was less convinced. "Eh. I mean, not everyone in the cast knows about this yet. Some of them are going to be seriously pissed. Vanessa's shit talk is really stirring up some anti-Alina feelings. Especially since the word is going around about that hook-up she had right when she was starting with *Southern Gods*."

Before I could ask about the hook-up that was now forcing my hands into fists, I saw Alina heading toward us with Candace in tow and two drinks in her hands.

"Here you go," she said, handing me a drink.

"So…" Candace drawled. "People are finding out about y'all and rumors are flying about what's happening next season. That story about you and You-Know-Who is getting some play again too, Alina. How are you guys holding up?" She gave me a measured up-and-down look, as if evaluating my worthiness to be with her friend. "Markus, you better be protecting my girl here or I will cut you with my stiletto."

"I-I-I…can't believe word is getting out so quickly. How? And what do people know — or maybe what do people *think* they know?" Alina's voice was hoarse with uncertainty.

"They think the worst, of course, it's human nature," Ethan said kindly. "Michael was 'overheard' on a call with the screenwriters talking about you two and your 'on-fire' chemistry. That it will be the main focus for next season and that it's 'fire' because it's real."

Alina's face crumpled. "It's not like that at all."

"I know." Rory put an arm around her and hugged her in commiseration. "It's going to be rough for a while, but, honestly, they'll get over it."

"Yeah, we could probably neutralize all of this nonsense by starting some other rumors…" Candace offered.

"Like what?" asked Alina suspiciously. "You three going to release a sex tape? Are we going to drop the news about Terrance and Vanessa being deviant assholes?"

"Hmm, the sex tape idea has merits," murmured Rory. Both Candace and Ethan, without missing a beat, turned and punched him hard in the arm. As he doubled over he cried out, "I'm kidding, kidding! Jesus, you people have no sense of humor."

Alina turned to me with a hand on her hip, trying to recover some swagger. "Do *you* care? It's one thing to make an appearance here that's suggestive, but coming out as a couple—especially with the show news and so soon after the word dropped on you and Kate—is going to be a whole different ball game." She was trying to act tough, but her voice was high-pitched and still a little shaky.

"No, I absolutely do not care if we're linked together. If you do, I understand, but I'm not ashamed of us," I said as emphatically as I could, and the anxiety racing across her face seemed to slow.

"Fine," she said and gave me a decisive nod. "Let's do it. Seriously, fuck them all."

The lights flickered down and up, indicating that it was time to start the show, and I placed my hand on the small of her back again as we entered the theater flanked by Candace, Rory and Ethan. As we walked through the crowd, people automatically stepped aside to let us pass, and I could hear the murmurs and feel the veiled glances.

As the lights flickered a second time to indicate that everyone should take their seats before the show started, I leaned over to whisper in Alina's ear, "Do you want to leave before the end of this? No one said we had to stay and Michael seems to be avoiding us."

She nodded then leaned into me to whisper back, her breath tickling my ear, "Yes, please."

I pulled out my phone and texted David to meet us around the back by the staff entrance in fifteen minutes. Leaning over again, I murmured, "This is all going to pass, hang in there. You're doing great. And you say you're not an actor." I dug my fingers into the knots at the back of her neck as she rolled her eyes at me.

"Come on. He's here," I whispered, pulling her up from her chair when my phone buzzed a few minutes later. While almost everyone was fixated on the screen, a few people looked up with narrowed eyes as we slid out of our seats and tiptoed out the doors. Alina kicked off her heels and knotted the ankle ties so she could wrap them around her wrist, and we raced through the empty hallways, finally able to breathe deeply, before diving into the car.

As David drove off, her breathing got ragged as the full impact of our decisions and her colleagues' reactions hit home.

"Come here," I said as David pulled away from the curb to join the nighttime rush of L.A. traffic. She slid onto my lap and I tightened my arms around her while she tucked her head beneath my chin.

I flattened my palm against her back and rubbed slow circles around her shoulder blades while she worried. "This is going to be far worse than I thought. Why did I even consider this acting business? I don't know if I can do this publicity thing, who knows if I can even actually act. Fuck, my head is killing me."

I hummed something sympathetic and the circles I was making expanded down to the velvety soft skin of her lower back as she continued to fret. "Yeah, it's not going to be much fun at first, but we've got each other, and Rory, Candace and Ethan. The hype will blow over. Think about your endgame. What you're getting out of this."

David cleared his throat from the front seat. "Sorry to interrupt, but where am I taking you now?"

"Do you want to come over? Or I could come to your house if you want company? We can watch a movie or something." I groaned at my lame offer. It was ridiculous that I had immediate access to every entertainment option in L.A., yet my go-to was 'wanna watch a movie at my house?'

Alina shook her head and winced. "No, thank you. I would, but I get migraines, and the stress plus that drink are triggering another one right now. I need to get home to a quiet and dark place."

"You sure?" I asked as I reached out to stroke her temples, which had gone clammy. Her eyes shuttered as she leaned against me. "I could maybe help. Get you water, medicine, whatever you need."

With her eyes still closed she nodded and said, "Totally sure. There's really nowhere for you to sleep other than the futon or my couch, and I can't bear to have anything touch me if this goes full-on."

"Okay, but let me at least help you into the house."

She nodded again and the passing streetlights illuminated her face. Even with her eyes shut, the sharp bursts of light from the lamps made her flinch, her face screwed up in a rictus of pain.

We waited in the car while David took the keys to go open the door ahead of us. Then I swooped her into my arms and carried her in. She whimpered a little with every thump of my feet on the worn hardwood floors.

I set her down on the bed and she managed to slur out the name of the medicine she needed from the bathroom.

I stopped her from lying down and she cried out in distress. "Come on, let me get you out of this dress and into a T-shirt or something so you can be more comfortable." She moaned and pointed in the direction of her dresser. I grabbed the first T-shirt I could find and slid it over her head, then I unknotted the halter top and slid her dress down, covering her up with the long shirt so she was never completely exposed. Once it was off, she lay down with a sigh of relief. Her eyes cracked open and she reached out a trembling hand to stroke my cheek. "Thank you," she murmured.

"Rest, get better. I'll stop by tomorrow to check on you." I bent, kissed her forehead and tucked the blankets around her tightly. Even though every fiber of me wanted to stay and make sure all was well, I slowly backed out of the room. My last sight of her was her hair spread all over the pillow in those big curls, her body clenched into the tiniest ball beneath her covers.

"Back home?" David asked as I got back into the SUV.

"Yes, please." I laid my head back and closed my eyes.

I didn't bother with the lights when I got home. Headed to the kitchen for a beer then up to my room. Everything was packed in suitcases lined along the wall for my upcoming trip home. I sat at the edge of my tub, drinking the beer and flipping my phone around in my hands.

Given our very new status, I really didn't want to leave her for even a few days while I went to visit my family. The attention from the event tonight ensured that people would go looking for her, and I couldn't let her face that alone, since the exposure was largely because of me. Maybe I could stay with her, skip the trip. My family would understand if I explained.

I slammed the rest of my beer and restlessly got up to wander my empty, echoing house that no longer felt like home, not the way Alina's tiny beach house did. My life was careening off the rails again, but this time in a good way, because I felt centered and grounded for the first time in five years.

This was the power Alina already held, and maybe I should have been scared, because I'd been so adamantly against falling into another relationship. Yet here I was, contemplating cancelling my first trip home in ages to be with her because I worried that she'd need me if the press came for her. But the only alternative to cancelling that I could see was to bring her with me. And that felt terrifying in its rightness.

# Chapter Nineteen

*Alina*

A tentative knock on my front door pulled me out of my half-awake, luxurious dozing. Everything felt tender and only halfway healed after a migraine, and I was moving at the pace of an invalid who'd been bedridden for months. Slowly, I pulled on a robe and headed downstairs.

"Just a sec," I practically whispered from the vestibule as I peeked through the peephole to see Markus bopping from one foot to another while carrying a take-out bag and thermos. I spun the locks, wincing at the noise, and finally opened the door. I immediately regretted not checking the mirror and could suddenly feel the remainder of my expertly done smoky eye crusted beneath my eyelashes. He grinned at me before he could stop himself, then quickly smoothed his expression as I glared at him.

"Still not feeling so well?" he asked as he searched my pale, messy face for a clue. "I can go, I'll drop these off." He offered me the bag, shook it gently in my face, and the smell of lemon curd and almond paste wafted out in a tempting cloud.

It was a very sweet offer, but he was damn lucky that smells weren't triggering my gag reflex anymore. He had a lot to learn about migraines if he wanted to be with me.

"Oh, for heaven's sake," I grumbled and snatched the bag. I inhaled the heavenly aroma and squinted at him. "You're forgiven. I don't have any more pain, only a little residual light and sound sensitivity. So talk softly please. What's up?"

"If you're sure, I really don't want to intrude," he said uncertainly. I dug through the bag and waved at him to follow me to the kitchen, where I grabbed a paper towel off the roll and placed it on the counter beneath an almond croissant.

"Well, first I wanted to go through the publicity blitz from last night with you and see if you wanted my team to do anything. It's not bad," he hastened to assure me. "But we can do anything you want to squash rumors — my team is at your disposal until you hire your own people. And second, I have a proposal for you."

He stepped carefully around me and set down the thermos. I watched, bemused, as he immediately opened the correct cupboard and pulled out two mugs. He poured and added the exactly right amount of milk before handing one to me.

"What?" he asked, misinterpreting my look. "Did I get it wrong? I think that's how I've seen you take it."

I took a sip. It was perfect. I shook my head and smiled. "It's perfect. I didn't know you noticed."

He blushed and his ears went pink as he said quietly, "I notice a lot of things about you."

My turn to blush now and look away.

"So," I started as I swirled my mug like it was an indecently large goblet of wine. "Publicity review and a proposal, plus a lovely breakfast…"

"And I was really worried — you seemed so ill last night." He shrugged. "If you're feeling better, I was wondering if you'd want to hang out."

"Yes? But you're going to have to give me a bit to pull it together." I tapped my chin and took a sip of coffee as I mentally ran through options. "Also, how public do we want to be today? Did you notice anyone tailing you?"

"No, I drove today and I'm positive no one saw me leave. My housekeeper brought over the pastries when she arrived this morning and that's my own coffee. For today, we should be fine. Have you checked your phone at all yet?"

I held up my phone so he could see the black screen. "Turned it off before the Premiere and forgot to turn it back on. What about a walk on the beach? It seems pretty quiet here today and we can go through the headlines outside. I need some air."

"A walk sounds perfect." He grinned and his left dimple popped for the first time since our impromptu Koreatown karaoke night.

I left him downstairs with an order to clean up our breakfast and dashed upstairs to throw on some clothes. While I scrubbed off last night's makeup and brushed my teeth, I took stock of my situation. I knew I looked the same as always — wavy brown hair, green eyes with a hint of dark circles and pale skin that should have been tan, considering I lived at the beach and loved being outside. But somehow, overnight, it felt like everything had changed.

My boring same-ol' outside didn't match my newly scrambled insides. I threw on my favorite pair of jeans and hurriedly tucked in a white T-shirt as I glanced down at the bracelets on my wrist. Still beautiful and still there, they were a symbol of the weird in-between place I seemed to have found myself in.

"All right, let's head out," I called as I pulled on a hat and my sunglasses.

"Aw, my little incognito beauty," he said as he hugged me around the waist.

I wiggled free and tried to pinch his cheek. Laughing, he ducked away, and it struck me how happy he looked. He was quietly glowing and his eyes were lit up from within, little flecks of gold standing out so brightly that I couldn't understand how they weren't his most commented-on feature. He looked completely relaxed and comfortable. All the lines on his face had suddenly smoothed out.

I went up on my tiptoes to give him an impulsive kiss on the cheek. "You look pretty good yourself, my little low-key handsome movie star." I headed for the back door while he stayed frozen in front of the mirror, staring at me in utter bemusement.

"I can't believe you kissed me—like it's totally natural. I mean, being with you has always felt that way, but it's so shocking to have you kiss me like it's normal. Like we can do that now," he said as he reached for my hand while I locked the door behind us.

"I guess it's our new normal, isn't it?"

The smile that blazed across his face almost blinded me. "It is."

Holding hands, we push-pulled our way to my back gate, neither of us letting go of each other, and finally stepped out onto the beach. I was teasing him about a really campy film he'd made a few years ago when he tackled me into the sand in retaliation.

"Enough. My fragile ego can't take it," he groused as I spat sand at him. He rolled off, and I sat up and leaned into him.

"I'm sorry," I said, not quite contrite, while trying not to laugh.

"You aren't, but that's okay. It was a shit movie. Really shit. I only did it because my little sister had a crush on the other male lead and she wanted to visit me on set."

"Such a good big brother." I patted his cheek.

"I am. Except he wanted to get off with me, not her, and I'd started dating Kate a few months earlier. Not a great scene. Ella, that's my sister, was so sad."

"How much younger is Ella?" I gave up on brushing the sand off me and cuddled into him when he threw an arm around my shoulder. The morning breeze on the beach was a little chilly.

"Oh, she's two years younger. She has a twin brother, Max, who I'm not as close to. He's running the family wineries. We don't have a lot in common and my parents basically married him off to the daughter of another winery owner. I thought it was bullshit, but he's always maintained that it was what he wanted."

"And you have another brother too, right? The soccer player?" I idly sifted sand through my fingers, surprised when I realized that this was the first time we'd really spoken about his family in any detail. Also slightly embarrassed that I knew so much about him — like everyone else in the country, I drank in the celebrity gossip about him and a select few others with my daily coffee.

"Yeah, Matti. Matthias. He's a lot younger, twenty-six, seven years between us. Not unwelcome, but certainly unexpected, as my mother calls him. Rory actually reminds me of him a bit. Totally unapologetic about who he is. Operates on instinct mostly. Smart guy, but doesn't think he is."

"Interesting. You must be excited to see them."

"Definitely. It's been almost a year and we're — or we were, I guess — super close." He stared out at the water.

"Well, I'm jealous. I haven't seen my sister in a few years. We're estranged, you could say, ever since my parents passed away and she decided it was a good move to hook up with my boyfriend at the time. Out of grief, she said." My voice was even, but I held my eyes wide open to avoid the inevitable tears that always rose to the surface when I thought about the open wound that was my family.

Silence. I looked over and he was staring at me, stricken. "I'm so sorry, Alina. You told me that a while ago, but I don't think I ever said that I was sorry."

"It was a while ago. I appreciate it, but it's okay now." I smiled at him and awkwardly punched his bicep.

We sat and watched the ocean for a while before he elbowed me in the ribs.

"Ouch! What?"

"Get your phone, I need to show you the stuff from last night." He gestured to my phone like "come on already you twit, don't be a pussy."

After a brief pause, notifications burst across the screen. News, social media, emails, texts. It was an explosion of annoying chimes and *whoosh* noises. There were dozens of news alerts for my name, mostly from social media accounts and independent bloggers, although some had been picked up by the bigger publications like *Star* and the *Daily Mail*. I looked at those first. The conjectures of who I was, what Markus was doing with me and what Kate would think were to be expected, I guessed, but the sheer number of them was overwhelming.

I was arrested by the pictures. There we were, in living color, sharing a secret smile as we waved to the media surrounding us. Even I could see the smoldering, possessive look in his eyes and the desire in my own. I sucked in a breath and glanced down at my bracelets, touching one pensively. I looked up at him, and he was giving me the same look as in the photos.

It worried me, though, because I saw something that Markus didn't see — or maybe didn't want to see. The way we looked at each other, what was broadcast so clearly in both of our eyes, was more than desire. More than lust. Maybe it wasn't love, but it was definitely something *more* than what was implied by a casual "let's see how this goes."

"You see?" he said softly as he reached out to stroke the same bracelet, our fingertips brushing.

I didn't answer, instead looking back at my phone to screen the other notifications — hundreds of requests for comment and interviews, fan messages and scathing derision from fans of Kate.

"Don't read the comments," Markus said hastily, trying to grab my phone from me. "First lesson my P.R. agent taught me, and she was dead right."

"Knock it off, grabby hands. I wasn't going to, but I do need to lock down my accounts. Everyone can see the video Candace posted of me drunkenly doing karaoke to *Livin' on a Prayer*," I fretted.

"Well, they'll at least know that you have amazing taste in music," he said as a smile broke through his overly solemn demeanor. "What did you think, though, of our photos and the articles?"

"Um, I think we came off okay in the interview. Michael's probably thrilled about all of the rumors that are going to swirl around the upcoming season," I answered, looking around to make sure we were still alone, and mimicked him. "You know, Alina, any publicity is good publicity!"

"I suppose he's right, from a very specific point of view. Not necessarily ours though. But what did you feel when you saw us together? I know things got emotional last night, but look at how we started." Markus pointed at the phone open on my thigh, frozen on a still image of us from the red carpet, completely focused on each other and no one else.

I shied away from the response that I wanted to give, which was, 'We looked like we were seconds from tearing each other's clothes off and fucking on the red carpet in front of all of the photographers.' Instead I simply said, "It was nice. We looked really nice together."

He flopped back in the sand, staring at me disbelievingly, hand grabbing his chest dramatically. "You're fucking kidding me, right? Nice? Alina, I look like I'm about to slam you into the nearest wall and claim you in front of everyone. And you look like you're daring me to do it."

"Oh, that? Right," I said faintly as I tried to keep a straight face while a sudden heat wave swept over me and squeezed my legs together in a vain attempt to release the tension ratcheting up inside me.

"Unbelievable," he muttered. "Nice." He shook his head and pulled away slightly, shifting his hips as though the sand were burning him. I looked down almost involuntarily and saw the cause of his discomfort.

Following my eyes, he grimaced and pulled his knees up to his chest so he could wrap his arms around them. "So, do you want my team to go to work on anything? From my perspective, this isn't that bad. But I'm not you and however you want to handle this is good with me."

"I think I'm okay, if you are. All the stories are pretty vague right now, just the pictures with us," I said slowly. "Nothing's too terrible and it's not as bad as it probably could have been. I'll start looking into my own reps, though."

Markus smiled at me and leaned over to brush a soft kiss on my temple. "If you're sure, I'll tell the team to stand down. If you want, I can ask them for some recommendations for agents to call. You should definitely have your own."

I nodded and relaxed into his warm embrace as a breeze kicked up around us and a few gulls cried out overhead, relishing the fact that this was our new normal and that he seemed as happy to be lost in it as I was.

* * * *

"Alina, you're not playing fair!" Markus threw his cards at me.

"What? Because you're always drawing four?"

It was late in the evening and we were playing Uno. Markus hadn't realized that the 'draw' cards needed to be hoarded and played when his opponent was on the verge of winning.

He glowered at me from his spot on the floor. "Yes. That."

I laughed and threw my cards at him from the other side of the coffee table. "Suck it."

His grouchy mood immediately disappeared as he grabbed a handful of cards, dove over the low table and shoved them down my shirt. I couldn't stop giggling as I tried ineffectually to push his hands away from my body. "Stop, Markus! Gah! Fine, you win!"

He grunted as I kneed him in the gut and he pushed me off of him.

"Hey," he said softly once he'd recovered his breath.

"Is for horses," I replied, still breathless.

He groaned and rolled his eyes at me. "What I was trying to say is 'Hey, I had a lot of fun today'."

"Oh, yeah. Me too."

"And I was wondering what you're up to over the next few days, if you might want to keep hanging out?"

"Well, my schedule cleared up considerably once I signed that contract. Michael pulled me from all post-production work so I could start memorizing lines and stuff. He still hasn't lined up coaches for me — think that's supposed to start next week. And then we only have a few weeks of rehearsals before filming actually starts."

"Woah, he pulled you from post?" Markus frowned in consternation. "But that's your job."

"Yeah, but I've done post-production with him before and know how it goes. I'm more nervous about the next three weeks before rehearsals actually start. I mean, it's Monday today and I start working with coaches next week, most likely. Which means I'll only have two weeks with them before having to be an actor in front of everyone."

"Shit, that is really fast. We should plan on spending time running lines. Which is part of my proposition, I guess. I was wondering what you're doing over the next few days, see if you'd like to get out of town for a bit. We can run lines and spend time together."

"Normally I'd love to, but aren't you leaving the day after tomorrow or something like that?" I asked, confused.

"Yeah, I'm supposed to fly out to see my family, but I also think we might need this time together. I can move it out till you're working with the coaches. That will give us some time to get grounded in our characters."

"No! You haven't seen your family in ages. I'll be fine on my own. You're not moving that flight," I said wildly, alarmed that he would drop his family for me.

"I'm not skipping the trip, only putting it off for a bit, because we *do* need to work together," he muttered as he awkwardly swept up and shuffled a handful of cards from the floor.

"Markus, no. We're fine, we have all the time in the world."

He studied me closely in the low lamplight and I stared right back, neither of us willing to yield. His jaw clenched and unclenched, casting shadows on his handsome face.

"You're right," he said in a low voice, "but you're also wrong. I do need that time with them, but we definitely don't have all the time in the world. You saw all of that coverage today. That was from one event.

They're going to find you — find *us* — and soon. I feel like we're on the edge of something together and I'd like us to be prepared before the shit really hits the fan. I don't want you going into rehearsals blindly."

His voice softened a bit. "Believe me when I say that I want us to build something together before the public finds out and people try to push us apart."

I wanted to scoff or roll my eyes and remind him about all of this being 'casual'. But he'd asked me to trust him and I really had no idea how wild things would get for us or how either of us would react if the pressure got turned up this early.

My bangs blew straight up as I forced out a stressed breath. "Fine, what do you have in mind then?"

His shoulders relaxed down from his ears when he heard my agreement. "This might sound a little absurd, but why don't you come to Germany with me? We could chill, run lines, meet up with my family if you're up to it."

"I appreciate what you're trying to do here, but this doesn't feel super casual. Can I think about it? Call you tomorrow with an answer?" I stood and held out my hand to pull him up.

"Oh, come on. No sleepovers? I'm very good at casually giving out orgasms." He threw me a wicked grin as he pulled me in for a hug. I pinched his side and he yelped. "Kidding, I'm kidding. Call me whenever tomorrow, and I can figure out the details if you want to come with me. I hope you do."

As he finished speaking, he stepped back a half step while keeping me in his arms. I looked up at him and he dropped his forehead down to rest against mine. His breath tickled my cheek and played with my hair. "Thanks for such a great day. Sleep well," he said quietly, then placed a sweet kiss on my surprised lips, before he turned and left, closing the door softly behind him.

The minute the door closed, I had my phone out to text Candace.

*Help! Markus wants me to go to Germany with him, meet his family. Wtf do I do?*

She replied immediately.

*Uh, say yes? Free Euro trip? Why WOULDN'T you go?*

I rolled my eyes.

*Maybe because we just started this casual thing and this feels like the opposite of casual?*

She sent me an animated eyeroll emoji in return and the typing dots balloon rippled at the bottom of the screen.

*It might be the opp of casual, but it's a good idea. You saw the news today about you two? It's gonna get worse and more in your face after last night. And I kno you don't need a man or anything, but he might need you.*

I gingerly poured myself a glass of wine from an open bottle in my fridge, praying it wouldn't trigger yet another migraine.

*That's what he said too. Plus we need to read through the scripts together, start blocking things out. Maybe there will be time for that on the plane.*

Candace was quick on the comeback.

*Listen to the man. He's been through this and dealt with the press for a looong time. If you don't want to go to Germany, go somewhere else. But I think you both might want to be somewhere while this blows over here.*

My glass was empty by the time I'd finished thinking through the possible ramifications of going to Germany on a moment's notice. I swiped to Markus' text string and, before I could lose my nerve, sent him a short text.

*You were serious about the invite, right? I'm in, but not for the whole time. I need to be back in a few days to start working with Michael's coaches. xo*

# Chapter Twenty

*Markus*

The minute I got her text, I quickly pulled the trigger on another ticket and forwarded the info to Alina so she could finish the check-in process. Then I emailed the building manager for my apartment in Berlin and asked that he send someone in to get it ready for guests — grocery shop, clean, the usual.

While I wasn't inclined to tell anyone about Alina — it felt too fragile for sharing — I had to let Will know that she was coming with me to Germany so he wouldn't be blindsided when the Euro tabloids started posting pictures. He and Claire were already busy with the requests for comment on the photos from the Premiere. I shot them a message saying that the two of us were planning a quick trip to Berlin to get away from the American paps before we were both due to return to L.A. for rehearsals.

For their personal benefit, I added that the latest round of nonsense with *Southern Gods* had brought us closer together and that we were in the very early stages of seeing each other. I also stressed that info wasn't to be shared with anyone and requested that they send over suggestions for an agent for Alina. Mixing too much business with pleasure was a bad idea. While I headed outside to the pool area, agreement and congratulations came in, along with a promise to email her a list of agents that Will thought would be a good fit.

Filled with restless energy and fueled by too much caffeine, I paced the deck and called my sister to see if she would be interested in meeting in Berlin. Ella was, predictably, overexcited about the possibility of an escape from motherhood, but hyper-concerned about me jumping into a new relationship. She'd figured that out, despite my assurances that Alina was a friend who was looking to check out Berlin before heading to another stop on her European travels for work. I wasn't fooling anyone, even with thousands of miles between us.

After Ella, I dialed Max and got his voicemail. While I wasn't sure what he did on a daily basis, he always seemed busy.

*Probably out being a diligent wine guy and playing with his grapes.*

I left a message with the details and asked if he would like to come. His wife was, of course, welcome as well.

Not expecting a return call any time soon, or possibly ever, I called Matti. He answered completely hammered after his team's unexpected victory against their biggest club rival. I wasn't sure how much of the conversation he would retain, so I just asked him if he fancied a trip to Berlin and left it at that. I was pretty sure that he answered in the affirmative before he broke out in song, and the rest of the club right along with him.

I listened for a while, vastly entertained, until I heard an equally wasted female voice offering him and a few of his boys a good time. I shuddered at the thought of my baby brother having sex with anyone, then I hung up and shot him a text with details.

Almost instantly, a GIF appeared in the message string—a pornographic one with nothing but a guy drilling a woman from behind, with a "Yes, Yes, Yes!" caption. I burst out laughing. My brother was an absolute class act.

\* \* \* \*

"Fuck, keep your shirt on. I'm coming." Alina's crabby morning voice was muffled behind the front door.

I banged again and leaned into the frame. "But my shirt can come off so easily. And it's not fair to be hiding from me if you're coming all on your own," I growled at the still-closed door.

Dead silence. The door creaked open and a furious green eye slowly emerged. "You are so fucking ridiculous. I don't even know how to handle you—no! Stop! I didn't mean it like… You ass."

I stuck my foot in the gap when she tried to playfully slam the door in my face and she managed to stop it in time to save me from a very uncomfortable injury. A brief tug of war later and she appeared, gnawing her lip and fiddling with the hem of a gray T-shirt cropped above high-waisted bleach-splattered jeans that were rolled to her ankles to show off a pair of Adidas Stan Smiths. My bracelets were still on her arm, an incredible warmth rose up through my chest. She noticed where my attention had caught and smiled.

"You like?" she asked sweetly.

I nodded, feeling strangely proud, like we were both happy with the evidence of our relationship shining on her arm for everyone to see.

"Well, they're staying on until we find the screwdriver. Do you still have the case?"

"Not here. I'll have someone send it. Ready?" My tone was brusque as I started to turn away from her.

She laughed at my clear annoyance and stroked my arm. "Don't worry, sensitive guy. I love them and don't want them off right now or anything."

"I know. It's fine. Really. I like seeing them on you. Sorry if that came out like I wanted to pee on you or something."

"You're gross. Now help me with my bags." She tossed a duffle at me and dragged out a carry-on roller bag. Leaving it on the porch, she ducked back in then emerged with her beat-up leather tote and locked the house.

I took her hand as we walked to the car. "Ready for this? I'm so glad you're coming with and I can show you around my hometown."

She squeezed my hand in response, flashing me a quick grin. "Me too. And we're running lines on the plane, right?"

"Of course," I said as I let go of her hand and helped her into the car.

"Hey, David," she greeted my driver, and he nodded back as I climbed in to sit beside her. She immediately slid over to rest her head on my shoulder once I was buckled in.

"So, what activities did you come up with for this little getaway? Are we really meeting up with your family?" she asked as her fingers tangled in her lap.

"My sister will definitely be meeting us. She's coming from a suburb. Matti will most likely be there as well. Not sure though, since he was drunk when I asked. Max is a busy guy, so I doubt it." The vertical crease between her brows deepened and I did my best to reassure her. "It's going to be fine. Don't worry. We've got a day to ourselves to get over the jet lag, and I made sure that my apartment is ready for us."

"Apartment?" she asked uncertainly.

"Yeah, my apartment. I've got a loft in old East Berlin. It's in Friedrichshain. I'm rarely there, but it's the first property I ever bought on my own. My favorite too, if I'm honest."

"Hold up. I want to talk about what we're doing in Berlin more in a second. But your *first* property? I guess I never thought about it, but how many properties do you have?"

"Three. The apartment in Berlin, the house here in L.A. and a townhouse in London. I also have part-ownership with my brothers on a villa and vineyard in Tuscany, but I'm the money guy for that one and rarely go there."

"Three." Her voice was faint and she shifted as though she wanted to jump out of the car.

"Alina, it's just an investment. Not a big deal. I mean, you've seen at least one of my contracts."

"I know, I know. But it's one thing to know it and totally another to *know* it. You know?"

"That's a lot of knowledge you're trying to drop," I teased in an effort to lighten the mood.

"Never mind. This is still new to me—you're fucking rich and famous. It's weird. Remind me you're a normal guy when I start to freak out."

I hugged her tightly against me and she curled an arm around my waist as her head found that perfect spot tucked beneath my chin. "I promise. Now, do you want to talk about what our options are?"

She snuggled infinitesimally closer and her nod gently bounced off my jaw.

"We'll be getting in early morning tomorrow and can stick around my apartment or go into the city proper for tourist-type stuff. The day after, everyone will be coming in, so we'll have to have more serious plans or else we'll bicker about what to do. What do you think?"

"I really like the idea of alone time," she said as she toyed with the hem of my faded black T-shirt, sliding her fingertips underneath to drag across my stomach.

"Me too," I managed to choke out as she absently traced over my abdominal muscles, dipping intermittently beneath the waistband of my jeans. I'd never gone this long without sex and she was driving me out of my mind.

"Let's leave tomorrow open then. I'd love to go to a museum or wander around the city, but I don't know how I'll be feeling after the flight. What if we did a bike tour? Rent bikes and go from place to place? Could be fun."

"Want me to text Ella to see if she can set it up for us?" I responded. "Shit, we're almost at the airport. Do you have a hat and sunglasses? We're at the concierge entrance, but still…"

"I'll be fine," she said as she gave a quick glance to make sure the privacy screen was up before slinging a leg over me and sliding onto my lap. She plucked the phone neatly out of my hand and stuck it in a cup holder. "You can text your sister from the plane. Now get over here. I haven't even kissed you yet."

Her hands curled around my stubbled jaw and their warmth re-ignited the banked fire that never seemed to fully extinguish when she was nearby. It was a gentle, teasing kiss to start, but then her knees tightened around my waist and she thrust her hands into my hair, nails scratching lightly against my scalp as she angled my head the way she wanted me. I groaned into her mouth as I lifted my hips to press into the hot, soft core of her that was covered by altogether too many layers. A knock on the privacy screen brought me back to earth and I started making plans for the bed in our private cabin on the plane. Elaborate plans involving a very naked and exhibitionistic Alina, one-thousand-thread-count Egyptian cotton sheets and all the champagne we could drink.

# Chapter Twenty-One

*Alina*

It took David's repeated knocking on the privacy screen to pierce the haze that had built up as we kissed. Both of us were sporting wild hairstyles and Markus had some serious adjustments to make before we could leave the car. Denying how badly I wanted this man was having a detrimental effect on my headspace. We seriously needed to fuck soon or both of us were going to end up with the bluest of blue balls.

As he closed his eyes and leaned back against the headrest, I rechecked my reflection in the mirror and tweaked my ponytail a little. My eyes were bright and my cheeks and lips had the type of flush that can only be attained by messing around with someone or applying a very expensive stain. David hauled our bags and passports over to the agent, who began the check-in process.

"Alina? You ready? David's waving us out." Markus opened the door and stepped down to the curb, then turned back to me with a smile on his face as he held his hand outstretched toward me, echoing his gesture from the Premiere. "Shall we?"

And same as that night, I nodded and reached out. Our palms met and his long fingers wrapped securely around my much smaller hand. He pulled me beside him effortlessly and guided me to the counter where David was waiting. The agent looked at us, looked at the passports and handed us boarding passes.

"Mr. Shellenberg. Ms. Ferrous."

We thanked him and turned to David. "Bye, David, thanks so much for everything," I offered as I held my hand out for a quick shake.

"I'll see you in a few days. You've got my flight details, right?" Markus asked, and David nodded. He turned to me. "David can pick you up too when you get back, if you want."

"Oh, no. I couldn't impose."

"It's not imposing at all. I'll give David your info and you can call or text him if you decide you'd like a ride," he said, and David grinned from behind him, making a 'call me' sign with his hand by his ear.

I stifled a laugh as we went through the automatic door. We moved through security efficiently — celebrities really knew how to live with this concierge business. It was like TSA Pre-Check on steroids. We paused on the threshold of the airline's first-class lounge to glance at each other. I smiled while I held out my hand to him. This was our first real test, the initial foray into the public as a...couple. *Yeah, this is totally casual.*

"My turn. Shall we?" I asked him.

He grinned back, nodded and grasped my hand. We pushed through the doors together. "So, don't be mad at me —" he started as we walked through, immediately sidestepping a group of chattering, confused senior citizens.

"That is a shitty way to start a sentence, you know. Only thing worse is 'we need to talk', or maybe 'about that missing million dollars from our bank account—'"

"Those are not remotely equivalent." He spluttered at me in confusion.

"Kidding! But seriously, what shouldn't I get mad at you about this time?" I asked, elbowing him as we continued toward our gate from the lounge at an unhurried pace.

"Um, well. I might have upgraded you again, despite you calling it a pointless expense, because I didn't want to *not* sit together on this long flight. I mean, we're supposed to be practicing together. And I did it kind of without telling you because I was afraid you'd say no since this is all new and stuff," he said in a rush.

I patted his cheek heavily. "Markus, you shouldn't have."

His face paled.

"But I'm so glad you did, thank you. I'll buy you a drink tomorrow when we get in." I smirked.

He laughed and tapped my hand. "I'm going to hold you to that," he said with a wink. I adored flirtatious Markus, but with only one wink and a smirk he'd ruined my brand-new lacy underwear. He took charge of our forward progress and pulled me down the terminal's moving walkway. Apparently he was one of those people who actually walked down them.

I was always, obnoxiously, on the 'Stand' side of that yellow line down the center of the walkway, daydreaming about the trips people were taking—the family trip to Disney with the parents who already looked overwhelmed and ready to commit adultery, the woman in the white fur coat and enormous black sunglasses trying to entrap a Pomeranian that had escaped from its carrier. The stories their body language told about love and secrets, exasperation and dreams of escape.

We got to our gate as they began boarding first class, and Markus let go of my hand to rifle through his backpack for his passport. I ignored the gate agent's curious look as she held out a hand for my documentation.

She looked between us again and raised her eyebrows at Markus, scanned my papers and waved me through. "Have a lovely flight, Mr. Shellenberg."

"Welcome to the lifestyles of the rich and famous. The bold and the beautiful," he attempted to deadpan as we headed down the walkway. "Where everyone is convinced they know you and have the right to eye-fuck you."

"I don't know if that's so much a them thing or a you thing," I said without too much heat. "You're too pretty for your own good."

"Welcome aboard, Mr. Shellenberg, please follow us." The flight attendants smiled professionally and gestured for us to follow them up the stairs to the first-class cabins.

While the downstairs of the plane was well-managed chaos, it was almost spa-like upstairs. The lighting was softer, lo-fi electronic music played a soothing backdrop and the dark wood and gold inlay made everything feel luxe as hell. The floor lighting glowed and illuminated each scuff on my four-year-old Adidas. My bracelets, which one of the attendants gushed over as I walked past, felt like the only part of me that belonged in this rarified space.

At the door to the last cabin on the left, the flight attendant slid the partition open and gestured for us to enter. She quickly pointed out the unobtrusive call button embedded in the wall next to the door, clapped her hands softly to turn on the recessed lighting and backed out smoothly. I took in the streamlined leather loungers, built-in end-tables and sixty-inch flatscreen with wide eyes while Markus dropped his carry-on carelessly on one of the chairs and pulled my own from my shoulder. He set it aside to rest beside his own and gently pushed my jaw back up to close.

The attendant quickly returned with two glasses of champagne on a tray and passed them to Markus. "Enjoy your flight, Mr. Shellenberg. Let me know if we can do anything to serve you today."

I shut the door, hard, behind her and smashed my hand into a button that made a privacy curtain descend over the window in the cabin's door. The whole experience of flying like this, following Markus around and seeing how differently he lived his life compared to mine—up to this point, anyways—was overwhelming and it pissed me off how small I suddenly felt in comparison. While I was pleased with the plush settings, it was hitting home that I was about to go visit this man's family when I had taken great care to avoid any and all families since my own had shattered apart. My nerves went into overdrive.

*We're too different for this to work. All this casual nonsense is bullshit.*

I drained my glass of champagne and grabbed for his. "Thanks," I said. Nicely. Because I was a nice person. Not irrationally angry or scared at all. Nope.

Markus flopped down on one of the loungers and barely managed to get out between guffaws, "Oh my god. You're so incandescent right now. You know, if I wasn't completely certain that you wouldn't castrate me, I'd tell you that you're gorgeous when you're furious. I kinda want to — argh!"

I'd accidentally-on-purpose tipped my drink over his head. The champagne left sticky bubbles that trailed down his jawline and got trapped in the stubble that coated his cheeks. My momentary satisfaction faded quickly as I watched his eyes darken.

"That's it. You're going to get it," he growled as he stripped off his wet shirt, threw it on the ground, where it landed with a soggy plop, and came at me, long fingers flexing threateningly.

"Wait! Wait, stop, Markus. I'm not fucking around here, you're pissing me off." I pushed him back and he landed on the other dark leather chair, shirtless and stunned. I sat down more gingerly opposite him. "I don't like to be ignored and I'm feeling like you're three levels or more above me. I've never even met the family of someone I've dated. It's kind of all hitting me at once here."

"Fucking hell. I misunderstood, thought you were messing with me." He rifled through his bag and pulled out a dry light-blue shirt, shook it and slid it over his head. Despite my anger, I had an internal moment of mourning at the need to cover up all of that skin and lean muscle.

He came over to me and held out his arms and I stepped into them. "I'll be okay. Give me a second," I said in a muffled voice as I wrapped my arms around his waist.

# Chapter Twenty-Two

*Markus*

Alina's hands gripped my shirt and I could feel her kneading and worrying the cloth. She wasn't crying, but was obviously emotional, and I'd completely missed every signal. I inhaled deeply, willing my heart to return to normal, and rubbed small circles between her shoulder blades. A knock vibrated against the door.

"Yes? We're fine in here," I said, my voice slightly more gravelly than normal.

"Mr. Shellenberg? I need to do a pre-flight check. We'll be taking off soon."

"We're fine. Absolutely fine. And completely buckled in. We may want something to eat. Maybe some wine? Two bottles of water?" I was desperate to get rid of her as I glanced at Alina, who had pulled away from me as she ineffectually tried to straighten her hair again.

"Oh my god, are they trying to kill us with punctual service?" she said with a small, forced laugh.

"Here, let me." I grabbed her hair tie and tried to coax her tangled curls back into their ponytail. She hummed her thanks and stroked my forearm with a single finger that left a slow-burning trail of fire in its wake. I finally got her hair pulled into a messy ponytail as the attendant knocked again. "Sir, your food."

I looked at her. "You good?"

"Certainly, thanks to my excellent hairstylist." She wiggled her eyebrows at me.

"I used to try to do Ella's hair when I was small, but I'm a little out of practice." I quickly kissed her cheek as I heaved myself off of my seat to answer the door.

I tucked the bottles of water beneath an arm and took the trays from the two attendants' outstretched hands. "Thank you, ladies. We'll ring if we need anything else."

"Of course," they murmured as they stared curiously around me at Alina, who oh so casually ignored them while flicking through her copy of the script she'd pulled from her bag as she sat curled up on one of the loungers.

\* \* \* \*

We'd been in the air for about two hours, spending most of it running lines. We were about a third of the way through the season in terms of reading through our scenes together, and I could already tell that she was going to be fine. Whether she was a true natural talent or our vibe was simply that effective, I wasn't sure, but we were both developing a strong sense of our characters. I leaned against the wall and swirled what was left of my wine while I watched Alina read and toy with a loose curl.

"Hey."

"Hmm?" she responded as she continued to scan ahead in her script.

"Get up," I said impatiently as I rose to my feet. "You're about to see why we pay the big bucks for these seats."

She stood and watched with interest as I reclined both loungers and spun them so they aligned and formed a full-size bed. I pulled pillows and a down comforter emblazoned with the logo of the airline in gold thread out of the closet by the door and shook them out with a snap to settle on top.

"Your bed, madam." I gestured with a bow that would have been worthy of a Shakespearean actor.

"My hero," she gasped and flopped onto our bed. "This is unreal! How do they have such comfortable mattresses on a lounge chair? On a damn plane?"

"You can watch a movie if you want or keep reading, but I need to crash." I threw her the remote. She put it on an end table and flipped on one of the reading lights next to the side she had staked out.

"I'm fine. Give me a second to finish this scene." She looked up at me and her eyes narrowed as she watched me start to undress. "Hey, what do you think you're doing?"

"Uh, getting out of these clothes? My jeans are still damp from the champagne shower, and I'm not sleeping in them." I got the jeans in question off, shrugged out of my shirt again and slid under the quilt, ignoring the heat in her stare, although it made me smile internally.

I lay on my side and watched her read for a bit with my head propped up in one hand. Alina's eyes scanned quickly up and down the page and she snuck a look at me.

"What's up? Thought you were sooo tired," she said with a smirk.

"I am, but I like watching you. And I need to know if we're okay. This morning and everything else is a lot to take, a lot of pressure on something new. Am I doing enough to support you?" I reached out to stroke her arm, circling the wrist that wore my bracelets.

She set her script in her lap and turned and faced me fully. "Yeah, we're okay. If it's weird for me to date someone like you, it's probably weird for you to date someone like me."

"You're right. It is a little bit," I answered. "What about the family thing?"

She kissed the tip of my nose. "It's fine. Seriously, I should have talked to you about it earlier. As long as you're aware that this is strange for me, but I'm trying."

"I won't forget." I brushed her bangs away from her face and searched her eyes for the sincerity that low-key shone out at me. She grabbed my hand and kissed the palm before placing it back on my chest, over my heart.

"I'm glad we're on the same page. Night," I muttered as I turned over.

"Night," she said softly.

I hummed something indistinct and closed my eyes, so fucking happy to be where I was in that exact moment. We were going to have to have a talk at some point soon, because I was already past the point of casual with her, but she seemed determined to hang on to that fact. I listened to her flip a few pages before she gave up on trying to read and got up. A few seconds later, her jeans hit the ground with a jingle. The bed dipped again as she got in and clicked off the light.

She wiggled back toward me and sighed as I curled up around her. One of her hands idly stroked the back of my forearm that draped across her stomach. The last thing I heard before my eyes slid blissfully shut was a throaty moan as my thumb rubbed gently back and forth across the smooth skin of her bare stomach beneath her T-shirt.

\* \* \* \*

A few hours later, something woke me—a bright light and sharp click. The cabin was dark and quiet again as I sleepily took stock of Alina. She was facing me with her head pillowed on my shoulder, and I was turned slightly toward her, both arms clasping her close. Her leg was trapped between mine, and one of her hands had a death grip on my bare hip.

The first time that I saw her, I hazily recalled, the entire world had seemed to slip away, the ground beneath my feet disappearing, leaving only her face and voice as anchors that had kept me from flying into the void. What I felt now was that same sense of weightlessness. The body curled next to me was the only form of gravity holding me together.

Nothing else mattered. Nothing else existed. I swore that I could feel her heartbeat echoing and speeding up to synchronize with my own. I was so warm and comfortable. I kissed her forehead and drifted back off after deciding the flash of light that had startled me awake had been a dream.

\* \* \* \*

When I woke again we were lying facing each other, our foreheads touching and legs entangled. One of her hands was dipped into my boxer briefs. Her thumb gently swirled around the head of my cock while her other hand curved over the muscles in my chest, teasing mindlessly down my stomach.

My hands were anything but innocent, and one was wrapped around her upper thigh and ass to dip slightly beneath the fabric of her boyshort panties, soaking my fingertips as they glided through her folds. She was so fucking wet. My other hand was entwined in her loose curls. I pulled gently and was rewarded by a moan as she arched toward me, bringing her chest into blazing contact with mine.

At some point, one of us had pushed her shirt up high above her breasts, and the feel of her soft skin and pebbled nipples gliding across my chest had both of us panting as we ground minutely against each other. But so softly. And so slowly. The whole situation was completely unreal. The quiet, the dark, the plane's white noise and her warm body aligned with my own.

We continued the slow push and pull, finding a tortuous rhythm, as if our bodies couldn't bear to be separate entities any longer, as if we needed to be absorbed into each other. Her hand slid completely beneath the waistband of my underwear to grasp my cock, and I groaned as she began to stroke me with a fist that tightened inexorably as she jerked me off.

I opened my eyes, owning the moment and my need for her. Her eyes were already wide and questioning, looking to me for her answers. "Yes?" I asked gently and she smiled faintly.

"Yes," she whispered.

I dropped my mouth to hers and shuddered as her tongue swept across my lips. The faint taste of champagne lingered and the scent of her body wash rolled over me in waves of dusky sandalwood. My hips bucked wildly into her hand and I dragged my fingertips slowly up her bare back to tangle in her hair.

Her curls wrapped around my fingers as I cradled her head in the palm of my hand while she clumsily tugged down my briefs and worked to free herself from her own.

The slightly rough, laundered sheets of the plane's bed chafed my overly sensitive skin as I rolled onto my back, taking Alina with me. She leaned over me with her hands braced on either side of my face, her bracelets jingling musically in my ears while we stared into each other's eyes, both of us in disbelief about what we were doing, the liberties we were finally allowing ourselves.

"Arms up, sweetheart," I whispered as I gently pulled the shirt over her head.

God, she was gorgeous. Her tits were perfect handfuls, rising and falling above me as she looked down at where she sat with her pussy spread open over me, soaking me. She started to slide back and forth on top of me, coating me with her arousal.

I gently tongued one of the tempting, wine-colored nipples that hovered over my mouth until it tightened to a point. She gasped as I sucked hard, grinding down onto me as I thrust upward against her heat, almost but not quite sliding inside her. The next time that she eased her hips forward I brought a hand down to her ass, my fingers parting her slit as she moved backward, impaling herself on two of my fingers.

"Fuck. Fuck, that feels so good, Markus!" she hissed as she took over the pace, fucking herself on my fingers and angling her hips lower to rub against my aching cock.

My balls tightened up and lightning gathered at the base of my spine as I struggled not to come. She called out my name as she finally bore down, hard, moving faster and faster until her inner muscles tightened like a velvet fist around my fingers. "Fuck, Markus. That… that…that was—"

"It was," I practically gasped. I was still incredibly hard.

"Fuck," she said again. She moaned slightly as I jerked against her still-sensitive flesh. My teeth clenched as I fought to keep from thrusting up into her. Her breathing slowed and she lifted her head to look at me. I was in absolute agony as she smiled knowingly at me. She bent her head back to my chest and drew her tongue in a slow circle around my nipple. I blew out a harsh breath and she raised her head, nipping at the base of my throat. "You all right?" she asked innocently. "I feel amazing, so relaxed, pleasantly sleepy. Maybe I'll just…"

I groaned, not wanting to beg, grabbed a pillow and pressed it over my face to muffle my curses. She lifted it and kissed me gently. Her tongue traced my lips and I tried to wrap my arms around her and pull her back down on top of me. She leaned away and said, playfully, "Nuh-uh, not so fast. It's my turn to take care of you."

She carefully placed the pillow to the side and smoothly spun to crawl down my body, where she swirled her tongue around the head of my still-hard cock then down to its base to tease my balls. "Let me make you come," she murmured as her soft lips encompassed me.

Heaven. I was in fucking heaven inside her mouth, but I couldn't resist the beautiful sight of her ass and pussy so near my face. I wrapped my arms around her hips and pulled her toward me. God, she tasted so good, a perfect balance of sweetness and musk, and so Alina.

She moaned brokenly, her hips straining back to ride my face as she leaned forward and swallowed my cock when my hips inadvertently thrust against her mouth. I spiraled off the planet for a moment as we both chased our orgasms, and came to with her lying next to me, gasping. I was pretty sure I'd seen God. And she had given me a big thumbs up. Eventually I reached out a trembling hand to touch her hip. "Are you okay?"

"I have no fucking idea," she answered hoarsely. "I think I've been fucked into a new dimension. And you didn't even put your dick in me."

"Unless you're trying to tell me oral doesn't count, I definitely did. Shit, I've never gotten that carried away. Did I hurt you?" My heart rate was still uneven, and I barely got the words out.

"I'm okay." She swallowed audibly and shifted her jaw left to right. "I will definitely be feeling it tomorrow, though. Jesus. Sex has never been like this before. This consuming."

I nodded as I caught my breath and stroked her jaw. "That was so fucking amazing. Thank you," I murmured.

"You're not so bad yourself. Thank *you*." Then she booped my nose and snuggled back down into my arms. She was snoring within thirty seconds.

I could forget whatever I'd said about not wanting to put labels on shit or being casual. I knew I was going to marry this girl.

* * * *

It felt like no time had passed before the attendants were back, knocking on our cabin door. "Mr. Shellenberg, we're starting our final approach into Berlin."

"Uh-huh, I mean, yes, we're up. We'll be ready for landing," I managed to croak.

I turned to Alina, who was slowly waking up, and gasped as I pulled the covers off her. Both of us were marked up. Tiny scrapes from her fingernails stung my shoulders and she'd left a decent set of love bites on my chest. We'd made messes of each other.

"What?" she asked sleepily, swinging her legs over the side of the bed. "Where did you throw my clothes, you animal?"

I pointed at her underwear and T-shirt in the corner, then cleared my throat. "Alina, hold up. Look at yourself. Look at me."

She glanced down and gasped, looking up at me with humor in her eyes. "Well, you know what they say. 'Go to bed with a vixen.'"

I laughed, glad that she seemed unbothered by the whole thing. Secretly, I loved being marked by her, and the memory of my own fingers digging into her hips as she moved above me made me fiercely proud in a strange, caveman way. She owned me, that was all there was to it, and I didn't care who else knew it. By the time the plane taxied to the gate, we were seated and had the door cracked for the flight attendants.

"Have fun, you two? You're the most adorable couple we've seen in a while." They looked at us and smiled while we flushed and muttered something complimentary as we moved toward the exit.

Neither of us were paying any attention to the murmurs behind us as we strolled into the airport, both still caught up in each other. By the time we cleared customs and got to baggage claim, though, the attention was unmistakable. Alina kept dropping my hand to wipe her sweaty palms on her jeans.

"Listen, I know this is bizarre for you. Ignore everyone. We'll be fine — our car should be waiting for us," I answered as I took a step toward the baggage carousel to pull off our luggage.

She paused, a notification on her phone distracting her momentarily. Suddenly both of our phones were clanging like winning slot machines. "Oh shit," she whispered as her hand flew to her mouth.

I looked at her phone. "Shit," I echoed, realizing that the flash and click I had thought I'd imagined had been one of the flight attendants sneaking in and taking our picture while we slept.

The quilt covered everything important, and it was clear that Alina had a shirt on, but we had been captured in an obviously intimate embrace. They had snapped the picture and posted it on social media with the comment, "They couldn't keep their hands off of each other. Clearly in love and didn't care who knew it." A bunch of heart emojis followed, and my name was hashtagged. TMZ had then picked it up and embellished it with a bunch of other photos taken by people at the airports. The headline "Shellenberg finds a replacement?" made me furious. Those attendants were going to be fired by the next day if Roger had anything to do about it.

I risked a look at Alina and asked quietly, "Not great, but at least we're covered. You okay?"

She looked at me for a long time, and I couldn't read her. Then she blew out a strained breath, an exhausted look in her eyes. "Let's find our driver."

"Of course, but this is still only the beginning." I kept my voice low as we joined the flow of traffic toward the entry hall. "Can you handle this? I'll be right here with you, but this is what it will be like — at least at first." I'd thought she was aware of the risks and likely events that would happen if we started going out more publicly, but the look she gave me frightened me a bit. *Is she already over this?*

"Yeah, I know. Don't be ridiculous, Markus. We're *casual*, right? But are we going to come out officially as a couple? How do we play this?" She was fretting again, staring up at me while she crossed her arms tightly across her chest.

"Look, we don't need to do anything that you don't feel comfortable with, okay? Did you interview any agents yet?"

She nodded. "Yeah, I picked Vinny Esposito — should I have him call Will and they can coordinate?"

"Good choice, I think you'll like him a lot. Yeah, have him call Will. I'll text you his number and you can forward it on. If they want to do a conference call, we can do that at my apartment, or you can tell him to get it shut down and tell all of the outlets to fuck off." I grinned at her and was relieved to see a similar smile. *It's going to be okay.*

We made it to the last door into the last waiting hall. The final bottleneck was a metal detector people could only go through one at a time. We put our bags on the belt and stepped through into the crowded hall, following signs to the pick-up area where a young, incredibly fit guy with a buzz cut stood at attention holding a tablet reading "Collins/Ferrous."

Alina looked back and forth between me and the driver. "Collins?"

"Yeah, Phil. The maestro."

"Oh my god. You're such a geek. How am I hanging out with you?" she nearly howled as she shoved me. I quickly sidestepped her, laughing at her embarrassed-for-me face.

We hopped into the car and she curled up in her seat immediately. "God, I'm still so tired."

"Sleep. We've got an hour or so till we get to the apartment."

"Mmmhmm. Thanks, Markus." Her eyes fluttered shut as I brushed a hand across cheek.

When I looked down at the phone on my thigh, one last notification caught my attention. A text from Michael.

*Congrats on your newly minted relationship! Wanna let me know what the fuck is going on with you two? Going rogue?*

Immediately, I fired back an eyeroll emoji to Michael's congratulatory text and kept scrolling through the stories. I couldn't get enough of the photos, especially the slightly blurry ones taken by cell phones at the airports. Us holding hands. Me with my arm around her, pulling her in. Her laughing up at me. Me kissing the top of her head. We looked happy. *Fuck that, we* are *happy and we* will *get through this.*

# Chapter Twenty-Three

*Alina*

I woke up to Markus gently rocking my shoulder. We had pulled up to what looked like an abandoned factory, with the lower floors covered in brightly colored, incomprehensible graffiti. He took one look at me blinking at him like a mole emerging from her burrow and laughed.

"We're here," he said somewhat unnecessarily as he unbuckled both of our seatbelts then helped me out of the car. The driver ran around and pulled out our bags before dragging each one up the steps to the camouflaged door.

"Can I help bring these up?" he asked with a sharp jerk of his head toward the stairs that were revealed as Markus unlocked and opened the building doors.

"Please," Markus answered and led the way, the driver and me trotting along behind him.

We stopped at the only door in the entire hallway on the top floor of the building. I was embarrassingly out of breath from hauling my duffle and overstuffed tote up the four flights of creaky stairs. Our gym rat driver was barely breathing hard as he dropped the remainder of our bags on the ground. He held out his hand for Markus to shake, nodded perfunctorily and banged back down the stairs to the car.

"Remind me to get them to put in an elevator and switch to a keypad or something," he grumbled as he struggled with the lock in the dimly lit hallway.

The door suddenly opened and we stumbled into the most unexpected apartment. From the overly graffitied outside, I'd expected a total dump. I was wrong. Markus' place seemed to take up the entire top level of the building, which he'd told me was an old shoe factory that had been converted to apartments back in the late 1990s. The light that poured through the original casement windows reflected back on brand-new, top-of-the-line appliances off to the left in the open kitchen, and the white walls glowed softly in the early-morning sunlight.

An enormous rug covered a huge amount of the cavernous space. Muted reds, oranges and grays complemented the camel leather mid-century couch and club chairs. Floor lamps with eggshell shades and bronze stands made the entire place feel warm and cozy, while a few abstract canvases in complementary colors drew the right amount of attention to the fact that this was the home of a man clearly comfortable with himself and his own impeccable taste.

I liked how assured the space was and how he seemed to grow in confidence as he showed me around. This was home to him, and seeing him here in his own environment let me in further.

"Markus, this is gorgeous!" I exclaimed as I slid a finger over the buttery-soft leather of a couch and wandered over to the window.

"You like it? Like I said, I think this is my favorite place in the world. Come on. Let me show you the rest of it." He seemed shyly excited by my approval, like this was his tree house with a big 'Keep Out' sign that he'd taken down for my benefit.

"This way first," he said as he beckoned me down a short hallway to the right of the main living space. A bathroom and two extra bedrooms opened off the hall, one for guests and one that seemed to be a small office. I tried to stall in the office, where a huge chaise and floor-to-ceiling bookshelves crammed the space completely, making it nearly impossible to move around.

I started to read the well-worn spines, mostly speculative fiction and memoirs. The stories hidden within people's bookshelves were almost more telling than the ones inside a medicine cabinet. Markus was reflective, almost too self-aware, and deeply attracted to possibilities over reality. I was more grounded, needed the practical around me — order instead of ambiguity. Together we balanced each other out. Whether that would be enough when push came to shove was a different story.

"I need to check these out!" I protested as he turned off the lights and headed back into the hallway.

"Plenty of time for that later. Do you not want to see where the magic happens?" He winked at me. We re-crossed the open living space toward the kitchen, to a second hallway that I hadn't noticed.

"What is this, MTV *Cribs*?" I joked as he continued to lead the way down the hall lined with high-contrast, black-and-white photographs of what I assumed were cities he'd visited.

He paused in front of the single door at the very end, did a drumroll on the doorframe and swung it open with a flourish.

"Holy shit," I breathed.

We were, indeed, where the magic happened. Those same original windows from the living room continued into the bedroom, throwing shadows from the grids in the casements onto the scarred wooden floors. A massive platform bed was pushed into the corner and it looked like the hooks on each corner of the frame were linked to a rope system that led to a single hook in the ceiling, suspending the bed about a foot above the floor.

"Markus, is your bed set up for bondage or — "

He snorted. "It's a rocker, Alina. Although I haven't tested out the bondage potential with it. My decorator thought the movement would be soothing. Or maybe he was hinting at something? Either way, I'm the only one who's slept in it. Alone."

"Phew," I muttered, a bit overwhelmed by the dirty thoughts that immediately flooded my mind.

He completely misread my stunned musings and directed me hastily into the attached bathroom, which did nothing to tamp down the ridiculous fantasies. The room was black marble with stark white fixtures and brushed stainless-steel finishing. A huge modern tub with a curve like a burlesque dancer's waist posed in front of a glass block window that let in muted sunlight, and a walk-in shower with jets up and down two sides took up most of one wall.

"Nice, right?"

"I don't want to leave."

"Well, we can certainly spend some time in here later, if you want."

"Oh, I want. Like, really, really want." I attempted sultry but stopped as he laughed at my obvious eagerness.

"Later, I promise." He winked and smiled at me. "Now come on, let me make you some coffee."

I twirled around one more time with a silent, mournful goodbye to that beautiful tub and followed him to the kitchen.

"So, today," Markus said as he passed me a tiny cup of espresso. "What do you feel like doing? Still interested in biking around?"

I shook my head and buried my nose in the cup before answering. I'd done some research and I knew exactly what I wanted to do. After swallowing, I took a deep breath and asked, "Can we be complete tourists? Or is that privacy suicide?"

He looked at me without saying a word, measuring my intensity.

"Maybe it's ridiculous, but I really, really — like, more than anything — want to go to the Neues Museum and see Nefertiti."

He burst out laughing. "Seriously? We could do anything, and you want to go to one of the most crowded tourist attractions in Berlin?"

"Closet history geek here. Can we go?"

"Okay my, little nerd, let me call a couple of security guys."

My enthusiasm suddenly waned. I'd known that it was a likely possibility, but I'd also kind of hoped we could get lost in a crowd and be normal for a day.

He tried to let me down gently. "It's like going to the Louvre to see the Mona Lisa."

I shrugged and agreed, then went to shower and change while he coordinated with his security team. By the time I got out, he was wearing new clothes and waiting by the door, playing with his phone. As he looked up, that same awestruck look from the Premiere played over his face. "I don't know how you do it, but I swear you get more beautiful every time I see you."

"That's a tad excessive. I'm clean and wearing a top and short pants that are obnoxiously wide." The top in question was boxy and cropped to sit right at the top of my paper-bag-waisted, wide-legged pants. I grabbed my sunhat and sunglasses then dumped my wallet and phone into my smaller tote before sweeping his stuff up and dropping it in as well. "So?"

"Did you take my wallet?" he asked as his eyebrows rose up to his hairline.

"Yeah, isn't that okay?"

"That is easily the most couple-y thing ever."

"Shit." I yanked out his phone and wallet and threw them at him. His wallet smacked his chest and he narrowly caught his phone before it clattered to the floor.

He laughed and pulled on the strap so the tote gaped open and dropped them back in. "Now we're worried about looking like a couple? Please, take them. I like it."

I smiled up at him as he wrapped an arm around my shoulders and kissed me lightly on the forehead.

* * * *

We were on our way back to the car after the museum when a small group of people with professional cameras descended, shouting questions in rapid-fire German and English. The security team bulldozed a way back to the car for us and Markus clutched my hand tightly, muttering angrily. Suddenly he stopped and whispered in my ear, "They say they'll go away if we give them a photo. No need for a comment."

I nodded. What other options did we have?

He stopped the security team and shouted, "Hey, guys! Guys! This is a little much, yeah? You're getting a little close. Back off a bit, we'll give you a photo, then we all go on our merry way."

A clamor of voices asking more questions answered him.

"No! I said that we'll stop. You can take your pictures, then go. Please, respect that."

He was right—they did move back and gave us some space. Some started fiddling with cameras, but the guys with phones kept them out, still trying to ask questions.

Markus looked at me, big questions in his eyes, and I nodded quickly. I stepped closer, tilted my head so I could look up at him and tipped my sunglasses down to peer over them. He grinned faintly and, without turning away from me, instructed the guys that they could photograph us locked in this fake half-embrace.

It was so contrived, though, that I couldn't help digging my elbow into his ribs, so he shrieked and flailed around before landing on his ass on the pavement. I extended a hand and pulled him up.

"I'm so sorry," I heaved out in between giggles. "I really didn't expect you to fall over!"

He stood, turned to the laughing photographers, and bowed sheepishly. "Ladies, gentlemen, show's over. Run along, please."

He brushed himself off and clambered into the back seat of the Audi A8L without much of his usual grace. "Shit, I've got a bruised ass. If you've ruined my chances to be the next Batman, I don't know if I'll ever forgive you."

"God, Markus, I'm so sorry!" My apology was negated by my inability to stop giggling.

"Oh, you think this is cute?" He pulled me across his lap and hit a button on the door that silently raised the soundproof privacy screen between us and the driver.

I nodded emphatically, hiccupping a bit as he arranged me on his lap. His hands slid beneath the hem of my shirt. I could feel the rough skin from the light abrasions on his palms as he feathered his fingers over my ribs. One hand slid from beneath my shirt to wrap around my ponytail and tug my head back, opening my neck and collarbones for exploration by his lips.

"Still think this is funny?" His hoarse whisper tickled my ear, and the gold flecks in his eyes glittered at me as he dared me to say yes.

I shrugged nonchalantly and tried to lean in to kiss him, but he pulled harder on my hair, holding me back. A thrill went up my spine as he took control.

"Yes? How about this, then?" he demanded as he rolled his hips beneath me. An arrow of warmth shot through my body and I could have sworn it was possible to smell the desire thickening the air between us. I moaned and pressed against him, unable to move my head with his death grip on my ponytail.

"Or this?" He pulled my shirt down from the inside, stretching the neck to reveal the lacy midnight-blue bralette I had put on because it reminded me of his eyes. His pupils dilated and he licked his lips as he eyed the tops of my breasts and rapidly tightening nipples through the translucent lace. "Take your shirt off, now, Alina."

I shivered as his words reverberated through me and I slowly pulled my shirt up, taking my bralette with it. Markus shifted me to the middle of the bench seat and knelt on the floor between my legs, staring up at me in awe.

"You are so fucking beautiful," he ground out as he wrapped a hand around each of my thighs, spreading them wider, and leaned in to tease my left nipple with his tongue. The combination of the cool air conditioning in the car and his warm breath on my chest made me moan and arch my back toward him. He reverently cupped my other breast in his hand, stroking gently as he switched between the two.

I looked directly at the frosted glass of the privacy screen, wondering how much the driver might be able to see. Was it completely opaque, or could he see our silhouettes as Markus knelt between my knees? Not knowing was the ultimate turn-on.

I lifted my hips slightly as his other hand tugged gently at the button and tie on my pants then dipped beneath the loosened waist. He quickly established a slippery rhythm, sliding one finger shallowly through my pussy. "More, Markus, deeper," I begged as I worked my own hand down to rub my clit.

A car horn honked next to us and I flushed as I pictured the people around us possibly watching. They were stuck in traffic, trying to get home, completely unaware of the fact that two people were inches from fucking next to them. I moaned as I continued to touch myself, loving the fact that we were in public, so close to being caught. Every touch, every feeling was heightened with that delicious knowledge.

Markus batted my hand away and pushed me back to lie lengthwise across the seat. "This is for you. Now sit back and be a good girl. Stop trying to do my job," he growled.

As he yanked my pants and underwear down with one violent motion, I reached out a trembling hand to carefully unzip his jeans before inching them down and off to lie in a pile with my clothes. He shuddered as he took in the sight of us completely naked in the back of the hired sedan stop-starting its way through Berlin traffic, barely hiding behind the tinted windows.

A short lock of hair tumbled over his forehead and his eyes seemed to ask a serious question even as he leaned away to rustle through his pants for the condom in his wallet. Was this too soon for me? For us? Should we at least wait till we were back at the apartment?

"Please, I need this," I whispered and pushed him back, unrolled the condom over him and hovered over his lap. I bent to kiss him with open eyes that I hoped conveyed everything I felt for him in that moment, and he wrapped his hands tightly around my waist.

"Yes, fucking ride me, Alina," he hissed as he held me up over his cock. My head dropped back as I began to sink slowly down onto him, feeling the internal stretch barely on the pleasurable end of pain as he bottomed out inside me. My thigh muscles quivered as I started the long, torturous pull back. We both watched, mesmerized, as his cock emerged then disappeared back into my body.

"God, I love seeing us together," he groaned, and I could only whimper in agreement as I continued to set a slow, punishing pace.

The corded muscles of his shoulders and arms bunched as he held himself back from taking over. I rocked against him, teasing him as I circled my hips until he finally broke. In one smooth move, he spun me around to face the privacy screen and lifted my arms back to circle around his neck, instructing me to hold on and not let go. He wrapped one arm across my chest to hold me in place and I felt the slight burn of his sparse chest hair on my shoulder blades as he slammed into me from below. His other hand slid down between my legs to press against my clit. My entire awareness narrowed down to the single connection point between us, and the people around us, our driver, all of them disappeared.

"Fuck!" I shrieked as he hit a spot that no man had ever touched. "So fucking good!"

"God, I can feel you strangling me with your cunt. Come all over my cock, beautiful."

His filthy words in that sexy, throaty growl were all it took to knock me over the edge I'd been teetering on. After a few more body-wracking thrusts, I felt Markus finish with a groan. He gently unclasped my hands that were still clenched together behind his neck and pulled me off him to lie on the seat.

My body shuddered in the cool air as I slowly circled back to earth, idly smoothing Markus' hair away from his sweaty forehead. The car slowed and Markus managed to raise his head to see out of the window. "Shit, we're about five minutes away. Hate to break up the afterglow, but we should get dressed. But first—" He kissed me soundly. "We need to do a lot more of that very soon. That was incredible."

I yawned and reached for my shirt. "You think we can get a repeat in your amazing bed tonight? I'm also thinking dirty thoughts about that bathtub of yours."

His shoulders shook and he helped me pull my bralette and shirt back on. He whispered, "The things I'm going to do to you, Alina... Just wait and see."

# Chapter Twenty-Four

*Alina*

The next day, our second in Berlin, started with one of those conversations between family members that outsiders should never be privy to.

A light feminine voice with a slight accent chirped from the entry, "Markus! There you are. I thought you were probably asleep, but this asshole — *sshhht*, Matti. It's early. Show some respect for the neighbors — figured you'd be up and probably making love to your new paramour. Isn't that a delightful word? Paramour? I love it."

A gravelly baritone responded in a voice that was pitched only slightly below a shout. "For fuck's sake, Ella. No one gives a fuck about your fancy vocabulary. And why are we speaking English? Markus, move your tight ass over and let us in. Time to introduce us to your new friend."

"We're practicing for Markus' friend, Matti," hissed the exasperated woman.

I heard Markus grunt as something substantial hit the wall by the kitchen, and the unfamiliar masculine voice continued, "See, Ella? *Friend*. Why use stupid words when very simple ones work equally well?"

Muffled laughter let me know that Markus was happy to see his exuberant family, and the echoing hugs and back slapping told me that the feeling was mutual. Even through a few walls, their family togetherness was daunting. I chose to emulate a sloth as I slid a foot out of the perfect haven of Markus' bed. Parts of my body that hadn't been worked out in two years were deliciously stiff and sore, and I grinned as I padded over to my suitcase to pull out a pleated midi skirt that hadn't gotten too wrinkled, and a sleeveless denim shirt that I tied off in the front.

"Now, Markus." Her voice was much clearer now that it wasn't muffled by a door and hallway. "Tell us about this woman. Also, where's Max? Didn't you invite him? You know he hates being left out."

"He never got back to me," Markus said helplessly.

"Whatever, bro, listen. I've seen those pictures. Hot lady, Markus. Fuck, you've got excellent taste —"

"Matti, you sexist pig!"

"Yes, Matti, please, drop the chauvinism down at least fifteen notches or she's going to kick your ass. Alina is still sleeping, and I like her. A lot. So don't fuck this up for me by being an immature dick."

"Oh, don't worry, man. Just complimenting your taste in women and the fact that you're getting over Kate with someone who already seems far superior. I mean, she's here, which is more than we could say of Kate mostly."

Hearing a slap and a smack, I envisioned the high five, bro hug, fist bump most likely happening and rolled my eyes.

"Ugh. You two. Well I guess I'm not surprised about Max. He's always so busy. But, Markus! This woman! What's the deal with this? I mean, I did *not* like Kate, but so soon?"

"Ella, stop. Look, I invited you here because I want you to meet someone special. Yes, whatever is happening between us is new, but it's good. And it's real. She's real, and I've honestly never felt like this before. We're trying to take things slowly—"

"What! Where's the fun in that? Don't ruin a little brother's faith in his older brother's prowess."

"Matti, how do you even know what *prowess* means?" Ella sounded like every bossy older sister ever.

I couldn't make out the muttered grumbling that followed until I heard the other two burst out laughing and Markus gasped. "*You* listened to a romance audiobook?"

The guffaws ended in shrieks and smacks until Ella, I presumed, broke them up.

"Fine, Markus, she's real. As you say. But you better believe we're going to be testing this out."

I figured that this was my cue to meet the family and headed, nervously, out into the living space while I tied my unruly hair back. I was glad for my hands to have something to do as I eyed the tall, blond family members, two of whom seemed to be berating the third about his very immature tendencies toward women. Markus spotted me first and waved me over while the other two engaged in a whispered argument.

"Guys? Someone I want you to meet. This is Alina."

I stepped up next to him as Ella and Matti turned to face me. It was uncanny how much the three of them resembled one another, like messing around with those gender-swap, aging filters on social media.

*Jesus. What do his parents look like?*

I waved uncertainly as they remained frozen in place, looking me over. The big dude, Matti, broke first and bullrushed me. He swooped me up, twirling me around. With his size and viselike grip it was literally like being hugged by a bear. The guy was taller than his older brother by a few inches and jacked in the way that only professional athletes could get, with long dirty-blond hair pulled back in a messy topknot and full tattoo sleeves.

As he set me down after another bone-breaking squeeze, he looked me straight in the eye. "Hi, I'm Matti. I'm the baby and delighted to meet someone who isn't Kate and who seems to make my elderly brother happy. Should you decide you'd rather hook up with a professional athlete, though— *Oof.*"

Ella elbowed him again and hissed, "How many times do we have to tell you not to be a sexist asshole? And stop manhandling her. What is wrong with you?"

"Um, pretty happy with your brother, thanks," I said with a distracted nod. My eyes were stuck on Ella, who'd turned her piercing, light-blue stare toward me. She looked at me with narrowed eyes and a slight purse to her mouth, head cocked as she considered me, giving me the *Look* of every overprotective mama bear when her cubs were threatened.

I stepped away from both Matti and Markus, and held out my hand. "Ella, right? I'm so glad to meet you. Markus has told me a little about you and your family. Twin daughters, right? That must be a handful."

Ella gingerly shook my hand and continued her appraisal before finally nodding sharply. "Yes, they certainly are, and for today they're my husband's problem." She smiled like a shark. "Well, Markus hasn't told us much about you, but it's nice to meet you too. I'm so glad we get to know you before Mother does. Don't worry, we won't put you through the wringer too badly." She grinned gleefully, rubbing her hands together in anticipation.

My face got hot. I'd forgotten how intrusive families could get. "Thanks. I think the siblings is plenty, since we've only recently started seeing each other." I said the last to Markus, and he grinned faintly at me and shrugged with an annoying "what can you do?" innocent expression.

He came over to rescue me from their attention and pulled me into his arms. "Ella, Matti, no third degree, okay? I can send you home."

"Sure, Markus," they chorused.

"I still get to tell her embarrassing stories, don't I?" begged Ella with a smirk at me. I smiled back, my tense shoulders relaxing for the first time since I'd heard the new voices in the apartment. This was going to be fine. Female solidarity already.

She and Matti took up seats at the island and looked at Markus and me expectantly.

"Okay, guys. Alina and I were talking and planned out a good option. We found a guy who can take us around on a private brewery and distillery tour of East Berlin. It will be this neighborhood and a few others. We've got a driver, so it should be pretty relaxed. Does that sound okay to you? Ella?"

"Yes, of course! Can we FaceTime Max at some point today? I really miss him and doing this kind of stuff with the two of you doesn't feel right without him."

I suddenly remembered that she and Max were twins and felt badly for her. They were obviously the closest of the siblings and she clearly missed him.

"I'm in too. And, yeah, Ella. We've got to call Max. To bitch him out for never leaving his grapes and shit. Markus, lead the way!" Matti leaped from his stool and started doing an exaggerated warm-up routine. "I've trained my whole life for this!"

Markus rolled his eyes at his obnoxious brother and pushed me out of the room before he could say anything worse.

"You okay?" he asked quietly as leaned against the dresser while I pulled my toiletries and accessories out of my suitcase. "Matti is such a shit sometimes and I should have expected Ella to give you the third degree. Since she had the twins, her overprotective tendencies have gone haywire. If she tries to pry, tell her off."

"Yeah," I murmured. "I'll be fine. But it's weird, you know? Hanging out with a family again. It's not as scary as I thought it would be. I've missed it, to be honest."

"Good. Fine. Great." He punctuated each word with a kiss and pulled me back down onto the bed. "Thank you for meeting everyone."

I kissed him back and laid my head on his chest, listening to the *whoosh* of air through his lungs and the steady pounding of his heart.

Then Matti shattered the moment, charging through the closed door and leaping onto the bed with us, sending it swinging wildly. "Whoa, what the fuck,

Markus? This is new. When did you get into sex swings?"

Markus shoved a pillow at his brother and I rolled off quickly to avoid any physical damage as they continued to wrestle. I slapped on my makeup in the bathroom, going casual for the day with a little highlighter, mascara and gloss, along with a few layered thin gold chains and Markus' ubiquitous bracelets that were, apparently, never coming off.

When I left the boys to their bickering, I found Ella on the phone, standing at one of the windows in the main space. She saw me emerge and muttered a goodbye in German before smiling shyly at me. "It really is good to meet you," she said in a low voice. "I've been so worried about him and I'm sorry if I ask too many questions or dig into things that aren't my business."

I smiled back, equally tentatively. "I understand. I know you talk to him a lot, so you've heard about the shit he's gone through."

Ella nodded as I continued, "I don't know what he's told you about us, but we're trying to take things slowly. We've each got our own demons and the show makes things complicated, but honestly, he's amazing. I feel lucky to be with him."

She surprised me by throwing her arms around me and hugging me with unexpected strength. "He's coming back to us, to life. And if you're the reason that it's happening, you and I are never going to have a problem."

Even though the last was a little bit of an implicit threat, it was a kind one, and I hoped that someday we could be actual friends. At her thirty-one and my twenty-eight, Ella and I were almost the same age, yet miles apart in terms of life. *Or maybe not*, I thought as her face lit up when her two brothers came out together, punching each other in the arm seemingly as hard as they could. An equally blinding smile hurt my cheeks as I watched the man I loved —

*Shit, nothing to see here, just throwing* casual *out the window.*

\* \* \* \*

The walking tour went surprisingly quickly and all of us, unsurprisingly, got completely wasted. Matti was off singing football club songs on the street while Ella flirted mercilessly with the very earnest, twenty-something hipster tour guide. Markus and I floated in our own very tiny, self-contained world, smiling benevolently down at the other two.

FaceTiming with Max was a blur. He was yet another very good-looking man with Markus' sharp bone structure, but with dark hair instead of blond. Ella's twin seemed lovely, perfectly polite to a stranger and good humored in the face of his siblings' drunken ribbing.

I hoped I would get to meet him at some point, if for no other reason than because I desperately wanted to know if he dyed his hair to stand out from his fairer siblings. No family should be that good-looking, and he seemed to be the family's literal black sheep.

Matti eventually abandoned us to get on a long train back to Cologne to meet with his team. When it was my turn to say goodbye, he picked me up in another bear hug before soundly kissing me on the cheek and informing me that he was at my service should his 'elderly' brother ever fail to perform. *What a tool.*

Markus tore me away from him and Ella kneed him in the balls. He dropped to the ground in pain and we all stepped over him, ignoring the whiny baby.

Like Matti, Ella was still trashed when we made our farewells while Markus' driver waited patiently to take her home to her husband and children. With a final, one-eyed warning to me to be good to her brother, she threw her arms around Markus and whispered something in German before shoving off and tripping back to the car. We waved as they drove away.

"What'd she say?" I asked, half-asleep.

Markus chuckled and scooped me up in his arms. He carried me up the four flights of stairs and into his apartment, where he deposited me directly onto his bed. "You don't want to know," he answered, nudging me toward the bathroom. "Go get ready. I'll use the other bathroom and meet you back in here."

By the time I re-approached the bed, Markus was already out and snoring softly. He looked so handsome in the bright moonlight that he made my heart skip a beat. Seeing him with his family had unlocked a new side of him. The media scrutiny and Kate had closed him off, but he was tentatively opening up again, and I liked everything about this stranger emerging from his dark past. This new Markus was someone who I could envision forever with, if forever came without the pressure of a public life. It felt like I had finally slipped home. All of the puzzle pieces had lined up, satisfyingly locking together.

# Chapter Twenty-Five

*Markus*

The next morning's hangover reminded me of two things — first, I was old, too old to drink competitively with my shithead brother. And second, travel, even a short flight like the one to my parents' place, was murderous with a hangover.

Alina seemed to concur with that sentiment. She wrinkled her nose adorably, slapping a pillow back over her half-opened, bloodshot eyes. "I feel like I got hit by a truck. Do you think Ella poisoned me?" She sounded so feeble, but genuinely curious.

"Nah, pretty sure it would have been me she poisoned. God, I feel like hell."

"Maybe we should stay here," she offered weakly.

"Where's the American fighting spirit, Alina? C'mon, let's get cleaned up and some food in us. Both of us have flights to catch."

She groaned and flipped me off as she rolled out of bed and zombie-walked to the bathroom. The water turned on and I heard a moan of appreciation as she stepped into my shower. Grinning to myself, I headed to the kitchen to scrounge for food.

Looking pale but somehow still radiant, Alina appeared shortly after and flopped into a seat at my rarely used dining table. I handed her breakfast and headed to the bathroom to get ready.

By the time I got out, she had straightened up the apartment and her packed bags sat by the door. Looking about thirty times more awake than she had before, she reached for me as I lined my suitcases up next to hers. We stood entwined until a buzz alerted me to the car out front, ready to take us to the airport.

"You okay?" I asked. "You're awfully quiet. Still hungover?"

"A little. More nervous about what's waiting for me back in L.A., and—this is going to sound so stupid—I'm going to miss you." Her voice shook a little, and she refused to meet my gaze.

"You know I'm going to miss you too, but it's only two days, and I'll call you. Besides, Michael is going to be keeping you too busy to even think about me, most likely."

She winced at the reminder and reached up to touch my jaw. "I know, but well, I..." She paused for thought. "I care. You know?"

I nodded, because I did—more than I let on and more than I could even communicate right now.

* * * *

The short flight to Cologne, where my parents lived, was completely uneventful, which meant that I was able to recover from my hangover in relative peace and anonymity. Even though I had seen him the day before, I was still somewhat dreading dealing with Matti. He had a real gift for making a fool out of everyone, especially me.

Matti was the opposite of me. He was loud and brash and had been caught fucking women in some of the least-likely places on the planet. I loved him dearly, but his willingness to play the fool was infuriating. At some point, he was sure to lose his job when the club got sick of cleaning up after his antics.

Coming out of the tunnel, I found him exactly where I had assumed he would be — in the center of a crowd of media types and women. He was laughing, and I could hear him joking with the reporters and photographers. "No, no. I have no idea what my brother's sex life is like. If you want to know the truth, I'm pretty sure that he —"

"Matthias!" My voice echoed in admonishment as I yelled from halfway across the hall.

"Ah, there he is, gentlemen, ladies. Go ask him yourself. Now, if anyone is curious to hear the tale of how I scored the winning goal during the last game and then nailed two Australian tourists on the pitch later that night, I'd be happy to —"

"Matti, time to go!" I shouted as the horde started to turn my way.

He laughed and ran towards me, hurtling over a few tourists and their suitcases, leaving the press and crowds staring at his back. Grabbing both my suitcase and duffle like they weighed nothing, he turned toward the door and yelled, "Follow me, slow ass!"

I followed him while attempting to apologize to those in his wake. *Fucking irresponsible little shit.* But his effervescent joy was contagious, and soon my pace had picked up to a sprint as we raced through the airport and parking ramp, looking for his ludicrous car.

"I don't know how you can find it. A Volvo probably ate it," I joked, a little out of breath, as I caught up to him.

"Fuck, I swear I left that little bitch right here," Matti muttered, barely breathing hard after his steeplechase. "Ah, yes. Over there, behind the pillar."

Sure enough, behind the pillar was his pride and joy. A little souped-up hybrid Fiat 500. "Doing my part for the environment," he said.

I was positive he did it for the attention that he garnered as he shoehorned himself and any passengers in or out of the matchbox.

We somehow wedged my luggage and ourselves into the tiny car and he expertly reversed out and whipped down the ramp out of the parking structure.

"You know something? I think I forgot to tell you that I wouldn't ride with you unless you promised to pick me up in a car where we wouldn't end up sitting on each other's lap. This is fucking stupid. We look ridiculous," I grumped.

"Nah, we look hot as fuck. Do you know how many people are having awesome threesome-sex-in-car fantasies right now?"

I gave up. Matti would never change until he hit rock bottom. We paid the parking fee at the gate and started the race toward our parents' estate outside of the city. It was early afternoon, and traffic was light. Matti kept up a steady stream of gossipy chatter about his team, the season, Mom and Dad's latest cause and the women he'd been seeing.

"Speaking of women, I liked Alina a lot, by the way. Still can't believe you invited us to meet someone random though. You *do* seem a lot happier than you have any of the other times I've seen you over the last few years, but it's still weird as fuck."

"I know. Looking back, the relationship with Kate should have been over months, maybe even years ago. Remember how she never wanted to come here?"

He nodded in commiseration but continued with his dogged line of questioning. "And…back to my original thought. It's not like we had time to talk about it the other day when we were drinking our weight in fine German beer. But Alina? You met her on set of this show you're suddenly joining? We thought you were coming home and taking a break?"

I took a deep breath before explaining everything. "Nope, I'm staying in the US, doing this show, then hopefully marrying Alina, getting a dog and cat, possibly having some kids. She'd look fucking hot pregnant with my kid, don't you think?" I was only half kidding. Especially about the dog and cat. Those were a given. Unless she was allergic, in which case I'd sponsor a rescue group.

After a long pause I looked over to find him staring at me, jaw hanging open.

"Matti, eyes on the road! What the fuck, man? I'm kidding."

"I'm sorry. Did you inform me of your actual life plans? You, who have never shared? I'm very confused."

"Yes, did I stutter?" I asked.

"You've introduced one woman to our family. One. In thirty-three years. And now, out of seemingly nowhere, you've introduced a random woman to me, to Ella, even Max. I guess I assumed you were rebounding. Now I'm wondering if you haven't completely lost it."

"Yeah, yeah. I get it. She feels necessary, though, you know? A part of me and my life that I didn't realize was missing. And I wanted the other most important parts of my life to know her too."

We turned into the drive and Matti whistled. "I'll stop giving you shit. I liked her a lot. If you're happy, I'm happy, and I'll stop flirting with her."

I punched him in the arm. "You better."

"Ouch! Dead arm, asshole. Thank god I play football. Anyways, you think I'm bad, Mother's going to have lots of questions." He grinned in anticipation.

My mother and father were waiting on the front steps for us and came rushing down as Matti pulled up. My ridiculous mother was wiping tears from her eyes as she pulled me into an embrace, while my dad waited patiently behind her. It was like I was home from war or something.

"And what am I?" Matti asked, teasing my mother as he picked her up to swing her away from me in a hug. "Your second-rate son?"

She laughed and hit him upside the head. "Put me down, you oaf. I have no idea how I gave birth to such giants, but you can't manhandle your mother. I'm old and fragile."

I laughed. The last thing Maria Shellenberg could have been described as was 'old and fragile'.

My dad pulled me aside for a hug. "We're glad you're home, Markus. Your mother has been worried, and we've missed you."

Matti unloaded my suitcases and hopped back into the car before shouting a hurried goodbye. Things felt immediately calmer as my whirlwind little brother backed his clown car down the drive. Then the full weight of my mother's attention descended on me alone.

"Ah, my oldest child. My prodigal," my mother sternly announced as she grabbed my arm, dragging me inside. "Now. Come tell your mother *everything*."

I followed, resigned to my fate. My mother was capable of digging even the most minor secrets out of her children—it made no difference to her if we were ten or thirty-three. Everything was her business. It was part of the reason that I hadn't been home in a while. I hadn't wanted to face the firing squad of maternal concern.

"Markus, are you not hearing a word I'm saying? Do you think your mother is babbling to hear herself speak?"

It was bad when she referred to herself in the third person. I looked at my dad, who shrugged helplessly and looked on in amusement. I took a deep breath and, for what felt like the millionth time, relayed the story of the last month or so.

My mom listened, metaphorical smoke coming out of her ears. "I'll kill her," she said, of Kate, then demanded, "When are you bringing this new woman home? How dare you not come back for longer?"

"Maria, calm down. Markus' plans merely changed. And his new woman friend might not be meeting us anytime soon. It sounds like Markus isn't ready, despite the lovely pictures that we've both seen." Dad was trying.

"Oh, you've seen the pictures?"

They nodded. My dad murmured, "Lovely girl, Markus."

"What did you think?"

"Those pictures, Markus, tell the story of a man who has found his soulmate," she stated solemnly while I tried not to roll my eyes. Clearly I had inherited the drama gene from my mother.

"Mother," I started, placating, "Alina —"

"Lovely name for a lovely girl," my dad cut in.

"Yes, Alina is someone special. I don't know if I'm ready for you to meet her, but I did introduce her to Ella and Matti in Berlin. That's where I was for the last two days."

My mother gasped in outrage over being left out.

"Maria, hush. Markus, really? Is this serious, after all?" My father sounded faintly worried.

My mother wasn't having it, though. "Loren, stop. I for one think it's wonderful. Sometimes fate works in mysterious ways." She turned back to me and patted my hand. "I remember the day I met your father. I took one look at him and knew that this was the person I'd spend the rest of my life with, even though he was a bit socially awkward. And yes, even after I found out he had had the nerve to get engaged to someone before meeting me —"

"What? I never knew this part of the story!"

"Oh yes, your father stupidly asked his girlfriend from university to marry him during their final term. And they had been engaged for *five* years when he met me, never actually tying the knot."

I looked at my dad for confirmation. He shrugged and blushed a bit. "It's true. I was an idiot. I mean, things were done in a logical, proper order, and that's where Trudy and I were. We graduated, got engaged, lived together. The next step was marriage. Until I met your mother."

"I tried to kiss him, you know, got him all drunk on our dessert wines and tried to kiss him. He left the next day, but I knew he'd be back. So a few years later he called me up, both of us were single and that was that."

"You're joking. How have I never heard this part of the story?"

"Eh, son, no one likes to let their children know that their mother was a nineteen-year-old hussy and their father a blind idiot." My dad laughed and my mother reached over and slapped him on the ear.

"So you knew? The minute you saw each other?" I asked eagerly.

"Well, I certainly did," my mother said. "It took a little convincing to get your father in line, though. Is it, perhaps, the same for you?"

I shrugged uneasily. I didn't want to admit that I'd fallen so hard, so fast.

"Ah, leave him alone, Maria. I was right there with her, Markus, but I was too stubborn to admit it. Maybe that's where you're at. Anyways, son, whatever happens with this woman, this Alina, we're happy to see you happy. You know? We'll always love you and support you."

"Yes, Markus. I'll let you off the hook this time on meeting her, but you are bringing her home for Christmas, understood?"

"Yes, Mother."

*I need to get back to L.A.*

# Chapter Twenty-Six

*Alina*

Everything kicked into high gear as I navigated out of the door of LAX's international terminal and started searching for a cab. As I slid into the back seat of an older model Ford Crown Vic, my jeans snagged on one of the many gashes in the upholstery. The unpleasant smell of industrial odor remover burned my sinuses and I wondered how many times people had vomited, bled or sweated through layers of clothes right where I was sitting.

Riding with David had spoiled me, clearly, but I didn't want to call him and put him out. I wondered how Markus was faring back in Germany with his parents. His brother and sister had told me some legendary stories about Maria, their mother, and he'd once compared a conversation to her to a blindfolded interrogation in front of a firing squad.

Michael had only texted me twice since we'd left the country, a small miracle and probably never-to-be-repeated phenomenon, but the last one had popped through that morning and I still hadn't gotten back in touch. While some of his messages waxed rhapsodical, this one had been curt and to the point.

*Call me asap when you get in.*

Plus a grumpy face emoji.
I texted back quickly.

*In a cab leaving LAX. Will call when I get home.*

No sooner had it read as received than an incoming call shrilled out of the tiny speaker. Michael. There would be no rest for this weary traveler.

"Hello?" I answered tentatively.

"Alina, my favorite assistant producer, my muse and now my leading lady," he cooed. "So lovely to have you back. I hope you and Markus enjoyed your little European jaunt."

"We did, thanks, it was—" I started, excited to tell *anyone* about how cool Berlin was, how incredible Markus' apartment was, that I couldn't stop thinking about his dick, but Michael probably wasn't meant to be that person. He also wasn't paying any attention.

"So for training, I've lined up a personal trainer and an acting coach. Our goal, by the time filming starts in a few weeks, is for you to passably move like a supernatural being, maybe do some of your own stunts and make sure you can get through lines without looking like a nutcracker. Get it? Wooden?" He giggled at his cleverness.

He droned on with a litany of physical training sessions and a dietician-approved meal plan, but I wasn't picking up on most of it. Then he warned me that Markus and I would have two-hour sessions with coaches and choreographers every evening at the studio to practice together and that he would be dropping by every other day to observe.

"Michael!" I erupted. "That schedule is bullshit and you know it. There's no way in hell that I can pull all of it off in a twenty-four-hour period. The acting stuff, for sure, but all of that other training?"

"Negotiating, huh. Look, try it for a week. If it doesn't work, we can adjust. You can do this, though. I really think this is going to be a game changer for you and I'm so fucking excited to get the two of you on camera for a K-I-S-S-I-N-G scene. Oh, it's going to be unreal, honey!" He squealed, and I could imagine him squirming in his seat like a toddler with literal ants in his pants.

"Okay, okay, simmer down there, boss man. We'll give it a shot. Have you sent over that list of contacts that I requested before I left town? I want to start feeling them out." My knee started jigging up and down and my heart rate went all wonky as I imagined actually calling or emailing these people. The meetings that might or might not result in a life-changing offer.

"Ah, that. I knew I was forgetting something, m'dear. Will send it to you tonight. Now, go get yourself a massage and facial. Tomorrow is going to barrel into you like a ton of fucking bricks. Get ready to jump back on the train!" He faked a train whistle and hung up.

By the time I unlocked my front door and opened the windows to air out the house, Michael had sent the promised list and I kissed my phone screen in excitement. I drafted emails for the top two that I wanted to speak with, trying to clearly define what it was that I wanted from each meeting. What I hoped to get and what I could offer them. Then I reviewed my portfolio from the last two years with Michael and from my agency job back in Chicago, pulling the best of the work into a short reel with some voiceover explanations of my role in each segment. After finishing my laundry and a quick dinner at Forse, I sent the emails and portfolio links off with toes and fingers tightly crossed.

When both women responded within the hour indicating a willingness to meet and a few scheduling options, I started to dance. In fact, I did the whole *Risky Business* series of moves from my staircase to my patio door. Slide and all, with a full glass of wine above my head. Touchdown danced when I didn't spill a fucking drop.

I wrapped up scheduling with Carolina Hernandez, my top choice of the two female directors I would be meeting with, and finished tweaking my portfolio. I hoped that a meeting with them could transition to a crew spot of some sort—I'd take unpaid at this point—once I was done taping *Southern Gods*.

My phone lit up with a news notification as I finished brushing my teeth and I swiped it open and scanned through. Same as before we left, conjecture about Markus and me. Full-on exposé about the great Shellenberg love triangle with me and Kate playing tug-of-war with his heart, and someone from her camp was proclaiming loudly and proudly that I was nothing but a front for them getting back together. *Great.*

I texted him quickly to see if he was awake, but didn't receive a response. Finally, I took a Xanax to shut off my brain and slid under the covers, praying that a fast sleep would be enough to get through Michael's grueling schedule.

* * * *

That first day of training nearly killed me. Up to that point I had honestly felt pretty great about myself — happy with my body, comfortable in my own skin and somehow convinced that my active job left me in great shape.

I was wrong, though. So wrong.

Turns out that 'slightly healthier than the average woman in her late twenties' did not equate to being able to complete a boot camp session designed for eighteen-year-old recruits. Nor did it mean that being able to balance athletic endeavors with grown-up responsibilities was even a remote possibility.

During my first morning workout alone, Michael hit me up three times via text and one call, Markus texted me twice, Candace four times and I kept longingly looking at my phone. My coach's condescending look when my arms failed at twenty-five pushups didn't help and I almost wanted to drag him out to the climbing wall for a race and a "how you like me now?" moment.

After lunch and a second workout that was a combo Zumba and capoeira, which legitimately broke me, I had to scramble to get ready, looking somewhat professional, for a crosstown meeting with Carolina Hernandez. I was practically sweating through my nice white button-down as I trundled up the walk to her home, messenger bag in hand that was weighed down by my iPad, a mini-projector and all of the cords that I'd need if she wanted to see any clips on the spot.

Carolina met me at the door in a very glam kimono that opened over a pair of bleached cropped bootleg jeans and a skintight black tank that showed off abs that I would have died for. Her rock-hard gym body proved the fact that she was not only one of the top action film directors, but also one with previous stunt experience. She was a badass. Her lightly accented voice belayed her Dominican roots and she slayed me with her assessing stare. "Alina, welcome. Please come with me."

She led me through her open, airy home that was filled with exotic knickknacks and plants, through a sliding screen door and out to a lanai that was shaded by a small grove of palms. She gestured at a few pouffes and pillows that rested on a worn Persian rug laid out over the wooden slats of the deck and gracefully descended onto one with a bold chevron print. I took the splashy palm leaf one opposite her and set my bag on the low glass-top rattan table between us.

"So," she started. "Michael Burch says you come highly recommended. Not that I particularly care what he has to say, but I'm curious. Why did you want to meet with me?"

I liked this lady. No coffee or refreshments offered, but a straight up, "What do you want?" I could roll with this.

"I'm glad Michael had good things to say. I wanted to meet with you because it's my goal to move into action and horror films. As you've experienced, it's not exactly a common genre for women—much less in a directorial capacity—and I'd like to learn from you. I don't know if you're taking on mentees, but I'd be happy to take on any role you might need filled for an upcoming project if it will give me an opportunity to learn from you. Both your process and how you navigate this boys club. It's suffocating me." I hadn't intended to admit the last, but she didn't blink.

She stared at me in an assessing way. "And do you know how to make a Cuban coffee?"

"No, but I know where to get the best Cuban coffees in the city, and if driving forty-five minutes out of my way every morning to greet you with your favorite coffee is what it takes, I'll do it gladly." I was dead serious. To work with this woman was my dream and I'd walk over hot coals if it gave me even the glimmer of an opportunity.

Carolina laughed lightly. "I'm sure that wouldn't be necessary. Why don't you tell me a little bit about the work that you've done for Michael. You sent me your reel, which I reviewed this morning, so I'd rather we chat and get to know each other a little better. It's refreshing to have someone want to meet with me to ask about mentoring rather than demand or beg for a job."

I smiled uncertainly and shifted a bit on my pouffe, wishing for a back rest.

"Can I get you a coffee or water?" Carolina asked, and I nodded politely.

She called into the house, turned her laser stare back to me and gestured for me to begin. So I did. I explained how I'd met Michael through my old job in Chicago, where my team and I had created the opener and visual effects for *Southern Gods*. How our work had been so impressive that Michael had offered me a job, which I'd taken when I decided to move to the West Coast. That

I'd been working for him for two years, clawing and scratching my way to my current position as assistant producer in a record time thanks to his guidance and mentorship. I decided to leave out the 'muse' nonsense.

"And now?" she interrupted. "What's making you want to leave? Michael likes you. Why tie your star to someone new? You're clearly talented, work hard. This is not an industry where people typically move up so quickly. And I know you're not sleeping with him, because that's the first thing I asked when he approached me about meeting with someone."

I blushed, because of course it would be the first thing anyone would think. My rise had been fast.

"Frankly, I want to leave because of that reputation. It's not the truth, but often when you are a woman working for a man and you move up quickly it's everyone's assumption. It's toxic and I'm sick of getting looked down upon while Michael gets slapped on the back with a not-so-subtle thumbs up. And I want to work with someone who knows what this industry does to women, who's succeeded and kicked ass the way I want to — taking on action and horror films and representing your femininity without apology or compromise. You're kind of my idol."

"Well, thank you for that, Alina. Now, isn't that something — Alina and Carolina — almost sounds like it's meant to be. I tell you what, there's an opening for a personal assistant on my next film with Lionsgate — horror, but we're still working with the screenwriter right now to fine-tune. It's a step down from your current role, but it's yours if you'd like it. We'll treat it as a job as well as a mentorship or apprenticeship. Is that something you'd be interested in?" she asked with a glimmer in her eye that said that she knew there was no way I'd turn it down.

"Yes! When would it start? The thing is, and I don't know if Michael mentioned this to you, but I've agreed to join the cast for *Southern Gods* for next season. It's a long story that I'm happy to go into, but not if it affects the timing with this project." I took another sip of my scalding coffee and promptly burned my tongue.

"Hmm. Yes, Michael mentioned that. I wondered if you'd bring it up. The project wouldn't start until next spring or early summer. If necessary, you could miss pre-production and jump right into filming, but I think you'd appreciate the pre-production process. It's quite different for a film like this than a television show." The last was said with some disdain.

My mind whirred with arguments for getting my scenes shot early and leaving *Southern Gods* before the season fully wrapped. Markus could help. He had enough leverage, given his reputation.

"Yes, yes. I can do it. I'll figure it out," I practically shouted.

"Yes? Excellent." She stood up. "I will send you the paperwork and an NDA. Once you have signed, I'll send you a script. We can meet again in a few months and I'll introduce you to the rest of the team. I will expect you to not only do your job flawlessly, but to set aside time to learn and hone your craft. Do we have a deal?"

I nodded furiously and held out a hand. She shook it and shot me her first not-professional smile of the meeting. "And now I must apologize for my abrupt departure, but my mother needs me to take her shopping for the week," she said as she rolled her eyes a little. "Eighty years old and she bosses the shit out of me."

I followed her back through the house to the front door. "Thank you again, Carolina, I can't tell you how much this means to me."

"You're welcome, Alina. I'm looking forward to working with you." She grinned as she gently shut the door in my face.

I barely made it to my car before tears of joy slid down my face. Michael had come through for me with the connections and good word, but I had earned this. My first shot at the next step of my Plan had been successful. The sun glared off the screen of my phone, nearly blinding me as I tapped out an excited text to Markus. Celebrations were in order when he arrived that night. But first I had a date with a drama coach to help me figure out this whole acting thing.

# Chapter Twenty-Seven

*Alina*

At eight o'clock in the evening, I was sitting in a hard plastic chair in a conference room at the studio offices, reviewing my calendar for the next day and impatiently rereading the script for episode one. Not that we shot in order, but I wanted to try to get a feel for my character from the beginning.

A knock shattered my concentration and my sore-from-boot-camp muscles protested aggressively as I hobbled to the door. A thin woman dressed dramatically in designer clothing with impeccable makeup swept in. She introduced herself as Diana, my acting coach. Her pursed mouth and full-body scan immediately told me that this would be my least favorite hour of the day.

"Please, come in! I'm so excited to meet you and get started," I gushed as I tried ineffectually to straighten my hair to match her impeccable look.

"Yes, yes. Likewise, I'm sure. Let's get down to business." Her light British accent made everything coming out of her mouth seem even more condescending, and she sighed as if I were wasting the universe's time by merely existing. "Right. How much experience do you have acting?"

"Um. None," I mumbled as my stomach knotted in embarrassment.

"No school theater? Role in the church nativity play? Nothing?" Her level of disgust was palpable.

"Nope."

"Then, no offense meant, but how did you score this role? Do you know how many *real* actors would kill for your position right now?"

I took a deep breath, trying not to see red, and rolled my neck. "To be honest, I'm not completely sure. But here I am—with a role—and here you are—teaching me. I'm ready to learn, let's go."

She sniffed. "Very well, I suppose I can attempt to make a silk purse out of this pig's ear. Let's start with vocal warm-ups."

The remainder of our lesson went about that well.

\* \* \* \*

I'd barely had time to kick my shoes off when a text from Markus announced that he was back in L.A. and that he wanted to see me. Rather, he asked if it was okay for him to come over. *So considerate.* When he sent a picture of two cupcakes in a plastic container, I grinned. Cake and pastry were the currency I preferred to utilize and he was nailing it.

A familiar cadence on my door sent me racing to open it, where I discovered a very handsome, smiling man with a ravenous look in his eyes, carrying a bag of delicious sugary goodness and lurking on my doorstep. I swiped the bag from him, peeked inside, snapped it shut and waved him in. "You may enter," I said sternly before cracking and giggling.

He tapped me under the chin. "God, I've missed that laugh," he murmured then kissed me softly.

As the kiss was starting to deepen, he pulled back, breathing heavily. "Sorry. I didn't mean to come in here and maul you. How did everything go with the trainers? What was Carolina like?"

I nodded and yawned, jaw cracking, while he plated the two cupcakes and refilled my wine glass before pouring his own. "Well, the workouts and acting class today sucked massive balls. Carolina totally made up for it." I gulped some wine and shoved the buttery spun sugar deliciousness into my mouth. "She's fucking awesome and I want to be her when I grow up," I said with a mouth full of cake.

He laughed and threw a dish towel at me. "Good, I'm so glad. I haven't met her before, but I had a feeling it would work out for you. From what I've heard, Sherilyn is a bit more difficult. Carolina seems like a better match."

I relayed more details about the meeting and he offered a few thoughts on what it would be like working on a major feature film set versus the small-screen stuff I'd done before. Finally, a massive yawn took over his face and he scrubbed his cheeks with his palms. "I really want to keep talking, but it's practically three in the morning in Germany. Can we finish this conversation tomorrow? I'll make you breakfast," he wheedled.

"Are you sure? I have to get up so early tomorrow for more training."

"Let me worry about the early morning."

"You say the sweetest things." I sighed as I headed up the stairs to my bathroom. He followed me slowly, the sugar in the cupcake only having provided a momentary shot of energy.

He kissed me hard and gave my shoulders a quick massage. "Come on. Shower first, I'll do all the work."

* * * *

Several days later, Markus and I were sitting on opposite sides of a conference table at the studio, waiting for Michael to show and reading through the new scenes that had arrived earlier from the writers. A jaunty, one-two beat knock interrupted us. We looked at each other.

"Michael," he growled.

I sighed in agreement.

Michael and the choreography coach barely made it through the door before he started issuing orders, directing us to page sixteen of our scripts, where our characters had their first kiss.

"I want you two to run this scene without any embellishment. But make me feel it. Make me believe that this kiss has been millennia in the making. Got it?"

We nodded obediently and the butterflies immediately took off. Markus circled the table to take up the chair next to me, plucked the papers from my hands and set both of our scripts on the table. The choreographer moved us into place, talking us through the scene and where we'd need to touch, figuring out where our boundaries were, confirming that we were comfortable with each other's limits. She stepped back and Michael yelled, "Action."

We said our lines and he leaned in and brought a hand to my face, slowly pushing back a wave that had slipped from the messy knot on the top of my head. His hand curved around my cheek and jawline, and my heart rate became erratic as I stared into his eyes. The room fell away as his hands tangled in my hair and we moved inexorably toward each other. Little pants of air emerged from both our mouths as we fought for control, the tension reaching a breaking point. Our lips met and almost as one, our eyes closed.

"Open your eyes. We're losing it," he whispered in a hoarse voice with his mouth still pressed against mine.

The kiss deepened as we struggled to open our eyes, and I overbalanced, tipping into him, and he caught me. Both of our eyes closed then, and suddenly nothing else seemed to matter in the room. There was nothing but the two of us exerting an immense gravitational pull toward each other.

Our hands were starting to wander, fingertips skidding over ribs and abs, toying with buttons and zippers, when a massive splash of water hit me in the face. A second one hit Markus square on the chin. He practically threw me back into my chair, shaking his head like a dog to get rid of the water, and looked around in confusion. "Was that really necessary?" he asked peevishly.

The choreographer nodded and wagged a hand back and forth. "Kind of. Your chemistry is outstanding, but you both—"

"You two are going to be the death of me and this goddamn show," Michael interrupted as he tossed an empty water bottle aside. "That was a pretty basic stolen kiss, and suddenly you're practically stripping her naked. Jesus. I'm disappointed in both of you. I'll be back tomorrow."

Michael tore out of the room like a whirlwind, followed by the choreographer. The door slammed shut and Markus and I looked at each other with huge eyes.

The door crashed open again, springing back on its hinges. "Oh, and I didn't mention it because I don't want to encourage this shit, but goddamn, you two. If you made a sex tape I'd pay top dollar." He winked and scuttled away, shutting the door gently behind him this time.

Markus laughed so hard he had to sit down. I threw my script at his face and pouted. My clothes were soaked, we couldn't be professional even off camera and I felt like we'd completely embarrassed ourselves.

"Sorry, that was totally my fault. Are you okay?" His voice shook as he tried again to unsuccessfully stifle his laughter.

"Can we not keep it together for five seconds? To be honest, I'm not sure who to be mad at. Mostly Michael, because my clothes are all wet and I don't have any others here, but—stop laughing! This isn't funny."

"Aw. Come on. It is a little. We'll have to keep practicing, which sounds like a perfect deal to me."

"Ugh. You're impossible."

"And you're pouting." He hooked his index fingers into my beltloops to tug me over to him.

I sighed and wrapped my arms around his shoulders.

He kissed the top of my head. "I'm sorry. I know this means a lot to you—and to me too. Come over to my house tonight. We can go for a swim, sit in the hot tub. I'll call David and he'll be here in a few minutes."

"Fine, Markus, but we've both got to be better. There's a lot more riding on this for me than for you, and you know it." I pushed off him and started rummaging through my purse to find tissues to mop up my face. "Do you mind if I invite people over? I haven't seen Candace since the Premiere and was thinking we could have her, Rory and Ethan over."

"That sounds great, we've got wine and food — maybe ask if they want to come around nine-thirty?" I nodded and pulled out my phone to text Candace.

He grabbed the leftover tissues and wiped his own face. "You're right, you know, we do have to take this seriously. But you're doing amazingly with the scenes outside of the romantic ones. I can't believe how fast you're picking it up. Tomorrow will be better." He stood and stretched, then headed for the door, where he grabbed the top of the frame and swung through like a gymnast.

I followed him dutifully out the door with my feet firmly planted, plodding along completely earthbound.

He squeezed me tightly as we walked down the hall and whispered, "It's going to be okay. I promise."

# Chapter Twenty-Eight

*Markus*

Ethan, Rory and Candace met us at my place and helped devour pretty much everything my housekeeper had bought over the last week. It was so different, so normal to have a night like that. Friends hanging out, getting a little wine drunk and playing stupid games. I couldn't remember the last time I'd done anything like that. I'd been in the public eye for way too long and my life had literally been red carpet to club to red carpet to club. That or hiding at home, trying to catch my breath and maintain my sanity. It had never been me, but I'd handed the reins of my life over to Kate a long time ago.

At one point, Candace and Alina disappeared for girl time in the hot tub, leaving me inside with Ethan and Rory. They gave me shit for a solid twenty minutes about inviting Alina to meet my family after knowing her for approximately three seconds.

"Seriously, Markus? What the fuck were you thinking?" howled Rory as he rolled on the ground. Ethan hauled him upright while wiping a tear from his eye. I'd given the story of my brother Matti meeting Alina for the first time.

I rubbed my own eyes and grinned sloppily. "I don't even fucking know, man. I'm not even the same person I was four months ago. Not even the same person since that first day in Georgia. Everything is changed."

"Aw, kissy-kissy." Rory made fish lips at me, and Ethan, ever the mature one, socked him in the gut.

"He means," said Ethan self-importantly, "that we're fucking happy for you, man. This is good stuff. Alina is special and I like her a lot. She's kind of a sister to me and I'm glad she has you."

"What's this? I'm your sister?" Alina, followed by Candace, strolled back into the room with towels wrapped around their bodies.

Candace held out a hand at Ethan and Rory like she was training a pack of unruly puppies. "Stay, boys. Let's get ready to head home." They were inches from panting after her, but she stuck her tongue out at them as she ran upstairs to change.

Ethan rolled to his back and looked up at Alina with wide eyes and said sweetly, "Yeah, like my sister. The one who will never judge me for liking guys and girls, or both at one time. The one who keeps my secrets and helps me run lines when everyone else is busy. The one who sends me flowers when I'm sick, the one who—"

I cleared my throat loudly and Rory laughed. As Candace came down the steps, Alina yawned and said, "I'm heading up to bed. Michael's got me booked for a boot camp session at eight. Thanks, everyone, for coming over."

The whole crowd got up and sort of oozed their way to the entry. Candace was still sober and would drive them all home. Everyone hugged, kissed and promised we'd do it again sometime and, finally, the door was closed and they were gone.

I leaned back against the door and watched her ascend the stairs, thanking everything that was holy that I'd found her and that she wanted to be part of my life.

\* \* \* \*

The next morning, I woke her up with breakfast at six, complete with flowers that I'd run out for at five o'clock. This early bird caught the worm and her 'thank you' resulted in stems on the floor, a few broken plates and crumbs in odd crevices as I pulled her up from the island where she'd lain only moments before. We were both sweating and she was laughing as she kissed me.

"What do you have going on today?" I asked once I'd caught my breath.

"Training in"—she pulled out her phone and checked the time—"thirty minutes, so I've got a little time. It's a beach workout today and you, my friend, are more than welcome to join me in the torture session."

I shook my head adamantly and helped her down from the island. She waltzed to the coffee machine and poured for each of us.

"And after that I've got a session with Diana, plus we have something with Mic—"

Her phone rang, the arpeggio of chimes interrupting her reminder about our shared session with Michael. She drifted out to the pool area as she said, "Hello,

Alina speaking." She was using her boss voice, and it was doing wonders to revive my dick after its morning workout.

I finished my coffee and peeked out the window, where I saw Alina walking back and forth across the patio, gesturing wildly with an enormous smile on her face. She paused and clutched a hand to her chest, nodding furiously as she listened. Finally she dropped her hand and spoke again, briefly, into the phone and started walking purposefully back to the door. I backed away and heard her say, "Sure, yes, Sherilyn, I'll talk to him and hopefully we'll see you later today. Yes, thanks again for the call. Bye."

She carefully placed her phone on the counter and turned to me. Her eyes were electric. "You're not going to believe this. Sherilyn Holmes wants to meet with me. Well, us. She wants you to come too, to discuss a project. She never responded to my scheduling suggestions, so this is incredible." She launched herself at me and I barely caught her, swinging her around.

"Congratulations! I'm so proud of you!" I kissed her soundly on the lips.

"I know, it's so cool. Today, though? Can you make it?" she asked anxiously.

"Sure, when? I have to call in for a few radio interviews later this morning and early afternoon, but we can work around that," I said easily and shrugged.

"How about three-thirty or four o'clock?" she asked with one eye on her phone, her trembling fingers hovering over the screen.

"That works for me—let me know what Sherilyn says and I can pick you up at the studio and we can drive together."

She hummed happily and ran upstairs to my room to change into workout gear while I cleaned up the remains of our breakfast.

\* \* \* \*

"Alina, wait!" She was charging ahead of me, down a narrow, uneven path through a gorgeously landscaped yard. "Please, be careful!"

I caught up with her at the car. She'd already climbed in and buckled up. Her arms were crossed across her chest and her foot was tapping on the floormat. "Well, that didn't go so well. David, please take us back to my place." He nodded silently and we pulled away from the curb.

"Didn't go so well," was a gross understatement. Our meeting with Sherilyn Holmes had been a massive dud. A massive, manipulative dud. Apparently, she'd heard from Michael that Alina and I were together, and since Alina had called to see if she could schedule a meeting, Sherilyn had attempted to kill two birds with one stone. She'd ignored Alina almost completely, instead directing her comments largely to me. At the end of it she'd handed me a script and offered me a job. Alina received a limp handshake.

Alina pinched the bridge of her nose, closed her eyes and leaned her head back. Her chest rose once, twice, three times as she sought to regulate her breathing. She blew out a hard exhale and opened her wide green eyes again. No longer shooting sparks, they were banked to a low burn. "What a fucking bitch."

I nodded. "I'm so sorry about that."

She shrugged and stared out the window as she plucked the cross-body band of her seatbelt. "It's not you or your fault. It's not even Michael's. She's an opportunist and saw an opening. Honestly, if you want to take the job, I don't blame you. Sounds like a great role."

"Fuck, no," I said vehemently. "I have enough on my plate right now and I don't like how she handled that. She could have called Will and requested a meeting. I don't like being ambushed."

Alina sighed and rested her head on my shoulder.

"I know it's disappointing," I said as I stroked her hair. "But not everyone is like that in this industry, and it sounds like you and Carolina really hit it off."

"We did, and she sent me the script the other day. Thank you, by the way, for helping to convince Michael that we can wrap my part early so I can do pre-production with her."

It was the least I could do. I felt like all of the pressure she was under was my fault. If I hadn't waltzed into her life, she'd be working for Michael, moving up on her own. Instead her life was under a microscope as conjecture swirled around her. Yesterday her address had leaked, and photographers had been there waiting after we'd left the studio. We'd done an illegal U-turn and driven straight to my house instead of stopping to pick up a change of clothes.

She complained about feeling trapped into moving into my house because of the increased security, that we were breaking our 'casual' arrangement. I wanted to tell her that we were well past casually dating at this point, but she never seemed open to discussing it. Both of us were feeling the pressure, snapping at each other and falling all over ourselves to apologize. It was an exhausting cycle.

"Should we stop off at your house, see if the crowd has died down so you can pick up some stuff?" I asked. "I can ask David to detour."

"No, no. That's okay, I want to have a drink in the bath. It's been a long day." She sighed.

"Whatever you need. I had Claire pick up some things for you — clothes and toiletries — and they should be at the house. I wasn't sure if you'd like me to do that, but I also want you to feel at home there." I felt terrible for her privacy being violated.

"Thanks, that's really thoughtful," she replied and stared out of the window. A moment later, she reached back for my hand and squeezed it tightly, but it wasn't as soothing as it perhaps could have been under different circumstances.

* * * *

The proverbial shit hit the fan, for real, a week later when we barely scraped through a rehearsal scene with Michael. Alina was at her limit, completely wiped out from training, struggling to remember lines, and we were both running up against a brick wall trying to balance our romantic scenes together. They were either too much or not enough. We were in the back seat of my SUV and David was driving us back to my place from the studio, her place now being off-limits until the attention died down.

She was texting furiously with Candace, pausing every now and then to snort and shake her head, probably letting her know how awful tonight had gone and getting pissed when Candace tried to calm her down. Alina was never one to back down when she felt trapped, and we were both feeling like we'd been painted into a corner with no way out. I wondered if Ethan or Rory would want to meet up for a drink soon.

"You know? It's probably for the best he let us go early, seeing as how the last time we ran a scene with him we barely made it through without him throwing water on us. Again." Her voice was husky as she tried to maintain composure. She looked up at me and gave me an exhausted half-smirk.

"But we're getting so much better!" I reassured her with a sympathetic twist of my own lips. Neither of us were able to fully smile after that long a session.

Alina closed her eyes and laughed. "You're right. We haven't gotten water thrown on us in a few days. I'm done. Can we watch a movie or something tonight?"

"Stole my idea, sweetheart. You go shower or whatever and pick the movie when we get home. I'll go grab some food."

But it wasn't meant to be. Because Alina fell asleep on my shoulder in the car and I couldn't bear to wake her. I carried her into the house and brought her up to my room, laying her gently on the bed and tucking a blanket around her.

I realized it was a little cliché to watch my lover sleep, but I couldn't tear myself away. My mind started to race as I began to outline a plan for the next five days in which we could maybe escape the rat maze we were stuck inside.

My call to Michael must have been a little bit of a shocker given the hour and the fact that we'd gotten done dealing with him in-person less than an hour ago, but his greeting was only mildly affronted. "Markus, to what do I owe this late-night honor?"

"My 'get out of jail free' card option in my contract about rehearsals. I'm exercising it now and taking Alina with me. She needs a break," I stated so firmly that there could be absolutely no possibility of compromise.

Michael gave me a long sigh. "I know. She's at her limit and improvement stopped a few days ago. I'm sure the press isn't helping you two either. Go get yourselves on the same page and recharge."

"Thanks. And I'm sorry for dropping this on you, but you understand."

"I get it. Thanks for exercising that one-time-only option, though. I was about to recommend a change of pace for you two and call for a five-day break — now I don't have to." I could practically hear the smirk in his words. "Give me a call in a day or so, okay? Maybe bang a few times. Really try to get that out of your systems." He laughed wildly and hung up without saying goodbye. *Asshole.*

Feeling lighter, I rushed back to our room and threw a bunch of random clothes into my leather duffle bag. I took my time in the bathroom, showering and shaving, finally wearing myself out enough to sleep, and slid into bed, sighing with relief as Alina's body released from its tight fetal position. She snuggled back against me and I draped an arm over her middle. Everything was complete in that moment.

\* \* \* \*

The next morning, I reverted to my usual asshole ways and woke Alina up with a wet finger in her ear. She did not disappoint with her ungodly shrieks. Her retaliation tackle, however, took me completely by surprise, and the force of it rolled both of us out of the bed. We crashed to the floor, winded, with her on top of me.

"Hey," she wheezed. "What was that for?"

I lifted a finger, indicating the need for a moment.

She didn't respect it and started to poke me in the ribs. "Nuh-uh, you brought this on yourself."

"Hey! Stop that!" I giggled like a little girl at a sleepover.

"Only when you tell me why you chose to wake me with *saliva*?"

"Okay, okay, stop." I flipped us over, grabbed her wrists, held them tightly over her head and paused to enjoy her squirming beneath me. "I woke you because we're leaving. Everything is arranged. You need to pack a bag and we'll be off. We can get breakfast on the way. So— What? Why are you looking at me like that?"

"You weren't planning to ask me how I feel about ditching my job? What did Michael say?"

"Michael called a five-day break. We've both been worried about you. I probably should have asked but, since it's already organized...let's do it?" I gingerly let go of her wrists and sat back.

She struggled up to a seated position and got in my face, index finger tapping my cheek. "Never do that again. You're lucky you're so handsome and thoughtful. Give me five minutes in the shower, fifteen to pack and we're out."

I leaped up and pulled her along with me. Bowing deeply, I murmured, "As my lady wishes, so shall it be."

She snorted and rolled her eyes. "Not bloody likely. Ass."

# Chapter Twenty-Nine

*Alina*

I may have been irritated by the alpha move, but I had to admit that Markus had nailed his kidnapping maneuver. We stopped for breakfast at a little roadside rest area, then piled back into the Land Rover he'd rented for the long drive to Ojai, a small town north of L.A., where he'd somehow swung some VIP nonsense and booked a fancy suite at a luxury spa resort with security measures fit for paranoid royalty. Our view of the national forest was stupendous and the solitude and privacy were top-of-the-line.

"Alina?" he asked as we finished eating dinner. "What do you want to do tonight? If you want to head to bed, that's fine. Orrr...maybe we could revisit the soaking tubs on our balcony?"

The private spa tubs on the balcony had sold me completely on this plan when he'd showed me all of the amenities on his phone after he'd woken me up. Now that he was proposing immediately jumping in, though, my first response was that old wives' tale that said to always wait an hour after eating before any sort of physical activity. Although perhaps an exception would have to be made for scantily clad activity in a hot tub.

"I'll go grab my bathing suit." I was dreading forcing myself back into the damp Lycra, especially after such a huge meal.

"Why? It's only the two of us, right? And it's nighttime. Forgive me if I'm wrong, but I'm relatively sure that we've already seen each other naked." He shrugged out of his robe by the door and headed outside, completely, gorgeously nude.

"Well, crap. When in Rome, I guess," I muttered as I followed him out to the baths, clutching my wine glass like a lifeline.

It wasn't as though he hadn't seen me naked before. It was more that almost all of our sexual encounters since returning to L.A. had been exhausted, dreamy, middle-of-the-night sex in a dark room. The level of stress and pressure on both of us made everything fraught. We craved physical intimacy with each other, but it had been more comfort-seeking than lustful for the last few weeks.

Markus was already immersed in the water, with his head tilted back to look up at the beautifully clear starry sky, by the time I pulled it together enough to join him.

"Hey, you," he said, twisting his head toward me when he heard me pad out. "Get in here. I'm getting lonely."

*Why am I suddenly so shy?* I took a deep breath and set my glass on the wide ledge of the tub.

His eyes scanned me and he frowned at my hesitant approach. "Everything all right?"

"Of course. I mean, I think so. Is it weird that I'm nervous about getting in there with you?"

"No, I feel it too." His voice was so matter of fact that I immediately calmed. "We've been so busy and under so much ridiculous pressure that everything seems brand-new again."

The relieved butterflies settled further as I stroked the lip of the tub and considered him. It was still unbelievable to me sometimes that he was mine. That this mythically popular gorgeous man wanted *me*. I shrugged out of my robe and let it drop to the wooden planks. "Shove over, sexy beast. You're in my seat."

He scooted over and watched intently as I balanced on the edge before sliding in.

"Jesus, you're glowing," he uttered in a low voice. "Get over here."

His demands sent a shockwave of desire rushing through me. Bossy Markus was hot Markus, especially in the bedroom — or bath, as it might be.

"Give me your hands," he growled and grabbed my wrists as I raised them in supplication, dropping them behind his neck.

"That's better, but you need to be closer. Sit." That command almost undid me completely as he wrapped his hands around my waist and pulled me down to straddle his legs. The gentleness of his actions at odds with the demanding words.

His head dipped to my neck and he traced a line from my earlobe to my collarbone with the tip of his tongue. I shivered from his featherlight touch and mindlessly began to rotate my hips against him in slow, small waves. The heat built and combusted between us.

He pulled back with a groan and looked up at me, dazed.

"You are so fucking beautiful. You have no idea what you do to me, do you?" he whispered then brought his lips to meet mine.

The kiss started out gentle but immediately deepened and turned to something darker, more desirous, as our minute undulations started to speed up. It became wilder still as our teeth nipped and tongues stroked, fucking each other's mouths, until we were both panting with need.

He retreated a bit and it was my turn to lead and control the pace. I doodled patterns with water droplets on his chest and licked them up as I ran my greedy hands down his body. I reached his cock and began a slow stroke up and down his hard length. He shuddered beneath me and his hands clenched into tight fists as he fought to keep still.

"Let go, Markus," I whispered. "Touch me. I need you."

My words granted permission, and he surged up to capture my mouth with his. With more gentleness than I'd thought him capable of in that moment, he pulled me back to his lap, where he began to move my body against him, angling my hips to create a smooth, waveless pressure on my clit.

The sudden intrusion of two of his fingers into my channel electrified my every nerve ending, and I clenched around them as I gasped out his name. His hoarse breath on my neck as he kissed his way to nip and tease the peaks of my breasts made me want to scream.

Suddenly he scooped me out of the tub, my pussy screaming for him to let me come, and set me on the ledge of the tub. He smirked at me. "Something to say?"

"Fuck. You. Markus. Shellenberg." I whined as I squirmed against his tight hold on my waist.

"Say please," he ordered as he lowered himself into the water and dipped his head down to kiss my stomach.

"*Please!*"

"Please what, Alina?"

"Please fuck me with your fingers, now!" I begged.

"No."

My eyes shot open. "What?" I exclaimed.

"The next time you come, it's going to be on my tongue," he whispered in a dark voice as he bent to his task. He kept a smooth, swirling motion around my clit with the tip of his tongue, first slowly then building and building me up until he slid three fingers inside me and curled his fingertips in a come-hither motion that undid me completely. I saw the stars above us imprinted on my eyelids as I came, convulsing on his hand.

"You're too good at that." I shivered in the cool air as I came down from my high.

"No such thing," he responded as he held me tightly.

We sat there for a minute, or maybe an hour, watching the stars move. I pulled back from him and stroked his cheek and jawline with a trembling hand. "Let's go to bed."

He pulled me from the tub and wrapped me in a towel as if my liquified bones weighed nothing. Striding back into the house, he carried me into the nearest bedroom and laid me down on top of the covers. He crawled up next to me and sat back on his heels, taking in my flushed skin, pebbled nipples and sprawled legs. His dilated pupils and jagged breathing telegraphed the threadbare nature of his own control after making me come so spectacularly.

"I need you, Alina. Let me be with you."

"Oh?" I responded lazily as the temperature started to rise again. I ran my hands over my breasts, circling and pinching my nipples. "And how do you want to 'be with me'? With your fingers again? Maybe your tongue? Or is it something else you want?"

"My cock. I need to fuck you, feel you come all over it. Let me, please." His breathing intensified as we stared at each other for a long moment.

"Yes."

The words had barely left my mouth before he was on me, growling. He bent to kiss me, first on my mouth then slipping over to my neck, where he drew delicate patterns with his tongue as he made his way down my body.

"Now I need you inside me," I whispered as I wound my fingers through his hair and tugged on the still-ragged ends.

He groaned as he thrust home in one sure stroke.

"Look at me," he ordered breathlessly when he was fully seated inside me.

I watched him as all joking disappeared from his gleaming blue eyes, only to be replaced by the same surprise, pleasure and joy that overwhelmed me. The feeling of my body joined with his, my nails gripping his shoulders, was almost too much to bear, and tears start to well up in my eyes as he began to move.

"Me too, Alina. Me too," he whispered. He reared back and began to rock harder against me, the shock of the aggressive movement pushing me back up toward the headboard.

After a few more uneven thrusts, a bomb went off inside me as I convulsed, screaming his name. He made two more erratic, harsh strokes before he tightened and exploded inside me. He buried his head in the crook of my neck and his shoulders started to heave. *The asshole was laughing at me?*

I popped my head up in shock and managed to splutter, "Should I be offended? I don't think anyone has ever laughed at me after sex."

"Jesus, shit, Alina. I'm not laughing at you. I'm laughing *inside* you."

We both lost it, cracking up in the euphoric aftermath of the most intense sex I'd ever had. Markus propped himself up on one elbow and looked down at me, stroking my cheek, my nose and my chin. His eyes were soft now as he bent forward and kissed me as gently as a snowflake landing.

"I care about you," he said softly. "I know it's right after we had sex, so maybe that negates it for you, but I'm serious. I've known now for a while how I feel about you. That this is real, not casual, and I need you to know." He paused. "Fuck, this is awkward, I didn't mean to say it. It's just that I couldn't keep it together anymore without telling you."

"Don't be ridiculous, Markus. I care about you too. And now *you* know." I smiled through my post-orgasm haze and booped him on the nose in satisfaction.

He shook his head at me. "Seriously, I knew this was the forever kind of real when you booped me on the nose the first time."

I snuggled down into his chest and felt him slowly, soothingly stroke from the top of my head to the small of my back. When his hand faltered and lay still on my shoulder, I chanced a quick look up. He'd fallen asleep, turned toward me with the faintest smile on his face. His sharp left incisor had snagged his lip and he looked for all the world like he was a heartbeat away from his world-famous smirk and a tackle to kiss every bad or scary thought straight out of my head. I rested my head back on the firm pillow of his chest. We may not have said the big L word, but this was everything.

* * * *

"Jesus, how many notifications can you get at one time?" Markus' voice was exasperated when the pinging of my phone's alerts took off as we got closer to L.A. and regular cell service.

I snorted in derision, glancing up from my phone and rolling my eyes at him.

"Is Michael harassing you again?" he asked.

"Not Michael. Everyone and their mother, who apparently has seen photos of us at the resort in Ojai, writing obnoxious speculative tweets, blog posts and articles, then contacting me for comments about them." I was proud of how calm I sounded, very mature.

"What photos? Literally no one knew where we were and we had security."

"Well, they found us. I'm looking at the pictures now." The tension in my voice was unmistakable and he did a double take as he looked over at me. My hands started to shake and I almost dropped my phone as I saw the worst yet.

He craned his neck, attempting to see while still navigating the twisty backroad from the resort to the highway.

"Pull over, Markus," I ordered, my attention frozen on one very, very private moment immortalized on my screen for other peoples' benefit.

"Seriously? Now? How bad can it be?" he asked.

"Now!"

He pulled off to the side of the road and I wordlessly handed him my phone. Slowly at first, then more frantically, he swiped through picture after picture of us on our private vacation. Most were blurry, shot at a distance, and we were barely distinguishable from any other couple. Some, however, were closer, and they were the most concerning. A few from the lounge at the hotel showed us holding hands and laughing over drinks. Fine. But the ones shot with a telephoto lens of us in the tub on our private balcony were not fine at all.

He looked over at me hesitantly. "Fuck, I don't know what to say."

"No? How about, 'I'm so sorry, Alina. This is incredibly fucked up. I can't believe someone managed to photograph the two of us fucking in a hot tub and sold it to the world. Don't worry, I will get my crack P.R. team right on this, and those assholes will suffer!' That would be a great start."

He smiled at my admittedly terrible impression of him, then straightened up. "I *am* sorry, Alina. I should have done more to ensure security. We had a crew on site and that resort is known for its privacy measures. I'm not sure how these photos were taken." He frowned and pulled out his phone, started typing. "I'll text Claire immediately and have Roger file papers. We need to sue and he'll know who to target. Have you called Vinny yet?"

"Yes, I already texted him. He wants a call with your team to coordinate. Do it now," I demanded and sat in silence, staring out of the window as I waited for him to slap out a fast order to Claire to call Vinny and get on top of this story, have the pictures pulled wherever she could, as soon as she could.

"Claire says that she's on it already, as is Roger, and they're getting cease-and-desist orders out to all of the reputable outlets. She'll call Vinny and bring him in as well. Will is also going after the independents. Between them and Vinny, they should have a statement in a half hour for us to approve," he said after a relatively fast back-and-forth.

"Fine. Let's get back to your place. This will pass, right?"

He grabbed my hand and brushed a kiss across my knuckles. "It will, I promise."

The rest of the ride was quiet as we descended back into the real world. Hopefully the stories would flame out and life would get easier when we started filming. Our getaway already seemed to be in the distant past, and my memories were now tainted by the media's involvement.

The one or two photographers who had been hovering around the entrance to Markus' gated community had multiplied to a group of dozens, and I slid down in my seat as Markus navigated through the crowd and the guard let us in. I think we were both shocked by the increase, and neither of us spoke until we reached his house. Slowly, we unloaded the car, and he grabbed both of our bags to carry up to our room.

I immediately ducked into the bathroom for a moment of privacy, but I had barely sunk to a seat on the closed toilet when I heard a soft knock. "Is everything okay in there? If you're decent, can I come in?" he asked, his voice muffled through the closed door.

My eyes itched and watered with the emotions of the last couple of hours. "Give me a second. I'll be out shortly."

I had to take a few deep breaths and swallow hard before I could open the door, then I pushed past him, grabbing his hand and tugging him along with me over to the bed. We both sat heavily. "I don't know, Markus. Maybe it's that we've been really lucky, but the exposure we've dealt with so far has been annoying and a little upsetting, but mostly manageable. This is next-level privacy violations and I feel like we need to be more careful."

I lay back on the pillows and he followed me down, resting his head in his palm as he propped himself up. He jammed his other hand into his hair as my words settled in. "What does that even mean? 'Be more careful.' Become hermits?"

"That's not it at all, not what I meant. I— I don't know. This is hard." I curled up against him with my head on his chest and he wrapped his arms around me and kissed the top of my head.

"Tell me what you're thinking, what you want to do and what I can do to help."

I sifted through my thoughts and chose my words carefully as I said, "It's so many things, and I'm not sure where to start. This relationship happened so fast. I care about you—I do—but all of this chaos and exposure makes me feel vulnerable and unsure of what's real when it comes to you and us."

"What do you need from me to feel safe and happy?" His voice was almost as shaky as my own.

"To be honest, I'm really not sure. Maybe I need you to keep reminding me that everything is a moment in time, that security will not always be a standard accessory. It's weirding me out that rumors keep flying around about us, and then two minutes later that you and Kate are getting back together. I don't like feeling this insecure. I don't like *me* very much right now." I leaned back to look him in the eye.

He pulled back and frowned a bit. "I promise to do that, and hopefully make you laugh at the situation too. It's fucking ridiculous, right? We're two completely normal people. Why the fuck would anyone care about the minutiae of our lives?"

I forced a laugh. "Yeah, if they could see your jar of toenail clippings…"

"Toenail clippings? You're so disgusting," he said in an incredulous voice as he started to tickle me.

"Oh my god, Markus. Stop!" I couldn't help shrieking through my giggles.

"I'll stop when you take it back about the toenail clippings," he demanded.

"Never." I was gasping now, with tears running down my cheeks as he upped the tickling punishment by digging into my ribs. "Fine! You win. I take it back. I take it back! Happy?" He stopped tickling me and I pouted. I hated to lose.

As he rested most of his weight on his forearms propped next to my head, he reached out to trace my eyebrows. "Yes, very. You know you have nothing to worry about as far as our relationship goes. We're solid, right?"

"I think so. I hope so," I said quietly.

# Chapter Thirty

*Markus*

The next few days went by quickly and the press furor slowly started to die down as Alina and I laid very low, doing everything from her training and our rehearsals at my place. We spent hours lying on a lounge chair by my pool talking, telling stories from childhood, playing board games. It was our own private island, but it was hard to forget that we weren't there completely of our own volition.

We were starting to feel cautiously optimistic that the worst was in the past. Things were better on set and Michael was pleased with our ability to finally nail the choreography of our romantic scenes. He wandered around preening about his abilities as a talent scout. Seeing the hell that we were going through also brought the rest of the cast together. With the exception of one or two, they circled the wagons around us, and I was so incredibly grateful.

It was the night before our first full day of actual filming and we were lounging in a post-coital glow surrounded by of a nest of twisted duvets and loving words. Alina had dozed off and I had gone to clean up when both of our phones seemed to explode — her phone ringing and mine with a thousand notifications. I cursed softly as I scrolled through the alerts, pissed off that I had gotten complacent. Everything we'd built now seemed in danger of being torn down and I dreaded Alina finding out.

"Alina, hey," I whispered. "Candace is calling." I handed her the phone and grabbed my own to silence it. She pawed at it and barely managed to get it to her ear.

"Hello?" she muttered, then sat up, rubbing her eyes. "Hey, Candace, slow down. I'm barely awake." She listened for a bit, then jumped off the bed and shrieked, "*What?*"

As I clicked through the news items on my phone, I started to feel a wave of anger beginning to rise.

Alina broke in on what sounded like a frantic spiel from her friend. "Candace, shh. Quiet. You're hysterical. Some blogger is making allegations about Markus cheating on me and has proof? I may be minimally functional, but I'm ninety-nine percent sure that's total bullshit."

I had to admit to being slightly pissed that there was even a one percent question about my fidelity in Alina's mind.

"No, seriously, Candace, you don't get it. These claims have been happening off and on for a while, but they're all fake. Stop. Yes, this is bad, but Markus literally hasn't left my side in weeks. And you know that, you've been here with us half the time."

She turned into a statue and I could vaguely hear Candace's shrill voice urgently explaining something.

"Thanks for calling and warning us." She waited for another long pause, then followed it with a sigh. "Yeah, I know. You're looking out for me. Bye."

"Candace?" I asked somewhat unnecessarily. "I take it she's seen the news?"

"Yeah, you heard most of it. What is she talking about?"

"Well, it's a story," I hedged. "First, can I thank you? For standing up for me and trusting me."

She rolled her eyes at me. "I have to, right? Unless there's something else you're not telling me?"

"Of course not! Here's why she's freaking out." I handed over my phone and she started reading. "It's super fucked-up, but Kate took all of our old texts, plus made up new responses supposedly from me, and sold them all to one of the big outlets."

Alina's eyebrows rose as her eyes darted back and forth across the screen.

"They tried to get quotes from basically everyone on *Southern Gods* — no one talked, except Vanessa, who had a whole load of her own shit to add to the pile. They also dug up your old boyfriend and some people from Chicago. I'm not going to lie. It-it's bad." I stuttered to a stop.

Her face paled as she kept reading, her eyes getting bigger and bigger as they remained glued to the screen. Finally she dropped the phone and looked up at me. "Fucking hell," she breathed. "What are we going to do?"

"I've already messaged my team, asking for a conference call. You should bring Vinny in — I'm sure you already have a text from him." She nodded and I continued, "I want Michael there as well. I need to know he's on our side in this."

"What are we supposed to do in the meantime? Like, how are we even going to be able to get out of the neighborhood?"

"I think we ignore it and stay in, see if Michael can move start time." Even I didn't think that was viable and she snorted at my weak-ass response, swatting my arm like I was an annoying fly that had the gall to buzz bullshit in her ear.

"Whatever. I'm not sticking around here feeling like a prisoner when, A, there's no truth to this story, and B, we start shooting for real in a few hours. Let's roll. We can get to the lot before a ton of people show up. Crash in your trailer or something, it should be ready."

Alina jumped into the shower, and rather than join her like I usually did, I reread the article. There were a lot of allegations in it. Some were the truth, some were close to truth and most were outright lies. None of what they said about me really bothered me—I knew it wasn't true, and I'd been in the public eye for so long that it was easy to take it in stride. What was most concerning to me was the amount of dirt that they had dug up on Alina.

Vanessa's description of Alina as a scheming gold digger who had slept with her husband, another actor on the show, was especially damning. But it was obviously untrue. Given her background with a cheating ex, there was zero chance Alina would get involved with a married man. The story was clearly full of holes, but Alina had never dealt with this kind of shit.

The water was still running, so I went into the bathroom to see if Alina might want company in the shower. She had her back to me and her face in her hands. I quickly slipped out of my pajama pants and climbed in with her.

"Hey," I said as I enveloped her from behind. "I know this is so messed-up, and I'm sorry you're involved. How are you feeling?"

Alina turned within the circle of my arms and tucked her head into my chest. I could barely hear her over the rush of the water. "I don't know. A lot of feelings, really. Bad ones. There's also something that I have to tell you."

"What?" My heart started to pound erratically and I was afraid to hear her answer.

"Some of it's true," she said in a muffled voice.

"Which parts? Chicago? I knew about most of that."

She kept her head down, burrowed into in my chest, and didn't answer immediately. The walls started to close in on me.

"No. Terrance."

"What are you talking about?" I asked carefully.

Finally she met my eyes with tears streaming down her cheeks to mix with the gentle rain of the shower. "It doesn't matter. It happened a long time ago, right when I moved out to L.A."

"It does matter," I said firmly. "These stories involve both of us. I've been up front with you. What happened?"

Alina was full-on crying with her face buried in her hands.

"It's not like it's something I'm proud of. Terrance hit on me all night at an industry party Michael dragged me to. I'd been in town for only a few days and he said that he was separated from his wife. He was hot, I was lonely, one-night stand, you know? I didn't find out the truth until my first day on set, when I saw him all cozy with Vanessa."

"You should have told Michael then. Or quit."

Her voice began to rise as she moved inexorably toward anger. "Fuck that. I wasn't about to quit on my dreams because of a lying, cheating asshole. He cornered me that first day and swore up and down that he wouldn't say anything to anyone and begged me to keep my mouth shut too." She slapped a hand, hard, against my chest. "I'm sorry if you're mad, but this isn't about you. It was a poor decision on my part and I'm paying for it now. What else do you want from me?" Her voice cracked on the last question.

"What do I want? I want this to have never come up. I want you to never have fucked Terrance and given the media such a perfect opportunity to hurt me," I shouted, and knew that I was being completely unreasonable. It wasn't about me.

"Hurt *you*? Yeah, I totally slept with a guy two years before I met you just to fuck with you. What about you? This shit with Kate? What am I supposed to believe?"

"You know that's complete bullshit—"

"Stop. Jesus, sometimes I wish I'd never met you. That I'd pushed back on Michael when he begged me to join the cast and save the show." She turned her back to me and leaned against the wall of the shower. "Get out, Markus. I can't stand to be near you right now. I'm done."

"You can't be serious. This is it? You're going to break up with me?"

She kept her back to me and didn't respond, letting the spray of water divide us further. I waited, hoping against hope that she would say something, anything, but her silence spoke for her and I stepped out of the shower and grabbed a towel. I disappeared into my theater room until an alert on the alarm system told me that she'd left the house.

# Chapter Thirty-One

*Alina*

Michael moved back the start of filming one day to give us time to run interference. Even though Vinny and Markus' team quickly got the article pulled and were investigating the sources behind it, we were still the center of a shitstorm of public opinion and gossip. Enough people had screenshotted the article or posted parts of it in other places that copies were still circulating. When I'd left Markus' house the morning the story broke, I'd taken a Lyft to a spot near the boardwalk and walked home via the beach in an effort to avoid the photographers camped in front.

My house smelled stale, musty. It had been too long since I'd been home. I lit a few candles to cut through the scent of abandonment and made sure all of the curtains and blinds were shut before running through my list of texts, starting with Candace's.

*ARE YOU ALIVE?!*

At least some things didn't change.

*Yeah. Just walked into my house. What's up?*

*WHAT'S UP? Only a few things. Like, what the fuck is going on with you and Markus?*

*...*

*DON'T GIVE ME THAT PASSIVE AGGRESSIVE BULLSHIT*

*Sigh. Fine. What are you doing? Can you come over? I don't want to do anything except get very drunk and cry.*

*YES. I can be there in an hour and a half. Order me lunch.*

*K*

*DID YOU JUST K ME?*

*K*

*OMG. You're near dead to me. Don't push it.*

*Can't wait to see you, missed your face!*

I dragged myself upstairs and plopped on my bed, ignoring my phone after a quick check revealed four messages and two missed calls from Markus. I was done with my life being on blast because of him, done with this acting bullshit. I was so fucking done with everything.

A few bottles of wine were still left in my rack, so I cracked one open and ordered a bunch of sushi for delivery from a neighborhood joint while I waited for Candace. Both the delivery guy and Candace conveniently arrived at the same time, which meant that I didn't have to continue my self-destructive bent toward finishing a bottle of wine on an empty stomach.

The delivery guy practically dropped the sushi and ran as Candace shrieked, "Alina, what the fuck are you doing? Get over here!"

We hugged as she gauged the level of liquid in the bottle. "Wait, how're you almost done with that bottle?"

"Sorry," I slurred lightly. "It'll be fine. Hand over the sushi and we'll make it better."

"Oh no. I did *not* come over to babysit. We need to talk."

"Give me a break, Candace. It's been a rough few days, weeks, months — whatever."

She looked contrite and went in for another hug. "Oh, sweetie. I know. But you're tough as nails. If anyone can handle this, it's you."

I shrugged as Candace swooped up the sushi and grabbed two plates, somehow gracefully balancing everything. I slid open the patio door to my small deck and plopped into a café chair as she stared at me encouragingly.

"Fuck, Candace. It's bad," I started. "Thanks for the warning."

She nodded furiously. "Of course. I'm so, so sorry."

There was so much sympathy in her eyes and I struggled not to cry as I tried to order my thoughts. My words wouldn't be pretty or approved messaging, but I needed to talk to someone about our argument and its aftermath. To her credit, she listened to it all — with her mouth hanging open — before responding.

"Jesus. So how many times has he called and texted since you left his house?"

"Hmmm, let me see, six texts and five missed calls — which is two more texts and calls than the last time I checked around an hour ago."

"Whoa."

"Yeah."

"Have you looked at them?"

"No. I don't want his apologies right now. When the story broke, he downplayed it. Got mad at me for never telling him about Terrance and never even denied the shit about him and Kate. I can't take it anymore, the pressure, the attention. It's too much and, right now, I don't know if he's worth it."

"I know, Alina. I know... But the guy is clearly floundering and super broken. Even I could tell when I met him in Georgia. Not to make excuses for him, but I wouldn't doubt his feelings. Despite the fact that he's being a dick for brains right now."

"And here I thought *we* were friends," I said, stung by her defense of him.

"We are. You know I'm on your side. Yeah, Markus has got some major shit to work through — but so do you. You've been ignoring this thing with Terrance for too long and have never come to terms with it. Your instinct to help Markus allowed him to suppress everything with Kate too, rather than deal with it full-on."

I was shocked that she'd read me so well, that she'd dare to call me out. It was all true, but facing my emotional baggage would mean I'd need to open up and be vulnerable. I was terrified of what would happen if I lost all control.

Candace continued, "And you're forgetting about the media — they're the real villains here. So what are we going to do to get the truth out? Once it's out and you've finally dealt with the narrative, then you can deal with Markus Eat-a-Bag-of-Dicks Shellenberg."

Despite the near constant tears, I laughed. She was right. Of the two, taking down the tabloids would honestly be easier to deal with than Markus. "What does my devious friend have in mind for taking on the entirety of the celebrity gossip machine?"

Candace rubbed her hands together and cackled like an animatronic Halloween witch from Costco. "Oh, Alina, I'm *so* glad you asked. Pour me another glass and let me school you in the ways of a petty bitch's strategy for revenge."

I poured. I was down for pettiness in a major way .

"First, we're going to figure out who all of the sources are. Then we're going to go after them, with a focus on Vanessa and Terrance. They're going down."

She continued to add more details, and I started to smile. I genuinely felt bad for Rory and Ethan if they ever tried to cheat on her — her levels of petty were off-the-charts.

* * * *

Thanks to my agent Vinny, a private investigator that Candace knew from high school, and Rory's agent, who had a slightly obsessive interest in true crime documentaries, we were able to track down and put a decent amount of pressure on the people who had made the exaggerated statements about me to the press. My asshole ex, in fact, showed us text messages from a blogger berating him for not saying worse things about me. That blogger had gone ahead and manufactured uglier storylines when he hadn't been satisfied with what he'd gotten.

Other than interacting with him at work now that we were shooting, I still hadn't talked to Markus since the day the news had broken, and refused to answer any of his messages or calls, which had tapered off somewhat. Perhaps that was immature, but I had decided it was an important bit of self-care. He wasn't even a part of my life anymore and the man still had the infuriating ability to whipsaw my emotions. I hated how he turned me inside out, that he'd refused to fight for me. My mind was descending into a by-then familiar whirlpool of depression and distrust when Candace called early in the morning and nearly tore my ear off in her excitement.

"Alina! Oh my god. It's done. Are you at home?"

"Yeah, what's up?" I sat up and scrubbed my face.

"Oh shit. I recognize that tone," she accused. "We're ready to drop those retractions and get the ball rolling on the new stories. The bigger tabloids have already fought it out for rights to the story and now we can go on a blogger blitz."

"It's over?" I asked, disbelieving that the forces that had shaped my life over the past few months were suddenly going to be neutralized.

"It's over, baby girl. The story is back under your control. And you know what you need to do now? You need to call Markus. You need to figure that shit out, because I know you still care. And you know he does too."

I nodded into my phone, even though I knew she couldn't see me.

"Yeah, lady, I heard you nodding. You know you need to fix this. Can I count on you to pull up your big girl pants and speak to him?"

"Yes, I promise," I muttered.

"One more time, louder for the people in the back," she commanded.

"Yes!" I hollered. "I'll call him, okay?"

"Excellent, chica, let me know how it goes, love you!" she chirped and hung up.

I'd lied, though. In the end, I didn't call him. Seeing him at work was hard enough, but trying to talk about this—about us—was going to be impossible, and I needed time to prepare myself. Finally, I settled for the coward's way out and sent him a text asking him to meet me at my house later that evening.

When Markus' hesitant knock tapped on my door a few hours later, I took a deep breath, straightened my shoulders, shook out my wrists and repeated my mantra, "You are a badass boss lady. You confront your problems head-on and kick their asses." I nodded resolutely, opened the door and drank in his disheveled state. It made me feel better, in a very shallow way, that his physical appearance—with his scrubby, patchy beard, purple circles under the eyes and wrinkled T-shirt—matched my insides. I'd tried to block out his slow decline in rehearsals as makeup worked overtime to keep him looking consistent, but it wasn't something that I was proud of and my heart shattered into a few more pieces every time I saw him.

When he looked hopefully at me with those bruised eyes from the other side of the threshold, I almost broke and reached for him. But he'd crushed my heart with his wild accusations. Sometimes it was a fine line between love and hate, and I was living right on it. I stepped to the side and allowed him back into my home.

"Come in, Markus. Thanks for coming," I said quietly.

He nodded stiffly and made his way into my living room, clearly remembering the familiar set-up of my house. I gestured to the couch as he hovered uncertainly. I sat down across from him, the coffee table a small but not insignificant barrier between the two of us.

"I've been working with Candace and a few others to get to the bottom of the stories flying around the media. Doing interviews and digging up retractions." I stumbled to a stop as his eyebrows climbed his forehead.

"What? Why?" he asked in clear disbelief. "I've been working with my team on this too and I think we're close to filing suit on a number of these outlets. Alina, I want you to know how sorry — "

"Markus, that's your team, not mine. I needed to take this on myself," I interrupted quietly.

"Okay, I get that, but why wouldn't you tell me?" he asked. "Can we talk about us for a second? I screwed up and — "

I didn't want him to finish, wasn't ready to talk about his feelings. He may have figured out where he'd screwed up, but he certainly wasn't listening to me or taking me seriously when I talked about how I had to be in charge of my own efforts to combat the press. He couldn't always protect me.

"Markus, I'm not talking about us right now — I'm not ready to make up or talk things out. And I don't think you are either. I wanted to share with you that I've been working with people to address the stories on my own. I don't need you—or your team—to constantly jump in and try to save the day."

He was stunned and sat there with glazed eyes, licking his dry lips over and over. "Okay, I understand."

"I don't know if you do," I said gently. "Your constant efforts to protect me and get me to rely solely on you broke me. Maybe it wasn't intentional, but you went from one codependent, fucked-up relationship to another without doing any emotional labor. Come find me when you've done that and maybe we can talk."

He stood up, still in a daze. "Is that it?" I nodded. Our conversation had taken all of ten minutes.

His face crumpled as he turned to leave. "Well, thanks for meeting with me and explaining in person."

"See you on set," I offered, not ready to commit to anything more with this man. The only way we'd be talking again about an 'us' was if he did some work on his own to fix his shit.

# Chapter Thirty-Two

*Markus*

I hadn't been completely sober in weeks, not since the day Alina had disappeared from my life. Somehow I'd been able to work—at least I waited until the evening to start drinking. My team and I were doing as much as we thought was possible to take down the false narrative, but it had taken meeting with Alina and having her call me out to finally break me from my spiral of self-pity. That evening, I called a therapist I'd hadn't seen since I first moved to L.A. and scheduled out a month's worth of appointments.

When *People* and *InTouch Weekly* finally brought forward their 'exclusives' with Alina and others to set the record straight, the public responded in a mad frenzy. Suddenly she was back in control of her life, while I was still wallowing in the muck of my own. I was working on better coping methods for my anxiety and new strategies for dealing with stress, but I still had a ways to go. I'd let my codependent nature warp me into a distrustful, closed-off person who had brought everyone down with me.

My brother's peppy 'Kool and the Gang' ringtone blaring out of my phone ripped me from another night of regret-fueled dreams a few mornings later.

"Ja, Matti?" I groaned as I answered the phone.

"No, fuckface, your other brother who you invited for a visit and is sitting at your front door. Come let me in."

"I invited you for a visit? When?"

"Not relevant, big brother. Now let me in before I kick down the door."

The little shit hung up on me.

"Markus!" Matti's muffled yell and loud thumps against my front door drove me out of bed in a mad scramble, and I almost ate shit completely trying to hurdle the stairs to yank open the door before the housekeeper lost her mind and finally quit on me.

"Brother." I stepped aside as he tore into my house.

"Ah, brother. Got a beer?" He nodded genteelly after the uproar.

I led him into my kitchen, where I glanced at the clock and saw that it was eleven o'clock in the morning. *Whatever.* I shrugged internally. I'd been living under airport rules for drinking for a while now and it was a day off for me. We cracked our beers and flopped down onto the couches in the adjoining living room.

"So to what do I owe the honor of this visit?"

"Are you fucking kidding me? You forgot that you invited me? I mean, I knew you were messed up over Alina, but how did you forget that you asked me to come out?"

"Maybe *you* forgot that I've been slightly busy lately, being stuck in middle of a publicity nightmare?"

"Oh, boo-fucking-hoo, Markus. That's a lame excuse. She's gone and it's your fault. You've been sulking and drunk, but it's all on you." He glared at me, daring me to contradict him. "For the record, you invited me a week ago. When I called you upset that I was being traded from Leverkeusen to a club in England."

"What? You got traded?"

"Oh, so we're not even going to talk about *your* elephant in the room. Let's talk about mine, right? Totally fair."

"Matti."

"Markus."

A staredown commenced until, finally, he blinked.

"Seriously though. Traded? What happened?"

Matti smiled grimly. "Exactly what you always warned me about. Management got sick of fielding calls from women saying they were having my baby. Oh, and one of those women might have been the niece of the owner, which I didn't know when I hooked up with her."

"Matti, Jesus. I'm so sorry."

He sighed. "Me too, man. Me too. I really fucked up. Mother is pissed as shit, tore me a new asshole and told me I need to grow up. Dad basically told me I shouldn't plan on coming home until I've grown up and learned how to treat women like people, not objects."

"When do you have to report to the new club? Which one is it?"

"Monday, three days from now, in case you were wondering what day it is, you lush. I'm off to Chelsea."

I winced. That team was mid-to-lower-Premier League. A huge step down. "How bad was it?"

"I don't want to talk about it. Let's leave it at it was bad and that I've been advised by my lawyers that I'm lucky no one is suing me. It's probably for the best though, you know? I need to do better and I've been a complete tool."

"Shit, Matti. I don't know what to say — maybe it's true, but I wish it hadn't happened this way."

"Me either. Let's talk about something better. I'm getting another beer. Looks like we're both thirsty today."

I didn't want to tell him that I'd been all too 'thirsty' lately, and simply waited for him to return with the beer. "Thanks, Matti."

"No problem. So, saw the covers of those celeb magazines. How'd you pull that off?"

"What? Me? I did nothing, Alina and her friends did all of it."

"Really? And how are you two?"

"Not speaking at the moment, other than when we have to at work. It's okay though, I don't think I'm ready to, and I've been working with a therapist to learn how to manage my issues. Until I've fixed myself, I can't go back to her. She deserves more."

"Good for both of you, but I still can't believe you fucked that up. You two seemed so solid in Berlin."

"I don't want to talk about it. I'm working through it."

"Markus, I think you need to — with more than a therapist. Your family is here for you, whether you want us to be or not," he said gently. "Tell me, what happened?"

"Me. I happened."

"Don't be fucking dramatic, jackass. What happened?"

"I screwed up, badly. Tried to wrap her up in cotton wool to protect her, not support her or lift her up, worked it so she was overly reliant on me and then dropped the ball big-time when the shit hit the fan. Told her she was being ridiculous and bitched her out for hooking up with a guy before we even met to hurt me." The last was nearly whispered.

"You didn't."

"Oh, I did. Like I said, I fucked it up. Big time."

"I promise not to tell Mother or Ella," he said solemnly after a moment's pause.

"Thanks." My laugh sounded like a creaky door.

"Anyways. What are you going to do about it? I mean, you love her, right?"

I sighed again. "Yeah, I do. More than I ever would have thought possible. She's — I don't know how to say it. Central to me? Like gravity or some other force of nature. Like breathing."

I dropped my head to my hands and finally admitted the truth. "The shit of it is, I knew the minute I saw her that she was it. But I denied and denied, we barely talked about our status beyond casual — even though I *knew* we both knew it was more. She deserves someone who will fight for her, and I stood back and let her walk away when the press came in and turned up the pressure."

"Markus, I've never heard you say anything like this before, and god knows I've never felt anything like what you're talking about. What are you going to do to try to win her back?"

"She won't answer my calls, respond to texts. I've stopped though — I'm trying to respect her space while

I work on myself. I think I'm ready, or at least much closer, to doing that now. To be the right person for her."

"You're still a fucking moron and you need to stop being such a pussy. I hope you're planning something big."

"What? Why? If I could get her to listen, I could easily explain—"

"Markus, Jesus. How are you this stupid? She's a woman, the love of your life, who you've royally fucked over. There's no reason for her to listen to you. So what are you going to do to fight for her? How will you show her you've changed?"

*Ah. The old deeds-versus-words distinction.* I was an idiot.

"Truthfully? I have no idea. Got any suggestions?"

Matti rubbed his hands in glee. "Oh yes, I might have a few. But first, tell me. Does she have any single friends?"

\* \* \* \*

"All right, gorgeous. See you this afternoon!" My brother grinned as he tucked his phone back into his pocket and gestured for me to stop pacing and sit down. "She's in. I'm picking her up at three and we're getting coffee. If all goes according to plan, we'll meet you at the observatory around five. Cool? And stop biting your nails, man. It's unbecoming."

I nodded and slid into the chair opposite him. My bouncing leg immediately started shaking the end table.

"You really think this is the best idea?" I asked.

"Well, good idea or not, she's in and it's happening. So you better be bringing your A-game, big guy. You'll need it."

My little brother was a force of nature with all of his plans and schemes, but step one had worked. Well, actually step one-point-five, since step one had really been to get her to answer the phone and stay on long enough to convince her to meet him for coffee.

"Okay, Matti, okay. We're doing this your way, but if it backfires, I'm stealing your first paycheck."

"Bah, fuck you, Markus. She loves you. You love her. Both of you said some things that you shouldn't and she freaked out about dating an uber-celebrity." He shrugged with his arms spread wide. "It's all understandable. That pressure from the media blew everything out of proportion—but it can't hurt you guys anymore. It's up to the two of you to make this work. If you want to, that is."

"You know I do, more than anything." I blew out a stressed breath and tried to channel my inner light. Or whatever the fuck my useless meditation app called it.

"Then stop whining and go get yourself ready to win back the woman of your dreams. Get a haircut and a manicure while you're at it. You look like death."

I lurched up and tackled Matti, holding him down while I poked him repeatedly between the eyes. "I. Am. A. Fucking. International. Sex. Symbol. I will never look less than gorgeous."

He twisted and flipped me onto my back. "You. Look. Like. Shit. Take. A. Shower." He was howling by the end as I punched him in the kidneys till he rolled off me.

"Thank you, Matti, for coming here and kicking my ass," I finally got out when I could breathe again.

"And for being your co-conspirator, right?"

"Obviously. I owe you big, little brother. Huge."

"Ah, yes, yes you do. And if Alina decides that she'd rather run off with me than meet you at the observatory, I promise that I'll invite you to our wedding."

"Bastard!" I gave him another punch in the gut for being an annoying little prick and leaped to my feet. Matti's groans of pain were the sweetest soundtrack for my escape.

# Chapter Thirty-Three

*Alina*

"Candace. I have a serious code red. Call me!" I don't know why I bothered leaving a message.

When the unfamiliar German number had showed up on my phone on my day off, I'd answered out of instinct—I was finally ready to talk to Markus, but it wasn't him. Apparently his baby brother was in town and wanted to meet up. Something about someone wanting him to read for a part and he wanted to talk about it with me?

And now Candace wasn't answering or returning my calls. I needed perspective. Quickly. As well as a makeover from her so Matti would tell Markus that I looked gorgeous and was doing fine without him, which he already knew since we worked together, but—

*Stop, you love him. Admit it.*

Candace: Sorry, on set. Can't talk now. What's up?

Me: I may have agreed to meet up with Markus's little brother. He's in town and called. I answered.

Candace: WHAT? WHY

Me: Because... I don't know. Are you busy around lunchtime? I need a makeover.

Candace: I'll be free, but need to be on set. Come here, and we'll get you ready. K?

Me: Thanks. I'm losing my shit.

Candace: Same, girl, same.

I was struck by a weird sense of déjà vu as I drove onto the lot, like nothing and everything had changed since my first day in L.A. on a real set. Even Candace was the same, bouncing around like a caffeinated jumping bean as she waited for me at the gates.

"Oh my god. Get over here. I only have—what? An hour to work some magic so you can turn Markus' brother's head and he can then tell Markus that you're doing fine and he'll come groveling?"

She was too good, and I rolled my eyes at her. "Obviously."

"Are you going to—dare I say it—take him back?" She was full-on harpy screeching and people were staring. I grabbed her by the arm as we hustled down a hallway.

"No. I don't know. He's stopped leaving me messages, texting, everything. But it's so him, right? Besides, you've heard the rumors. Apparently he's out every night, partying like he's a frat boy on spring break."

"And...you're meeting his brother why?"

"Because. When Matti called it was like a massive kick in the ass. Markus Fucking Shellenberg didn't break me. I need to prove that. To him and to me."

She scoffed. "Oh, Alina. Stop lying to yourself. If he hasn't realized that over the last few weeks working together, then he's seriously not worth it. But you're still in love with him, aren't you?"

My eyes overflowed with tears out of nowhere. "Yeah, I am," I answered softly. "He was so imperfectly perfect—for me. I'm still so pissed at him, but I don't think our relationship ever had a chance with the media pressure and neither of us being ready for it. The feelings were the only thing that were real, but everything was built on trembling fault lines."

Candace sat me down in a makeup chair and smiled at me in the mirror. "I know. Everyone could see it on set. It was like watching a chemical reaction. Every time you were in a room together, nothing else mattered but the two of you. It was so obvious."

I sighed as she started to mess with my hair and dabbed a bunch of cream on my face. "I can't believe we thought we were getting away with anything. But we both still have a lot against us and some major issues that we need to work through."

"Yeah, you do, but you also have something special between you two." Candace paused mid-brushstroke to look me over. "Oh my god! What if it's not Matti that shows up today, but Markus!"

"Is it terrible that that's what I'm kind of hoping for?"

Candace laughed in my face. "No, maybe that's what this is. And maybe I'm styling you for your happily ever after."

She finished up, twirled my chair around and whipped off my cape. "Ta-da!" Our eyes met in the mirror and I took in my no-makeup makeup and easy-breezy beachy waves. We both grinned. Today was going to be a good day.

\* \* \* \*

"Alina! Hey! Good to see you. Thanks for coming!"

I looked around the crowded coffee shop, hoping to see a different hulking Viking — *my* Viking — behind the six-foot-five, tatted-up berserker struggling to un-wedge himself from the little café table.

"Oof. Fuck. They need to make bigger tables," he muttered as he almost upended it in his effort to crush me in an enormous hug and enthusiastically buss my cheek with the ubiquitous Euro cheek kiss.

"Matti, good to see you too." I was still craning my head, hoping against all hope that Markus was hiding somewhere.

Matti caught my action and grinned slyly. "He's not here, pretty lady."

My cheeks heated up. "Ha, ha, who? I mean, duh. Not looking for anyone. So...you. You're here...in L.A. What's up with the show?"

He laughed in my fucking face. "Uh. Huh. Got it. Noted that you are absolutely not looking for my brother."

"Shut up, Matti."

"Ah, I missed you. It's unbelievable that we only met for a day. Anyways, yeah, so, I lied."

I rolled my eyes, not even remotely surprised. "There's no show, is there?"

"Nope." He popped the *P* in the most ridiculous younger-brother fashion, and I almost slugged him.

"Why did you call then? Is everything okay with your brother?"

"Oh, him? We can talk about him? He's a bloody fucking mess. Working on himself, though. You'd be proud."

"Cool." I sounded like a Valley Girl.

"But as to why I'm here... I was naughty and got kicked off my team, and now I've got some downtime till I need to report to my new club in England. So I decided to come visit my brother, who has truly been making a mess of his life."

"You're not kidding," I muttered. "Oh my god, though, sorry. Sorry about your team! That completely sucks."

"Yeah, it does. Not why I'm here today, though." He cleared his throat loudly and proclaimed, "In case you didn't figure it out on your own, I'm here on behalf of my idiot brother. I mean, where else would I have gotten your number?"

"Ah, yeah, I was wondering." I retreated to sarcasm, my only defense against Matti's determination.

"So, you two. I'm concerned, you know? He really fucked things up, from the sound of it. Both with you and not dealing with some pretty severe emotional issues. He's done a bang-up job."

I nodded.

"Anyways, I am here to relay a message from He Who Will Not Be Named. He's sorry."

I snorted.

"More than that, though, he's cleaning himself up. He hasn't had more than a drink a night since I've been here—which actually pisses me off. Like, how can he not take his hot brother out to clubs and introduce him to his single friends? What the fuck, Markus? Am I right?"

"Not. The. Point. Matti."

"No, no, it's not." He sighed theatrically. "Anyways, like I was saying, he hasn't been out even once since I've been here, and has been meeting with that therapist he started with when he first moved here. Like, every day."

"That's nice, Matti. Really nice to hear that he's working on himself and that the rumors of him partying all the time are bullshit." I meant it, even though I was super underwhelmed with the direction of this meandering conversation. Markus had been suffering a lot when I'd first met him, and it was clear that I'd been a Band-Aid he'd slapped over some very deep wounds.

"Fuck, I'm really cocking this up. I'm only here as a messenger. Sorry, I'm terrible at this. The gist of it is this—he wants to see you, if you would be willing to meet with him. Hear him out."

"I've heard him out. All these words on voicemails, texts, DMs. So. Many. Words. But no actions, you know? I don't know if I can take any more words from him."

"But you care about him, right? A lot, if I'm not mistaken. God forbid Markus confide in me, but he's obviously very deeply in love with you. He knows you might not forgive him right now, but maybe you'd be willing to give him a chance?"

I sat, silently staring at the imploring face of Markus' little brother, gauging the truth behind his words. "I—I...yeah. I would be willing to give him a chance. How?"

Matti slumped back in his chair, a look of total relief sliding over his face. "Oh, thank god. I really thought I was fucking this all up for him. He would have killed me. First time he ever trusts me with anything more important than picking him up at the airport and I crash and burn. Whew. Thanks—"

"Matti, stay on track. How am I supposed to give him another chance?"

"Oh, that. What time is it?"

"Four o'clock. Why?"

"Shit. And it's probably rush hour, right?"

"Yeah... Why?"

"We've got to go! You ready for a kidnapping?" I didn't get a word out, but managed a nod, and he whooped as he threw me over his massive shoulder then started sprinting toward a black sedan with tinted windows.

"Matti! Put me down, you asshole!" I was laughing as I smacked him in the back, but he wasn't budging, and people seemed to be way more interested in my attractive kidnapper than me, the obvious victim. My fellow citizens were really dicks about passive observance.

He dumped me in the car and shouted at the driver, "On to phase two!"

Despite my annoyance, I did kind of think it was cute that well-intentioned kidnapping was apparently a family trait.

# Chapter Thirty-Four

*Alina*

"If I trip and fall off a cliff because of you, Matti, I will come back and haunt your ass forever. Swear to god." I was stumbling around, arms outstretched, with a blindfold on in what felt like an enormous cavernous space.

"A little to your right, Alina. Yup, you got it. Now nine steps forward." His voice boomed from somewhere to my left. Music was playing at a low volume.

"There, I mean, no. One. More. Step." I slammed into something warm and solid that grunted when we connected. "There! Stop, you're good. Okay, I'm going to head out. Peace!"

"What the actual fuck, Matti?" I tore off the blindfold and looked right into the face of the very person I'd been secretly hoping to see for days. His trembling hands wrapped around my biceps, steadying me, and his breath *whooshed* out in relief.

"Alina."

"Markus."

Was this it? We were going to stare at each other and say our names over and over? It was like we were both under a spell, locked into each other, unable to move. Finally, I shifted back a bit to get out of his immediate reach and noticed the song playing. Phil Collins, letting us all know that the air tonight had some extra special feelings going on.

"Send your brother to do your dirty work so you can set up your very own Lloyd Dobbler moment?" I asked sarcastically, trying to hide a grin.

The corners of his lips quirked up. "Sort of. It worked, though, didn't it? Sorry it's not Peter Gabriel, had to go with my maestro. Plus, couldn't be a total cliché, right?"

Markus' tiny smile was like sunshine after the grayest, coldest February on record, and I could feel my frozen heart unfurling toward his warmth.

I smacked his arm. "I'm still so mad at you. And you sent your annoying brother to do all the heavy lifting! I expected public groveling."

"Annoying? Not cool!" came Matti's muffled voice from...

*Somewhere?* I looked around suddenly. We were in the vast entrance hall of the Griffith Observatory. One of L.A.'s famous landmarks and usually packed with tourists. Yet we were all alone. Although apparently we still had a voyeur of sorts.

"Time to go, Matti!" Markus yelled, not taking his eyes off me. Like he was afraid I would evaporate if he shifted his avid attention for even the slightest moment.

"Going. See you at home?"

"Matti, get out of here!"

"Fine, but I'm telling Mother that you were a shit host!" The door to the building clanged shut as he raced off in a huff.

I started laughing as Markus pinched the bridge of his nose. "He's something, isn't he?"

"Something tragic, that's for sure."

"Oh, I wouldn't say that. I mean, he got me here, didn't he?" I stared at Markus for a long moment, observing him as he did a similar visual search.

"Fuck, Alina." He exhaled loudly through his nose. "I was almost too afraid to hope that he'd convince you to come. In fact, I was maybe eighty-six percent sure that he'd pull in alone and we'd get blind drunk and lie on the floor listening to Phil Collins' greatest hits while I cried."

"Well, I'm here. Want to tell me why?"

He stepped forward and grasped my hands, like touching me would keep me tethered to him. His thumbs slowly circled the backs of my hands as his stare somehow became laser focused. On me. He gulped and closed his eyes for a count of three. I could literally see him counting, head nodding, one…two… three times.

When he opened his eyes, they blazed down at me. "Well, it's like this," he began slowly. "I'm sorry. So very, very sorry about everything that happened between us."

I tried to wrench my hands away. Not more words. "Markus, we haven't even talked to each other in a month outside of work…"

He clung tighter. "I know. I guess I mean from before that. From the moment we met. I was self-absorbed and afraid of losing everything at once. I was afraid to be completely open with you and never thought about what you needed versus what I needed from you."

"Oh, yeah. That," I muttered lamely.

"Yes, that. I've fucked this up. Said shit out of fear and paranoia that I can't take back. There are so many things I regret."

"Do you regret it all?" I asked in the world's smallest voice.

"*No*. Never. Not in a million years do I regret the shit that led up to and resulted in me meeting you. Because—and I don't know if I ever told you this—but I *knew* the minute I saw you that you were someone important."

He paused for a moment and blinked heavily before soldiering on. "You are absolutely everything to me. It frightened me how intensely I felt, how easy things were between us, and I'm embarrassed to admit that I used you. Used the ease of things like a security blanket, but still kept you at arm's length with all of that talk about keeping things casual."

He dropped my hands and started to pace in a small circle. "It was like concentrating on this brilliant, new, shining thing that sprang to life between us gave me an excuse to sweep aside all of the turmoil in my life. I'm sorry for that, that I didn't work through my own problems before basking in this. Because it led to our downfall, I think."

I grabbed his hands and pulled him to a stop. I needed him to listen now, to hear the hard words that I'd been thinking about for the last month. "It did, but I'm partially to blame as well. I went into our relationship feeling unbalanced. Feeling like I was backed into a corner. And on one hand, it wasn't so bad because you were there with me too. But on the other, I felt like you were also the one who put me there."

"I'm so sorry for that." He frowned at his toes. "But if it's not completely obvious, I love you. I loved you from the first time I saw you, and I love you even more now, while you're looking at me with more fear than I'd ever want to see in your eyes."

"Markus…I know. I love you too. I missed you even more, but you're absolutely ridiculous." I was crying and hiccupping as I tried to get the words out.

"So…" He looked at me so hopefully through his own sheen of tears. "Can we work through this? Be together? It's not too late?"

*Moment of truth.* It wasn't even a hard decision to make. In fact, that decision had been made for both of us months ago in Georgia.

"It's not too late for us. You're mine, I'm yours and I'm afraid that's going to have to be that." I threw my arms around him and pulled him tight against me. "I love you, you stupid weiner schnitzel."

He threw his head back and howled, "How long have you been waiting to call me that? I love you too, and now…"

He fidgeted with something in his pocket, and a few moments later I heard the muffled, booming whirl of a helicopter roaring up to the observatory to land on the promenade outside. Which was totally not in the slightest an over the top and unnecessary gesture.

"Now is when I ask you to come with me. Let me make everything up to you, prove to you that my words are meaningful. That I'm truly trying to be better than the man you first met."

"Markus! That is the stupidest speech ever. What is this?"

"I'm kidnapping you. Again."

I grinned at him then, through my tears, and started dragging him away from the sound of the spinning rotors, deeper into the building. "What is it with everyone trying to kidnap me these days? Seriously, call off the helicopter, you ass. It's totally unnecessary."

Markus pulled me tight against him and smiled. "Thank God, I hate helicopters. They make me piss my pants. I'll text David right away. Grand gesture successful?"

I reached over and booped his stupid adorable nose again. "Yes. Just, yes."

# Epilogue

*Two years later*
*Markus*

"You ready yet? I swear, you take longer than Candace's drag friends to get ready for a party." Alina was leaning against the doorway to our bathroom, looking otherworldly gorgeous in what she'd dubbed her "fancy goddess dress".

Her makeup was light and glittery, her lips were a perfectly pouty pink and her tits looked fucking fantastic. She eyed me up and down. "Got to say, though, whatever you've been doing in here looks good on you." She winked and laughed.

I straightened my sleeves, shot my cuffs and gave her a debonair smile as I held out my arm. "Come, my lady, our chariot awaits."

"But of course, Mr. Nominee. I'd be delighted to ride you—I mean, ride *with* you."

We took a last look in the mirror and she whipped out her phone. "Smile for the fans."

I dipped her and she took the shot upside down. That was the shot, of course, that went on social media. *Our* social media. Which was completely weird — *we* had our own following, not each of us individually anymore. It was, and always would be, us controlling our own narrative.

I helped Alina into the car. Her green-and-ivory pleated chiffon dress had an empire waist so she could move around easily and, as she put it, "hide a multitude of sins". It wasn't, however, a good one for climbing in and out of cars since it would tear so easily. I slid in behind her and sat back, thinking about our last two years together.

After Alina had forgiven me, a fact that still managed to humble me to my knees, we'd made an escape to the South Pacific during our mid-season break in filming. She'd wanted to see Fiji, and I'd wanted to see her naked on a deserted island. We'd compromised — as one did in all grown-up relationships between equals. Or so I was told.

Upon returning, we'd jumped back into filming together. Her season on *Southern Gods* had gone better than expected, and as Michael had hoped, ratings went way up. Apparently, people tuned in for our bullshit, and even though it had only been one season, it had bought Michael some breathing room to figure out where to take things next.

After the show, Alina had taken on the job with her mentor, Carolina. Of course, she'd impressed the shit out of Carolina and the project was set to release in another year. Alina had been offered an A.D. credit on the next film in the franchise and was more than ready to get started with it. I'd asked if she wanted me for a part because, holy shit, I'd always wanted to do a good jump scare, but she'd smacked me and told me that she'd rather order me around our house than a film set.

I'd ended up deciding to take the role with Sherilyn, after Alina agreed that it was the right thing to do, even though we were both unhappy with her underhanded methods for getting me to the table. But now I was done for a while and we were both looking forward to bit of a break.

We pulled up and I looked over at her. "You ready?"

She smiled as she said, "After you."

I climbed out first, waved and reached my hand back into the car to help her out. We paused and smiled for the cameras once before strolling away arm in arm and ignoring the rest of the gauntlet. Neither of us gave a single shit anymore. The pictures would say enough. They always did.

Inside, I grabbed us drinks and we took our seats next to some of the other people from Sherilyn's film. My nerves were starting to jangle. If I won, Alina was probably going to kill me. In fact, I knew she would. I looked up to the balcony and strained to see if everyone that I had invited had made it, but it was too shadowed.

We sat through boring speech after speech, musical act after musical act, barely paying attention and existing in our two-person world. She made me laugh all night and I made her squirm, telling her all of the new ways I'd been thinking about stripping her naked and making her come in our outdoor shower. Until, finally, it was time.

Some up-and-coming action film guy made weird, inappropriate jokes with a former Disney star, then the tone changed altogether as he announced, "And the

Award for the Best Actor goes to...Markus Shellenberg."

For probably the first time in my life I'd actually hoped to lose, because I had made another stupid bet with my brothers that I would propose to Alina during my acceptance speech if I won.

I was planning to propose anyway, after the ceremony. That was why I'd flown all of our family and friends in, and every one of them was sitting in the balcony. *Shit, shit, shit.* Now I was going to have to do this in front of a live audience at a televised event.

"Markus! They called your name! Get your ass up there." Alina was laughing at my shell-shocked face.

I looked at her, pulled her close, kissed her hard and whispered, "No matter what, remember that I love you. And that I take really stupid bets sometimes."

"What?"

I kissed her hand and stood up. Buttoning my jacket, I walked to my certain doom. I thanked the Disney star, shook the action guy's hand and accepted my award. I leaned over the microphone and took a massive breath. "First, I want to thank everyone who worked on this film with me. Director Sherilyn Holmes, the rest of the crew and cast, I wouldn't be here if it weren't for you. But most of all for the woman who has made everything possible — Alina, thank you."

I paused for clapping and looked over to the wings, where I nodded at the backstage crew who'd arranged for this surprise. They dropped the lights and a spotlight moved through the crowd and landed on Alina, who looked surprised, then amused, then concerned when it didn't waver.

"Alina, remember what I said before I came up here?" I could barely see her silhouette nod. "Could you please come up here?"

Music started to play and the entire crowd turned around, rustling and murmuring. At first she didn't move, frozen to her seat. When she did get up and began her march toward the stage, it was like she was walking to her execution.

As she joined me, I said into the microphone, "This is probably not the greatest idea, but I've had worse." As the polite laughter of the audience washed over us, I dropped to one knee, pulled a small box out of my pocket and grabbed her trembling left hand.

The entire room gasped as one entity as everyone realized what was happening.

"Alina, you are everything to me, and I'm nothing without you. Every morning that I get to wake up with you is the best of my life. Regardless of wherever we are in the world, whatever we're doing, I know that I'm home, because I'm with you. I love you, more and more every second, minute and hour, and can't imagine being without you. Will you marry me?"

When she didn't kick me in the balls right then and there, I had some hope that I hadn't made yet another moronic relationship decision. She'd definitely looked like she wanted to kill me when my knee hit the ground and she realized what was going on. As I continued to talk, we both started to tear up and she made me wait an uncomfortable amount of time before nodding, one hand over her mouth.

The applause was overwhelming. She pulled me up from the ground and in for a hard kiss and whispered in my ear, "You are a complete. And utter. Asshole." Each word was punctuated with a nip to my earlobe.

I laughed and directed her offstage. She'd barely gone two steps before she saw them. My parents and brothers. Ella and her family. A few friends from Chicago. Candace and Rory, who were also newly engaged. Ethan and his latest boyfriend. Everyone who mattered to us was there.

Her hand over her mouth, she whirled around and punched me in the chest, making the audience laugh harder. Then she grabbed me by the shirt and dragged me off, landing us in the biggest group hug in the world.

"You're going to pay for this, Markus. So. Hard."

"I know," I sighed. "But I'll love every second of it. And so will you."

"Always." She smiled through tears. "Always."

Want to see more from this author?
Here's a taster for you to enjoy!

# The Shellenberg Brothers:
# The Game
## A.B. Wilson

## Coming Spring 2022

### *Excerpt*

*Abby*

Air horns, club songs and pile-ons from teammates.
Confetti raining down in the drizzle, sticking to our
hair and rain-spattered, grass-stained jerseys. I would
never forget the moment that the F.C. Chelsea women's
soccer team won the championship. Never, ever in my
life had I felt the level of exhilaration that the men's
team must feel after the average game, because that's
how many people had crowded into Stamford Bridge
stadium to watch us win — a sold-out crowd.

All around me my teammates had torn off their
jerseys to trade with our opponents and were battling
tears with sloppy hugs. Something magical happens at
the closing whistle of a hotly competitive match that the
average person never feels. The way in which your
direst enemy suddenly becomes your friend, happy for
you in your happiness. There is that solidarity amongst

female athletes where those congratulatory moments mean something, and I'd been dreaming of this one since I was five years old.

Up in the manager's box the entire men's team was cheering us on. And there. Right in the middle of the crowd, if I could be bothered to look, would be my nemesis with his dirty blond hair trapped in a messy top knot, nice dress clothes most likely all rumpled with his sleeves rolled up his massive, tattooed forearms.

His electric-blue eyes would be crackling above his stubbly, chiseled cheekbones and jawline. Probably waving his hands theatrically, acting the fool and everyone loving on him. If he were American instead of German, I'd have bet money on his tie being wrapped around his head. Matti Shellenberg, a man I'd wished a bad case of jock itch on more times than was probably healthy.

Knowing he was up there was enough to make my blood boil. My eyes shot straight to him — like there was a magnetic force between the two of us — even at this distance. To my complete shock, he wasn't in the mix with his teammates, instead he was sitting all alone in a corner of the box — him, the man who was never still, never at rest, never less than one hundred percent positively on. The center of attention and master instigator. Now he sat slumped in his chair like a puppet with his strings cut, head in hands.

*He's probably pissed we're getting all of the attention.*

One year later, I could still feel the mashed potatoes crusting in my eyebrows and long auburn hair that I'd curled so carefully the night of the fundraiser for pediatric cancer patients. Those hyperrealistic plastic spiders he'd stuck on my chair that made me scream and flip my plate, launching a shower of food down on top of me and my tablemates.

I could still see him in my mind's eye, doubled over in laughter, wiping tears of hilarity off his flushed cheeks. Could still hear his delighted slow clap and taunt, '*You gonna come after me with that steak knife, Stabby Abby?*' I hated nicknames, but I had to admit that 'Stabby Abby' was one I could get behind. *That clever jerk.*

The confetti storm had finally settled in colorful, sodden clumps and the team's owner and head of operations strode through the tunnel and out onto the pitch for the trophy ceremony. I winced as I wound my way through the crowd, my bad knee was twinging like a motherfucker after a tackle from Porto's defender that had knocked me awkwardly onto my ass. Hopefully I'd only twisted it, nothing more serious.

My co-captain, Teresa, wrapped an arm around my shoulders and started tugging me toward the hastily erected podium at midfield. The team song was still blaring through the stadium speakers and the emotions of the day were catching me. I'd won a gold medal with the U.S. Women's National Team, but this was somehow bigger. Better, because it was unexpected. Times like this reminded me that every sacrifice I'd made to play professionally was worth it.

Tears pricked my eyes as Teresa hugged me close. "We did it, chica. Can you believe it?"

I hugged her back and we wiped each other's tears and laughed. "You get up there first," I encouraged. She hopped up on the stage and pulled me up behind her. Together, we walked to the podium to accept the trophy. The owner and manager were tag-teaming a self-congratulatory speech about how delightful and historic the moment was. Teresa and I exchanged a

Look. This moment would have come a lot sooner if the club had bothered to invest in its women's side the way it did in the men's.

The owner handed us the trophy, almost bobbling it as he attempted to kiss our cheeks. The smell of whiskey flowed off of him as he leered at us. Teresa and I did our duty, ignoring the foul, smelly man as we smiled and raised that trophy high above our heads. Not even a lecher could rub the shine off of this one for us. I kissed the cool, damp metal that smelled like blood and fresh grass. That too-brief kiss was, without a doubt, the greatest in my entire history of kisses — not that that history was particularly long or interesting.

I jumped down with the Cup, wincing again as my knee protested the action, and passed it off to my teammates. Teresa and I stood back from them, arm-in-arm as we watched the celebration continue. The men's team would be rushing the field soon because they could never handle the women's team having the lion's share of attention. I had no interest in being out there when Ratty Matti showed and turned to Teresa. "I'm going to the locker room, need to hit the ice baths before we have to get ready for the party," I murmured. "Cover for me?"

"You got it. Guess we all need some extra time to look our best tonight after this, huh?" She winked at me.

"Ugh, totally. But if I don't get in an ice bath soon, I'm not going to be able to stand in high heels." My tone was rueful and she slugged me in the shoulder, jerking her head in the direction of the locker room.

I took one last mental picture of my still-celebrating teammates, and the fans who hadn't stopped singing our song, and started for the bench to scoop my warm-up. As I maneuvered around the celebrants and the men's team clattering up from the tunnel, I glanced back up at the owner's box and got one hell of a shock. Matti was still up there, not down with the rest of his team trying to steal our glory. No, he was still in his seat with his head in his hands. *Curiouser and curiouser.*

The locker room was empty, but the training staff were there and ready with congratulations and help tearing the tape off from the brace around my knee. I'd suffered an ACL tear not too long ago and coming back had been an excruciating journey.

The physio helped me into the tub and one of his assistants started dumping in the ice. The cold burn of an ice bath was something that athletes supposedly got addicted to. Me, though, I was dreaming about tropical beaches and a solitary walk on white sand with the ocean curling in to tickle my toes as I shivered uncontrollably while buried in the tiny cubes.

"McKinnon, your mobile's ringin', darlin'! Says 'Sylvie'. That's your agent, right?" The head physio shook my shoulder as he showed me the screen of my phone. I sank back into the tub and managed to get out through my chattering teeth, "It can wait till I'm done here, probably a congratulations."

"I dunno, darlin', this is the third time she's called in five minutes. You're about done, let's get you out of there and you can take the call." He hadn't even really congratulated me. Nor had he asked me if I was okay, given the slight limp I knew he'd seen with his laser-like focus on all of our working extremities. My stomach hollowed out and my shivers got bigger and stronger as I accepted his hand and let him haul me out of the tub.

What did he know that I didn't?

I grabbed my phone and headed back to the locker room with a newfound sense of foreboding and sent a quick text to Sylvie that I'd call when I was out of the shower. I resolutely ignored the immediate buzz of a reply and the repeated chimes that indicated an incoming call. All I needed was one more moment to bask in the feeling of winning, of being a winner, of finally, *finally* achieving my dream before the real world could intrude again.

The water speared into me and I could barely hear the shouts and laughter of my teammates finally coming off the pitch over its spray. Our ancient locker room was about to turn into a pre-party while we all got ready for the huge end-of-season shindig thrown by the club's owners.

A bunch of us wanted nothing more than to go home — including me — but one simply did not skip this event. No matter how tired, no matter how injured. You went, you gladhanded the shit out of everyone, and you pretended to have the best time. Every year, I dreaded it. This year, though, things would be different. We were winners and I was trying to shake my salty reputation — my contract was up for renewal in the off-season. I cranked the water to cold to rinse out the last of my conditioner and practiced my biggest, most pleasant smile. My cheeks hurt already.

With my team all around me, their chatter echoing off the cinderblocks that needed a new coat of paint, I felt like I was in my safe space. Safe enough, at any rate, to call Sylvie back. The insulation of their enthusiasm made a little bubble around me as I waited for her to pick up. I snorted when her voicemail kicked in. That was so Sylvie, harass me for hours then pout when I finally did what she wanted — probably thought she was teaching me a lesson.

Joke was on her, though. I'd grown up in the most passively aggressive toxic home with a mother who knew how to wield silence as a weapon as easily as a backhanded compliment. In a small Midwestern town in southern Wisconsin where everyone knew you and your business.

Shoving thoughts of Sylvie aside, I forced my attention to making myself up to appear as photogenic and approachable as possible. Most of the other girls had completed their transition from sweaty athlete to debutante and were starting to file out to the hired cars that would take us to the Fairmont Hotel for the celebration while I was still winding a final section of hair around my curling iron.

One of my nineteen-year-old teammates had taken me aside earlier and thrown away my makeup bag with a theatrical grimace. With the rest of them around her chanting our names, she'd proceeded to make me over so thoroughly that it would take me an extra thirty minutes to make my hair look as good as her makeup. I waved at Teresa in the mirror.

"Want me to make sure there's a car for you when you finally finish?" she asked with a small smile, knowing how much I hated the schmoozing that went along with our captain's badges.

I waved my curling iron at her. "Nah, no big deal. Just need to make sure Sam's work wasn't in vain. If I miss the last car, I'll cab it."

Teres shrugged, unconvinced, and gave me a tiny finger wave as she pushed through the swinging doors. "Your funeral if you miss it."

"I'll be there, don't worry."

My stick-straight dark-auburn hair was behaving after much overspraying while wrapped around the hot iron and the big pin curls were fantastic in contrast with my pale, freckled skin and gray eyes. I looked like a dolled-up gladiator in my dark-green dress with the black lace overlay and admired the way it hugged the smooth muscles I'd sacrificed so much to build and hone. I was taking a last dab at a slightly overcolored spot on my top lip when my phone finally rang.

And like every time it rang without me immediately being able to see who was calling, my brain shouted hopefully, "Mom?" I castigated myself for still believing in the impossible. She hadn't come around to my profession or my love for the game in twenty-three years. There was no starting now. I flipped my phone over and saw my agent's face with her badass shark grin and tapped the screen.

"Sylvie," I said without further greeting. Sylvie hated that perfunctory nonsense.

"Abigail Jean," she returned grandly. Never mind that that wasn't my middle name. Sylvie changed it up every time and first- and middle-naming me was the way she showed her affection.

I rolled my eyes. "What's up?"

"Did I feel you rolling your eyes at me, young lady? Because I got a distinct vibe from that—"

"Sylvie, cut the crap. What's going on that you had to blow me up like this tonight of all nights?" I asked impatiently.

"My dear, I know. I know. While I would love to let you rest on your laurels, I unfortunately can't." She sighed and my stomach knotted again as she continued, laying it out bluntly and with no sugary sweetness to cushion the blow. "The team has decided that they'd like to go a different direction next season. They have some kid from South Korea on scout who is basically you pre-ACL tear on performance-enhancing drugs."

I couldn't speak or breathe. Now? After six years and a championship. Had they seen me limp around after my knee got torqued to hell?

"I know, dear, this is a lot to take in and it feels like it's out of nowhere," she said with no small amount of sympathy. "I was shocked too. Completely taken by surprise. Between you and Matti, Chelsea is —"

"Matti? What happened to Matti?" I asked, my voice higher-pitched than I would have thought possible. Sylvie managed both of us and he was a recent sign for her when his last agent cut him loose after yet another one of his infamous house parties had turned into a cocaine-fueled orgy. Management hadn't been fond of those pictures.

"He's being cut. Only the team had the grace to actually tell him in person, unlike this fiasco."

"When did you find out about us?" I asked, wondering if they'd already decided they wanted someone else before they'd seen me win the game for the team, before they might have spotted the slight limp.

"Well," she prevaricated. "Here's the thing, they called me right at kick-off. Matti was told at your half-time. I don't want you to worry. There are going to be a lot of teams interested in you after today's win and Matti is always bankable. I've already had a few calls for each of you."

She paused and I could tell she'd popped in a square of nicotine gum as I heard the aggressive chewing noise. "I know how you feel about him, but I need you to do me a favor and keep an eye on him tonight. He's not answering his phone and when he drinks, bad things tend to follow. I need you two to be on your best behavior while I negotiate."

"Sylvie, I'm not his keeper and tonight's going to be crappy enough. You know how badly he embarrassed me back at that fundraiser," I responded through a clenched jaw.

"You don't have to talk to him—although maybe it wouldn't be such a terrible thing if you could pull that stick out of your ass and drop the grudge. I've always thought the two of you would make such a cute couple." She muttered the last part and sighed heavily, like I was the one who made her life difficult and not the eternal man-child. Who, yes, was super hot, but oh my god was he an awful person.

"Please, Abby, get him in a cab if he gets too unruly, I'll text you his address," she begged.

I groaned and felt a headache start to form behind my eyes. "Fine, but I want a cut from his signing bonus for doing you this favor."

Sylvie ignored my sarcastic comment. "I'm flying out from La Guardia tonight, will be at Heathrow tomorrow morning. We'll meet then and can start talking about your options."

I sighed and slumped back onto the bench, feeling completely unmoored. My options. Six years, the peak of my career as an athlete, and they'd '*decided to go in a different directio*n'. The pendulum had swung back and the price I'd already paid to play the sport that I loved, the only thing that had ever mattered to me, now seemed indecently high. *Fuck this beautiful, fucking game.*

*Who even am I without soccer to define me?*

Home of Erotic Romance

Sign up for our newsletter and find out about all our romance book releases, eBook sales and promotions, sneak peeks and FREE romance books!

# About the Author

Amanda (A.B.) Wilson is the pen name for a heat-seeking librarian from the upper Midwest. Long after her sassy five year old and long-suffering husband go to bed, she writes steamy, escapist contemporary romances about celebrities, athletes, and billionaires—with a twist.

Amanda loves to hear from readers. You can find her contact information, website details and author profile page at https://www.totallybound.com